TOUCH WOOD

A Girlhood in Occupied France

Renée Roth-Hano

FOUR WINDS PRESS
NEW YORK

Acknowledgments

I would like to give special acknowledgment to the playwright Philip Freund, who gave me my first encouragement, and to Jack E. Koechley, who supported my beginnings.

I also feel very indebted to the faithful members of my writing group, whose unflinching support forced me to forge ahead week after week: Barbara Tallerman, Rita O'Connor, Michel Magee, Flora Hogman, Frida Weinstein, Pascale Retourné-Raab, Maxine Marc, and Mary MacBride.

My thanks go to Meredith Charpentier, my first editor, whose strong faith kept me going and without whom this book would not have come about, and to Cynthia Kane, whose keen sensitivity and understanding helped keep intact the emotional overtones of my writing and helped to give it its final shape.

Last but not least, I would like to give special thanks to my husband, John, whose warm support has seen me through my highs and lows.

Copyright © 1988 by Renée Roth-Hano. Frontispiece map designed by Andrew Mudryk. All rights reserved. No part of this book may be reproduced or transmitted in any form or by any means, electronic or mechanical, including photocopying, recording, or by any information storage and retrieval system, without permission in writing from the Publisher. Four Winds Press, Macmillan Publishing Company, 866 Third Avenue, New York, NY 10022. Collier Macmillan Canada, Inc.

First Edition. Printed in the United States of America.   10 9 8 7 6 5 4 3 2 1

The text of this book is set in 11½ point Bembo.

Library of Congress Cataloging-in-Publication Data. Roth-Hano, Renée, date. Touch wood. Summary: In this autobiographical novel set in Nazi-occupied France, Renée, a young Jewish girl, and her family flee their home in Alsace and live a precarious existence in Paris until Renée and her sister escape to the shelter of a Catholic women's residence in Normandy. 1. Roth-Hano, Renée, date—Juvenile fiction. 2. Holocaust, Jewish (1939–1945)—Juvenile fiction. [1. Roth-Hano, Renée, date—Fiction. 2. Holocaust, Jewish (1939–1945)—Fiction. 3. Jews—France—Fiction. 4. World War, 1939–1945—France—Fiction. 5. France—History—German occupation, 1940–1945—Fiction] I. Title.

PZ7.R738To 1988 [Fic] 87-34326

ISBN 0-02-777340-X

*To my sisters
and
to the memory of
my mother and father*

This is not the work of a historian. I have drawn on my childhood recollections to tell the story of what happened to me and my family during the German occupation.

I chose the diary format as the best way to portray the climate of the times and the escalating terror that we felt. I tried to keep the entry dates as close as I could to the events as they occurred.

Many years have passed since I was a girl in occupied France, bringing inevitable lapses and inaccuracies. But the essence of my emotional memories has been captured, with its tragic, cruel, and tender moments.

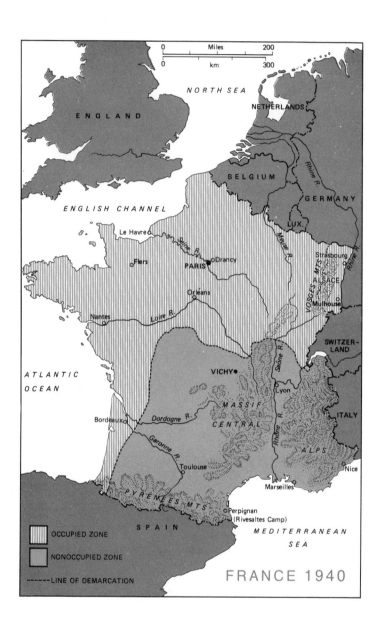

I

PARIS

1940

"Don't be so obvious!" Maman scolds—for the hundredth time, it seems—as I look out of the window into the courtyard, straining to make out my favorite tune.

I bristle. The courtyard is the best thing that's happened to us since we left our home in Mulhouse, in Alsace, to run away from the Germans, and settled in Paris a few weeks ago. I like to rest my chin on our fifth-floor window bar and look down at the narrow cobblestone courtyard and watch the people come and go. The yard has no tree, but it shows a big piece of sky. It makes up for the cramped quarters where my parents, my grandmother—Maman's mother—my little sisters,

3

Denise and Lily, and I have to squeeze. Above all it allows me to hear the neighbors' radio when the weather is nice enough for the windows to be open.

I sorely miss not having our own radio. We can't be *that* poor! I sometimes tell myself, recalling the large one we had to leave behind. But I keep my thoughts to myself: Papa, Maman, and Grand'mère have more important things to worry about.

"What did I tell you?" Maman scolds again, her voice a bit sharper. "Don't you have any pride? What if your sisters were to do the same thing?"

I turn around to face my mother, who has now come out of the kitchen and is wiping her hands on her apron.

She is very pretty with her delicate features, hazel eyes, and short wavy chestnut hair—much prettier, I think, than my sisters and me. But all I see now is her annoyed expression.

I am getting annoyed too. Can't she understand that I don't like pretending, that it makes me feel like a beggar to have to listen to someone else's set? Don't I have the right to listen to Charles Trenet too? His songs make you so happy to be alive!

"So what? Why can't we have our own radio, like everybody else?" The question is out before I can stop it.

"Because Jews are not permitted to have any, that's why!" Maman snaps.

I feel the blood leave my face; my knees grow weak. Not permitted? That's a good one! Didn't we come all the way to Paris because we were told it was safer for the Jews?

Maman's expression softens. She walks toward me and cups my chin in her hand.

"Don't look so sad, Renée! Doing without a radio isn't

the end of the world. Nothing worse should ever happen to any of us!"

Maman doesn't understand. She just can't see that the good spirits I have struggled so hard to rebuild in the last few months have vanished again. "What does it mean, exactly, not permitted?" I ask her.

"It's very simple: There's a law now that forbids Jews to own a radio—and requires that they turn in the ones they already have. That's why we never bothered to buy a new one."

"But why can't we have one?"

"Frankly I have no idea. None of their laws and decrees makes any sense. I've stopped asking why. This is the way it is, period."

"And what makes it a law?" I demand.

"The fact we'll get into trouble if we don't go along with it."

"And who made this law?"

For once Maman doesn't mind my many questions. "The Germans, I suppose. I'd like to think that the French are only following orders!"

"But how would the Germans know that we own one?" I ask, puzzled.

"You never know! Someone may denounce us to the police!"

"What are they going to come up with next!" I explode. "Are they going to ask that we turn in our roller skates and our dolls too?" I think of my doll, Jackie: There's no way I would give *her* away! I hate Maman's resigned look. I'm worried all over again. Does this mean that the hostilities against the Jews are going on here, too, right under our very noses, even though things seem calm on the surface? I ask myself.

We are, to my knowledge, the only Jews in our building. What would happen if—God forbid, as Maman would say—things got rough for us? Would our neighbors—the Chavignats; Mme Lelièvre; our concierge, Mme Giroud—forgive us for being Jewish?

Maybe it isn't the end of the world for Maman, I think. But it is the end for me, right now!

I slam the window shut in anger.

I no longer want to listen to anyone's radio. Ever.

"After the war," I mumble to myself, "I'll have a radio in every room!"

It was a radio that started the whole trouble. I count on my fingers. It's eleven months, now, since it all began. . . .

————

We were in Villers-sur-Thur, a little village in Alsace where we'd been spending our summers. Nothing in the air had warned us that the day was going to be different. It was warm—just like the day before and the day before that. *Summer* always seemed to me to be the most beautiful word in the whole world. It meant the chirping of the birds greeting us in the morning as Maman threw open the shutters and the sun flooded the room; fragrant, warm air; a passing train in the afternoon drowsiness; freedom from homework; and above all, late bedtime.

We were gathered around the large dining-room table, finishing our lunch. There was Papa; Maman; my sisters, Denise and Lily; and our hosts, M. and Mme Peters and their son, Seppi, short for Joseph.

The radio was on. As usual I wasn't listening—it was always so boring. I was much more interested in convincing Lily that I had more lemonade left in my glass than she did in hers, even though I'd taken more sips from mine. With the three years I had over her—I had just turned eight, and she was five—it was still easy to fool her.

Suddenly M. Peters spoke in a loud, rushed voice, pointing his finger to the radio. I didn't know what was being said, but I sensed panic. Within minutes our host, Papa, and Seppi had their ears practically glued to the set. The volume had been turned up by now, and it was impossible not to pay attention. In the jumble that came out, I registered only five words: *war with Germany* and *massive mobilization.*

What's so unsettling about this announcement? I had wondered. In school earlier in the year I had learned about some of the wars France had fought over the centuries. Germany was now our most feared enemy. Alsace had been French territory since 1918—the end of the last war—but I knew Alsace and Lorraine had gone back and forth between France and Germany for years, depending on who won what war. I loved the many songs and tales recounting these heroic times, the War of 1870 and the Great War. "The Last Class"—which told of the last French class in a small Alsatian school on the eve of the German occupation in the war of 1870, where all the village officials and many grown-ups turned up—was my favorite story.

I almost stopped breathing when Papa, M. Peters, and Seppi left the room and ran out to the street. They didn't wait for their usual coffee. Papa even let his Celtique burn in the ashtray, robbing Maman of the opportunity to make her usual comment about how he smoked too much.

Mme Peters and Maman rushed to the street, too, the three of us girls trailing closely behind. Before long, men and women from neighboring houses had joined in and gathered in small groups. They were getting excited—raising their voices and moving their arms. That's when I heard Papa's voice mentioning distant cities like Nancy, Strasbourg, Lyons, Paris.

Did that mean that he would have to go far away to fight the war? I asked myself.

I had to know. I rushed over to him, trying to catch his eye, but he didn't even see me.

Disappointed, I decided to walk back to the house. Standing by the open door, I looked at the familiar room. The cuckoo in the clock next to the bookshelf came out of hiding and struck the quarter hour.

I loved this little house and this area of Alsace—the well down the street, the river Thur flowing quietly under our very window, the daily garden-fresh lettuce and tomatoes and the mounds of *crème fraîche* served at every meal.

Would the war keep us away from here? Would it last as long as four years, as the Great War did? Would Papa have to join the Army as he did then, even though he had a family now, and we needed him?

I thought of our life at home in Mulhouse: our Friday evening meals with heaps of *tartines*, buttered slices of bread sprinkled with paprika, which Maman could never resist nibbling from; her fragrant apple cakes; Papa's Sunday morning card games at the Café de la République.

And I remembered our long walks to Salvatore Park or to our famed zoo, and especially the picnics on the banks of the Ill. I loved the ride to the beach, in a streetcar that was wide open during the warm season. I always feared falling over to the street below and made sure that Maman sat near the edge, fully confident that her bulk would offer a reliable protection.

I ran over to the radio and banged it with my fist. "That'll teach you!" I raged. "You mean thing, you!"

I tore outside to look for my sisters, but they were playing with a hoop, untroubled. Lucky them, I thought. At least they are too young to worry about anything for very long.

Standing between my troubled parents and my busy sisters, I suddenly felt very lost. I knew that things would never be the same again.

My sisters erupt from the bedroom, where they were keeping Grand'mère company, bringing me forcefully back to the present. I am grateful for the interruption.

"It's your turn to do the dishes today, isn't it?" Denise asks. She always looks pretty, with her perfectly round face and her huge brown eyes. "Lily insists it's mine."

I sigh and nod. We never seem to agree about who is to do what chore.

"One of you better set the table. Papa will be here any minute now!" Maman reminds us from the kitchen.

"The bell! It's Papa!" Lily exclaims. She rushes to the door, recognizing, as we all do, his distinctive set of rings.

Papa looks tired. It seems as if his face has become more drawn, his hair thinner, and his shoulders more stooped since we left Mulhouse. But you can tell that he's happy to be home. He is now working for a raincoat manufacturer; sometimes he brings work to finish on his sewing machine at home—we had to buy one in a hurry—but not tonight. I'm glad. Papa is much older than Maman, sixteen years, and I am always afraid for his health.

He kisses Lily first—he always does—and hands her his newspaper and raincoat. Then he kisses Denise and me.

"What's for dinner, Mancsi?" he yells out to Maman. Mancsi is a Hungarian nickname for her full name, Marguerite. "It smells so good! Let me guess: chicken paprika?"

"Yes. Surprise!" Maman answers.

"Where's Grand'mère?" Papa remembers to ask.

"She's in bed, resting. She doesn't want to eat tonight," Maman explains.

I busy myself getting out the dishes, glasses, knives, and forks and begin to set the table.

It's not my turn to do it, since I'm doing the dishes later. But tonight I couldn't care less. Tonight I've learned that we are not safe, no matter where we go.

Tuesday, August 27

I put down the net bag containing the carrots, cabbage, and apples I've just bought and throw my jacket on the chair nearest me.

"Hang up your jacket! Maman will have a fit!" Denise warns me. She hardly lifts her eyes from the card game of Nain Jaune she's playing with Lily on the round dining-room table.

I don't even bother to answer: I get too mad for words when she is so bossy, since she's a good two years younger than me.

"Hurry up! Make up your mind. We've only got a few minutes left before dinner!" Lily grumbles.

But I know that Denise will not budge and that Lily will have to wait until after dinner to finish the game.

Grand'mère is sitting next to Lily. Hers is the only upholstered chair with a loose back pillow that we have—and the only piece of furniture we bought. She is grating carrots. She always wears drab-colored dresses, as if she didn't want to be noticed. I hate them. I also hate the kerchief covering a mass of hair which, I can tell, is too dark and too full to be her own. In the family they say that old ladies sometimes wear wigs for religious reasons. What those reasons are is unclear to me, but I suspect they are why Grand'mère wears her wig.

She busies herself constantly. When she isn't grating carrots, she's peeling potatoes or shelling peas, all the while looking aimlessly ahead of her. She is blind.

According to Maman Grand'mère has been blind for a long time. "Will you get blind too? And Denise and Lily and I?" I asked once.

"Of course not. It's not hereditary, if that's what you mean," Maman replied with a shrug.

Grand'mère's condition, she had explained, had started around her "change of life," a mysterious state which she always pronounced in a hushed voice, as if it brought bad luck. The affliction was also called cataract, she said—a word which, I vaguely knew, also meant "waterfall." All this was very confusing, but I thought it best to ask no more questions. They were sure to cause

Maman to throw up her arms and raise her eyes to the ceiling in an exasperated gesture meaning, "Will this child ever stop asking questions?"

But no one seemed to make much of a fuss about this state of affairs—least of all Grand'mère—so I stopped worrying too.

"Where are the eggs, Renée?" Maman asks from the kitchen.

My heart skips a beat. I remember how I got so distracted looking at the window display of the charcuterie that I rushed home and forgot to stop at the Durands' dairy store.

"I forgot all about them," I admit sheepishly.

"I knew it! How many times do I have to tell you to make a list? Your head is always in the clouds. I should've sent Denise!" Maman scolds.

Leave it to Maman to make me feel bad.

"I'll go down again. . . . It'll only take a few minutes," I promise her.

"Never mind now. It's almost dinnertime. Papa's home, finishing some sewing he has to do. We'll do without them."

I should never have been the oldest, I think as I go to hang up my jacket and return to watch my sisters' game. How can I set an example for Denise and Lily when I am always the one who trips, who soils a dress on the first day, who gets the key stuck in the keyhole, or coughs at the movies, and—worst of all—the one who gets flustered when scolded.

Now, I know I am very bright—I am always at the head of my class—but it is difficult to shine when Maman gets so impatient every time I fumble and when my sisters tease me nonstop. They tease me about everything: about my humming the latest songs, or moving to the beat the minute I hear a band on the neighbor's radio, or my shameless love for my doll, Jackie—not to mention the way I burst out laughing when reading about the misfortunes of Bécassine, the simple country girl.

It's a good thing that no one knows about my sucking my thumb in the dark once in a while when I feel really misunderstood. God knows, it's embarrassing enough!

I have an idea why Maman is always after me: She worries about my future.

"You'll never catch a man with potato peels that thick!" she says deploringly when I rush through the chore to get back to my reading. "How can anyone afford you?"

I panic at the thought, but not for very long. I know perfectly well that I can peel potatoes or work as hard as the next person, but I simply refuse to give in. If my getting married depends on how well I peel potatoes, grate carrots, or the rest of it, then I am not interested.

Besides, marriage is a long, long way off. Why worry about it now?

I study my sisters, each so different.

Denise and I are on the plump side—as are Papa and Maman. It is a definite plus in Maman's eyes: She sees it as a sure sign that she's a good mother.

Shortly after I had started school in Mulhouse, someone had called me a *grosse patate*—a fat potato. I had rushed home, utterly crushed. But Maman had consoled me promptly: "Don't you listen to what they're saying! You're healthier than those string beans any day!"

Until then I had thought that people were born with a certain shape—some tall, some short, some skinny, some fat—and that was that. But the insult I had just swallowed brought home the fact that what we believed at home wasn't necessarily what the rest of the world thought.

Denise is definitely the most beautiful of the three girls. Since she smiles a lot, people often say of her, "What a happy child!"

More important: She never gets her clothes dirty, and she keeps her things in such disgustingly good order that Maman automatically forgives her for being such a slow-poke.

Lily is made of a different fabric altogether. First of all, she's all legs and bones. Unlike Denise and me, she's always been a picky eater. I remember that when she was still a toddler, Maman had to run around the table to catch her and try to force-feed her. She didn't always succeed.

My littlest sister is also very clever with her hands and has an incredible understanding of mechanical things.

"I don't know who she gets it from!" Maman would wonder, half admiring, half in awe, after Lily had managed to change a fuse. "Certainly not from Papa or me!"

Sometimes I think that's why she is Papa's favorite. She definitely is: He often takes her for hours at a time to play cards at the Schriffts'. And sometimes, when she is not hungry, she is allowed to sit on his lap and to nibble from his plate.

I have long known that Papa has always wanted a boy—you can tell from the names Denise and I were given. But when our little sister was born, everything got turned around: She got a real girl's name and managed to get Papa wrapped around her little finger.

Deep down I love my sisters very much, and I shouldn't get so annoyed when people comment on

Denise's winning smile or Lily's precocious mind. Is it maybe because I can't find anything special about me?

I know only too well, no matter what Maman says, that my good looks vanished after my third birthday. Now, whenever I am forced to look into a mirror, I find my hair too curly, my eyes too small, my lashes too short, my teeth uneven, and the rest of me much too round.

I count on the passing time to straighten things out.

Monday, September 2

"See this? It's all the bread we're going to get for the month!" Maman explains as she puts a batch of booklets on the table.

There's one booklet per person. Denise takes the one bearing her name and opens it up: Inside is a page of ration stamps.

"They look like postage stamps, don't they?" she says.

"The quantities look rather small to me," Lily comments. "Fifty to one hundred grams. It can't be very much!"

"How much bread do you think it will come to?" I ask.

"The way we go at it in this house, I'm sure it won't be enough!" Maman predicts.

Like everyone else in Paris, we've had to go along with the new restrictions and get food stamps from the local school on Rue Turgot.

"It was to be expected," Papa says, putting down the newspaper which he sometimes likes to hide behind. "I was just reading about it." He explains that with France split in two—the German-occupied zone, where we are, and the Free Zone, where our Government has resettled with Vichy as its new capital—there's bound to be trouble. And, he says, the war has wrecked many areas in our country: Roads and bridges have been destroyed, trains and transportation stopped, trade interrupted. It will take time before supplies are available again.

"What about the Germans? I don't know how many there are in France right now, but I am sure that they're helping themselves to whatever we have!" Maman remarks. "I guess we should consider ourselves lucky to have had a break since we got to Paris. Other areas in France were not so fortunate!" She always remembers to count her blessings. "And it's only the beginning!" Maman continues. "I heard people talk about rationing milk, cheese, and God knows what else."

Slowly I pick up my card. It reminds me of Zainvillers, where we stopped on our way to Paris: Coupons meant that we were always hungry. Now I'm sure that we haven't really escaped the fear that made us flee Alsace.

The day we left our town of Mulhouse, we'd heard that the Germans would be there in just two days. France was now at war with Germany and was losing ground fast. The Germans wanted to annex Alsace and had ordered the Jews there to leave.

My parents had had some time to make plans for us. We would pack our belongings and head for the border town of Kruth, in Alsace. From there we would find some transport over the Vosges Mountains and travel to Paris, where Maman had some childhood friends, the

Schriffts. They were convinced that Paris was the best spot for us: It was a big city; Papa could find work, and so far—"touch wood," Maman told us—at least they'd left the Jews alone.

It took Maman a very long time to find a truck in Kruth. Jewish families were already gathered around the Grand'Place when we got there, sitting on their valises, hoping, as we were, to find some means of transportation across the mountains to the safety of the French side—the "Interior."

Three times we saw Maman disappear in the crowd, looking for someone with a car, a van—anything on wheels. Three times she walked back, as if the few moments spent with us gave her the courage to start all over again.

The fourth time she was not alone: She had managed to convince a French military officer to come to our rescue.

A middle-aged heavyset man, ready to burst out of his uniform, he greeted us with a stiff but friendly salute.

"We're not permitted to take civilians in our trucks, you understand," he explained, as if deploring the strict rule. "But as an officer, I have, of course, a little leeway."

"Please, help us! We won't make any noise, I promise!" Maman begged. "No one will know that you have anyone in the back of your truck!"

The man remained silent, but his eyes moved slowly from one of us to another. He stopped at Lily, and, walking toward her, he said as he patted her cheek, "I have a little girl just about your age."

"Please, God. Someone make him hurry," I prayed silently, aware of the clock ticking away our precious time.

"Let's go!" the man finally said, pushing us forward, his voice suddenly imperative. "We must hurry. My truck is parked near here."

But there was one catch: Only four people could fit in the tightly shut, windowless back of the van if we were to take along our belongings.

Before we knew it, Maman, Grand'mere, and my sisters were lifted by strong arms into the recesses of the truck, and the doors were slammed shut. There had been no time for hugs and kisses—only the promise that somehow Papa and I would join them in the tiny village of Zainvillers, many miles away on the other side of the Vosges Mountains.

Which left Papa and me to our own devices.

We waved and waved until they were just a dot that was swallowed by the road.

"*Eh bien, ma grande,*" Papa said, calling me his big girl. "We've got a long day ahead of us."

Funny how conveniently our parents treat us like little adults when it suits them! I *did* feel rather grown-up, though. Wasn't I, just like Papa, facing the unknown? The walk itself didn't scare me; I had been on many outings in the mountains before. What was unsettling was that this was going to be no ordinary trip: Our lives would depend on it.

I looked at Papa. Except for the canvas bag he was carrying, he didn't look different from any other day; he wore a striped three-piece suit. His shoes were well-polished and made of fine leather—an unlikely outfit for a long hike. But then, Papa has never been one to dress casually.

I took a quick reading of his face. Perhaps he would

have preferred to be with Lily? Or surely with Maman? But I noted the full lips, the dark hair like mine. They were a definite bond between us.

He pulled his Omega watch out of his vest pocket in a familiar and reassuring gesture.

"It's eleven o'clock," he said. "We'll stop for a bite around two. Maman gave us some bread and cheese for the road. What do you say?"

I nodded in agreement.

"Ready?" Papa asked.

"Ready!" I replied.

Should I give him my hand to hold? I wondered, facing my first decision. Hardly, I told myself: It wouldn't be very grown-up.

"This way, then!" Papa said, pointing to the road sign reading COL DE BUSSANG.

He took my hand, deciding for both of us.

The sun was warm, the air smelled of the familiar pines of the Vosges, and the surrounding mountains were so peaceful.

I couldn't leave; not like that. I had to stop to take a deep breath—to take in all I could. I looked longingly at the majestic, strong pines, at the passing birds. Will they be forced to sing in German, I wondered, just like the little boy of "The Last Class" did?

"Come on, Renée," Papa urged. "We must get going!"

I broke away and leaned to the side of the road to pick up a fallen twig. Then I ran to catch up with Papa.

As we began to walk I took a last glance over my shoulder. It seemed hardly possible that only miles away there could be something so wrong with our world that we were leaving it behind—never, perhaps, to return.

The bell rings. Three impatient, shrill rings.

"It's me, Raymond!" a voice says across the door.

We are sitting around the table, having barely finished our lunch. As usual, unable to bear the sight of crumbs and soiled dishes, Maman has been hurrying us along, and ignoring our "Don't-rush-Maman-we-have-all-afternoon"s, she has started to collect our plates.

"Impossible! It can't be Raymond!" Maman remarks, startled, like me, by my cousin's appearance. She rushes to open the door.

It *is* Raymond—and his younger brother, Fernand.

"Raymond! Fernand!" Maman exclaims. "What on earth are you two doing here? Where are your mother and father?"

Then she catches sight of my aunt and uncle coming up behind them. The boys walk in, followed now by Uncle Maurice and Aunt Fanny, all loaded down by bundles and valises.

"Let me sit down first," Aunt Fanny sighs, collapsing on the chair I have graciously vacated for her and forgetting to thank me.

Questions and answers are now flying in all directions.

"Let me do the explaining," Uncle Maurice says, covering the noise with his baritone voice. "I know . . . I know. . . . We were supposed to settle in Grenoble. . . . We tried—at least for a few weeks. . . . It's a clean, pretty town, surrounded by beautiful mountains—but it was hard to get used to it. We didn't know anyone there. . . . Fanny was worrying about you, I couldn't relax and get settled, so we decided we'd probably be better off in Paris, near all of you—and we made sure we could get here before school starts. . . . So here we are!"

"God knows, I'm all for it!" Maman cries. "But what are we going to do? There's ten of us now. Why didn't you let us know that you were coming, Maurice?"

"Relax, Marguerite," Papa says. "We'll work something out!"

"I'm sorry," Maman says, apologizing and taking Aunt Fanny's hand. "Of course, we'll work something out. At least we are all well and together. Paris has been good to us so far—touch wood."

I can understand Maman's panic, but only for a moment: I'm too busy greeting my favorite uncle.

I can't figure out why Maman doesn't like him. So what if he isn't the world's handsomest man and his eyes don't look at you at the same time? I suspect that she resents his plying my sisters and me on the sly—against her orders—with white chocolate, which we love.

There's no doubt: Uncle Maurice likes to spoil us. I could swear that *he* at least would have welcomed a daughter. I also know that I am his favorite; I can tell by the many nicknames he makes up especially for me, and the way he suddenly rubs his bristling cheek against mine when I least expect it.

It's easy to see that Aunt Fanny is Maman's pet. She's Maman's baby sister; like my mother, she's plump with short, wavy hair, and I think Maman prefers her to the three of us. It's so obvious! Maman is so much more patient with her. She never tires of explaining, time and time again, how to prepare stuffed peppers so that they remain firm and doesn't mind answering any of her many questions. In turn Aunt Fanny worships Maman. They make a perfect team.

Our aunt is far from being so easygoing with us: In

fact, she is rather bossy. I try very hard not to take her too seriously. I know that, deep down, she is just a little child in a grown-up's body.

Our cousins—thank goodness—are not typical boys of six and eight who like to roughhouse. We will get along, I know.

"We'll manage for a couple of nights," Maman concludes. "We can always pull out an extra blanket and let the children sleep on the floor. But tomorrow we'll have to help you find a place to stay."

Maman does wonders. She finds out that there is a vacancy coming up in our building. My uncle, aunt, and cousins will stay at a nearby hotel until they can move in.

Thank goodness, I think when I hear this news. Ten people are too many for our apartment. Still, it is interesting to watch my aunt and my mother together. I know that sisters and brothers don't always get along when they are young. But I hope that when Denise, Lily, and I are grown up, we will be nice to one another, just like Maman and Aunt Fanny.

Thursday, September 26

"Girls!" Maman says, addressing Denise and me. "We need tomatoes, potatoes if you can find any, and some sausage for tonight. Why don't you two go to the market on Rue de Clignancourt and get yourselves some fresh air? And while you're at it, get half a dozen eggs and a hundred grams of butter."

Maman knows perfectly well that, though we grumble about cleaning the house or doing the dishes, we never need to be told twice about going to the market.

Daily marketing is a necessity. Maman does her best to come up with original ideas to keep our food fresh, like keeping the butter in cold water on the windowsill in the back bedroom—always cool because it doesn't get any sun—or preparing dishes that last for two or three meals. But for the most part food has to be eaten immediately.

It's so different from what I remember of Mulhouse, where we had Charlotte to help Maman with the cooking and the cleaning and to run most of the errands. On Thursdays—our day off from school—Maman would take my sisters and me shopping in Rue des Maréchaux. There we would stop at the butcher for some special cuts of meat, and at the grocery store nearby, the only one that carried Maman's favorite green peas and noodles. I liked the old wrinkled lady who took care of us: She never failed to give my sisters and me a mouse-shaped candy with chocolate covering.

I slam my book shut now and get up from my chair, ready to go, grabbing the vegetable net from the doorknob while Denise looks for some money.

I don't even mind taking along Raymond and Fernand—Maman's orders—to show them the neighborhood.

"Just don't let go of Fernand's hand!" Aunt Fanny warns. She needn't worry. While he's Lily's age, he is not half as independent. As long as you let him take along his miniature car, he'll follow you anywhere.

As for Raymond, he's always in the best of moods. I know he'll insist on carrying the grocery bag.

Denise and I have worked out a certain routine whenever we go marketing: We first steal a glance at Mme Petit, the proud owner of the fancy fruit-and-vegetable store right next to our building. We are sure to find her sitting at her cash register, and we try to contain our giggles while we watch her glasses about to fall off her nose as she adds long columns of figures in a large green ledger.

"Look at the tomatoes! They're beautiful! Let's buy some here," Fernand suggests.

I know I'm turning as red as a beet and I want to disappear into the ground. "We can't. We can't afford these kinds of prices," I whisper in his ear, pulling him firmly away.

We catch up with Denise and Raymond and walk by the Durand dairy store; the Michelet bakery, where day in and day out we get our bread; and the wine store, where on special days Papa buys some *vin ordinaire* from a dribbling tap.

We finally go past the *droguerie* and I suck in with delight the distinctive whiff of paint, shoe polish, Marseilles soap, and turpentine.

We have now reached the terraced café of the crescent-shaped Place du Delta.

"See the big white church up on the hill? It's the Sacré-Cœur," I explain to my cousins as the building comes into sight. "You can spot this Place when you look down from the terrace."

Strange how proud I suddenly feel. I must sound as if I owned it all.

But in a way I do. Just like the other people in the area,

I have come to consider this street as "our" street, and the stores as "our" bakery, "our" dairy store, "our" drugstore. It's becoming "our" neighborhood, and it helps me to miss Alsace a little less. And when we reach Rue de Clignancourt—crowded, noisy, alive—I realize how much I love the sight of the many colorful carts and their clever vendors.

"Won't you taste the best cheese in Paris?" one asks as we pass. "It's that much less that the Germans will get! Don't be afraid, mesdames. . . . Take advantage of the offer while you can. The way things go, there may not be any tomorrow, and you'll be sorry you didn't get any!"

I'm glad they can still make us laugh, in spite of our misfortunes.

Monday, September 30

I toss and turn, biting my pillow to keep still. My stomach cramps are getting worse. I can't help being a bit nervous: School starts tomorrow.

All I do is wake up Denise, sleeping next to me.

"What's the matter?" she inquires. "Are you sick?"

"I've got to get to the toilet—fast!" I whisper, suddenly feeling the call of nature. Grand'mère is asleep in the bed near the window, and we don't want to wake her up.

"I'll get the flashlight and keep you company," my sister offers.

"If you want. . . . But you know, there's hardly room for one person in there, and the floor is always so damp and slippery."

"We'll manage," Denise assures me.

I am grateful for my sister's concern, but I must concentrate on getting into my slippers and don't even take the trouble of putting anything over my pajamas. Time is of the essence.

We tiptoe through the small corridor and the living room, out the door, and across the hall.

I'll never get used to our toilet, I think as we creep along. To begin with, we must share it not only with the other two families on our floor but with the three families on the floor below as well.

I hate to keep constant vigil behind our closed door to wait for the signal—the flushing chain—so I can run to the toilet before anyone else beats me to it.

I also hate the whole idea of having to do without a seat. "Squatting is more sanitary," we are told.

We are in luck—the toilet is lit. One of the Chavignats must have just used it: Our neighbors have devised a clever way to light it directly from their apartment with a time switch. But I know the light will go off in a few seconds.

It goes out before I have a chance to get settled.

"Hurry! I need some light! The silly *minuterie* just went off!" I yell in panic, afraid to slip on the slanted damp floor as I struggle to get positioned on the footrests in the dark.

"I'm here, don't worry," Denise says from the hall. "Everybody's asleep at this hour, so you can leave the door open."

I relax as she flashes ample light in my direction.

As usual, I make sure to rush away right after flushing the chain. I don't want to get sprayed!

"I can't stand these toilets!" I rage once we're back in

bed. "Sometimes I'd rather not go than be bothered!"

"If only they were clean," Denise whispers. "Some people don't even take the trouble of flushing the chain enough! It's disgusting!"

Denise seems just as wide-awake as I am, so I settle back to talk with her.

"In Mulhouse at least we had our own toilet . . . and we could keep the light on all night if we wanted to," I whisper. "To tell you the truth I'm a little disappointed in Paris. Aren't you? The best thing was getting here. . . . Like when Papa and I walked across the Vosges Mountains. You should have seen the little house on the road where some old, very old people invited us to spend the night. They had a grandfather clock that chimed every fifteen minutes—and the bed where Papa and I slept had four posters and a fat eiderdown!"

"You mean, you slept with Papa?" Denise asks, almost loudly. She has now raised her head, and her eyes are sparkling in the dark.

"There was only one bed in the room—but it was so huge, three people could have slept in it. I don't even remember falling asleep: Papa says I was drunk from the wine they wanted me to taste."

"You're right. . . . Even Zainvillers was nicer than this!" Denise agrees, reminiscing. "Do you remember Sister Marthe? She was so good to us—even though we are not Catholic. She tried so hard to scrape up bread and chocolate for us and the other children of the youth center when there was so little food around. Why, there must have been fifteen of us!"

"Frankly I couldn't see why they all made such a fuss about Paris," I say. "To begin with, we were forced to spend the night at the police station because our train got in after the curfew—as if it had been our fault! And then we wound up in this small apartment—a fifth-floor walk-up to boot!"

In my excitement I am speaking faster and louder.

"Hush!" Denise reminds me.

"But it's true!" I can't help protesting. "And to top it all we can't even have our own radio!"

"Enough now!" Denise whispers loudly, poking me with her fist.

I stop myself short from hitting her back. "Yes . . . we're going to wake up Grand'mère—and Papa, Maman, and Lily in the other room—if we carry on this way," I say, agreeing.

"All right. Good night, then," she says, giving me a peck on the cheek. "Just don't wake me up again!"

"Good night," I echo, returning the peck.

———

I wake up in a sweat. It's still early; the daylight is seeping through the closed shutters. I look for the familiar blue dresser, the large bay window, for my doll, Jackie, and our teddy bear, Alex, resting in the fat velvet armchair of my room in Mulhouse.

But my eyes fall on the narrow room, the shabby wallpaper, the bare window. We are in Paris.

Tuesday, October 1

It's the morning recess. I am glad to get away from the classroom to stretch my legs in the yard for a few minutes.

I am glad, too, that Maman walked my sisters and me to school this morning. It's our first day.

Now, I've always loved school, and I'm not at all worried about spelling: I know I can easily get a hundred. I'm not concerned about math either; I've never had any trouble figuring out such dumb questions as how long it takes for two trains traveling in opposite directions to meet. No, what bothers me is the idea of having to speak in front of twenty-five or more classmates in a French still colored with Alsatian inflections.

There are girls from other upper-grade classes in the schoolyard. I miss my sisters—I don't know anyone else yet—but I'm told that the girls from the lower grades have their break at a different time. The yard isn't large enough to hold everyone.

I like the yard. It's smaller than the one in Mulhouse—but then everything seems to be smaller in Paris. It has a few trees, and we are allowed to play ball and to run around within a certain area.

I also like the smock I'm wearing over my dress—light blue with a pocket on each side. It is the rule. It makes me feel a part of the school, even if I am new to it all. And of course, Maman welcomed the idea: She is such a stickler about keeping our dresses clean.

A bunch of girls are playing ball. Our teacher, Mlle Serin, is keeping an eye on all of us. She, too, wears a smock. She looks silly with her tight curls and her crimson red cheeks as she rushes around on her spike heels. But there she is, watching over us and blowing her whistle the minute anyone gets out of line.

I don't like to play ball or to run around and make a lot of noise. I prefer to talk or to play at quiet games.

"Are you from Alsace?" a blond girl with braids asks

me. "I am. My name is Odile Muller."

I know she is not in my class. She must have heard me talk to someone.

"Yes," I reply, eager for a new friend. "I used to live in Mulhouse. Where are you from?"

"We are from Strasbourg, but we've lived in Paris for over two years now. How long have you been here?"

"A little over two months," I tell her.

"My papa came here to help his brother run a garage. Why did you move to Paris?" she asks.

I can't help casting my eyes down and lowering my voice.

"Because we're Jewish. We *had* to leave."

I wish she hadn't asked. I wish I hadn't told her.

"My papa says that there are too many Jews, and that the war is the best thing that's happened to Alsace," Odile says. She speaks without so much as a wink—a real parrot.

"Let's play *marelle*," she says in the next breath. "Come on, we still have time."

I swallow my hurt. What else am I to do?

I follow her and start to play hopscotch, but my heart isn't in it. I think of something Maman has said: As Jews, we are being forced into a war much worse than that between France and Germany. We can't tell our friends from our enemies.

———

Until we heard that the Germans were going to take over Alsace, my understanding of what a Jew was had been rather vague. True, I had always felt a warm bond with anyone whom I found to be "one of us," as Maman sometimes said. But above all, being Jewish meant being different. For example, unlike the other people of our town—who went to church for the most part—our family and friends went to the synagogue to celebrate the High Holy Days of Rosh Hashanah and Yom Kippur. How I hated being forced to sit with the children and the women—away from Papa and his friends! They had to drag me back more than once from the men's quarters.

In school, too, I was made to leave the class while everyone else was given religious—that is, Catholic—instruction. I also vaguely sensed that a lot of exotic food was forbidden to us for reasons I didn't quite understand, but that never bothered me. I was perfectly content with our home cooking, and I never trusted the looks of the lobsters, crabs, and shrimp displayed in the fancy shops. Though I did feel a little excluded from the Christmas celebrations; I was always terribly envious of our neighbor's musical tree.

There *had* been that unpleasant incident on Good Friday of last year. In the middle of jumping rope a little neighbor of mine had said to me: "You know, don't you, that it was the Jews who killed Jesus?"

Baffled, I looked at her for a couple of seconds. What's that got to do with me? I had wanted to snap, but I decided to continue as if nothing had happened. Of course, I had heard of Jesus; everyone knew he was very important to the Catholics. But I also vaguely knew that what the little girl was talking about had happened quite a long time ago and in a country far, far away—and it had to do with people who were total strangers to me. Besides, I quickly decided, it couldn't be *that* important since we had never talked about it at home. So I forgot about it.

Why all this fuss, then, I wondered, when Papa told us we would have to leave Mulhouse? It seemed as if nothing could be so catastrophic as to make us leave our home.

"I was hoping that the three of you would be spared the hardship your mother and I—and certainly Grand'-mère—had to go through in the past," he had explained to us girls at the dinner table on the night we learned we were leaving.

As Papa spoke Maman was nodding her head in agreement, tracing with her fork an invisible pattern on the tablecloth.

"Being a Jew is not just staying away from pork, or going to the synagogue on Rosh Hashanah," Papa continued. "It means never being totally welcome anywhere. Oh—how do you explain something that doesn't make any sense?"

Papa stopped and scratched his forehead.

"I think I'd better start from the beginning," he said, sighing. "You see, throughout the ages, Jews have always been blamed for the hard times, no matter where they happened to have settled down. In some countries their homes—sometimes their entire neighborhoods—were burned down. Everything that went wrong was their fault. Why do you think I left Poland—and then Hungary? The same goes for your mother. She left Hungary with her parents and sisters to find a freer, better life. Her two brothers were already married, so they decided to stay. Am I right, Sarah?" Papa asked Grand'-mère.

"Unfortunately yes. . . . God knows how often we have been accused of taking food from people's mouths, stealing their jobs, or causing them to be poor," Grand'-mère said.

"So why can't we just tell them that it's a bunch of lies?" Denise protested.

"It's not that simple, and there's nothing more unreasonable than people who are convinced that we're the cause of their bad circumstances."

I looked at Grand'mère in disbelief: She knows so much, and yet she is usually so quiet.

"France, you see," Papa went on, "has always been known to believe in freedom and equality, so we thought we'd be safe here—as did many. We were beginning to feel at home. When I bought my tailor shop two years ago, I guess I thought it would last forever. A Jew always hopes . . . and hope is stubborn!"

"It sure dies hard!" Maman whispered, as if to herself.

"We certainly didn't expect this maniac, Adolf Hitler, to rise to power and start trouble for us all over again!" Papa added.

"Who's Adolf Hitler?" Lily wanted to know.

"He's a dangerous individual who spends all his energy hating the Jews and spreading his hate around. For reasons that are beyond me he's managed to become a very important figure in Germany." Papa went on to explain about Germany's plans to annex Alsace. "They have asked that the Jews leave Alsace—for our own protection, as they put it. Now, isn't that solicitous of them?" Papa continued, his voice growing louder and louder.

"This Hitler sounds crazy to me! Why doesn't anyone stop him?" I insisted.

"Because he's dangerous only to the Jews," Papa said. "What's so disturbing is that no one seems to mind his kind of thinking. In Germany, as I said, he's very popular obviously, since he's practically running the whole country!"

"How can you tell a Jew from someone who isn't? We could stay here if we didn't tell anyone," Denise suggested.

"There are ways," Maman said. "They'll *find* ways, believe me. Besides, we've never kept the fact from anyone!"

"But why can't the French protect us from the Germans?" I questioned, more and more uneasy. "We're French and this *is* French territory, after all!"

"You're right, technically," Papa agreed. "But now that France is losing the war, the Germans want Alsace back."

Papa was beginning to look very drawn, so I decided to keep to myself the question that I was dying to ask: How could anyone force our family—and other families just like ours—out of the only home we knew?

It was *our* home! *Our* belongings! *Our* life!

What gave *them* the right?

Friday, October 4

Class has just started. I notice a girl sitting a few desks away from mine. She looks familiar. Have I seen her in the neighborhood? When marketing?

She is just as quiet as I am, I notice.

When, moments later, she turns her head and looks at me, I smile. She returns the compliment.

In the afternoon, quite naturally, we sit next to each another. She is pretty, with short, baby-fine reddish hair, a pug nose in a perfectly round face, and big brown eyes. Definitely *not* Jewish, I tell myself.

"What's your name?" I ask, gathering all my courage.

"Gabrielle Larmurier—but they call me Pépée. And you?"

"My name is Renée Roth," I say.

I find out that Pépée lives a few doors down from me, at the corner of Rue de Dunkerque. It *has* to be a good sign. I also learn that she is two years older than I, that she is good in arithmetic, that she likes to sing and to read—and that she plays the piano.

I have a friend!

I suddenly don't care about my Alsatian accent and the rest: I know I am going to like my new school. I am becoming a well-rounded Parisian!

At home that evening Papa tells us he's learned that while Mulhouse can pride itself on a city hall that is a historical landmark, a town gate that dates back to the Middle Ages, and its famous storks' nests, our Paris *arrondissement* contains no less than the Opéra, the Trinité Church, the Folies-Bergère, and the city hall—where Napoleon got married.

I know we are also within walking distance of the Sacré-Cœur basilica, the Place du Tertre made famous by so many painters, and the world-famous nightclub, the Moulin-Rouge.

We could have done much worse!

Saturday, October 5

I never miss an opportunity to wait in line at the food stores. In the absence of a radio set it is the best way to learn about what's going on. Besides, with the ever-increasing rationing, it's the only way to be sure to bring some food home.

The other day I was waiting for my turn at the dairy store. I knew it would be a while, as the store was still closed. Deliveries were expected any minute.

One of the housewives, determined to wait comfortably, had settled into the folding chair she had brought along and was chatting with her neighbors.

"Believe me, getting from the Occupied Zone into the Free Zone is no cinch! You need a pass, and they check your luggage and your handbag inside out! And do you know that it has taken every bit of two months for me to get a letter from my sister in Dax! Isn't it something?"

"No doubt," a lady next to her replied. "I'm not saying that things are running smoothly . . . but, as my husband says, we must be grateful that the Germans have agreed to sign an armistice and to occupy only half of our country!"

"Do you really think so?" commented a third lady. "Now that our Government has been transferred to Vichy, all of us are under the Germans' thumb, for sure!"

———

Papa shows me on the map the new boundaries of France, with Vichy as capital. And then what? I wonder. An armistice—how long is it supposed to last? Does that mean that we no longer have to worry about our enemy?

I try to read the paper, but I feel a little lost with all the complicated names and words I don't always understand. Besides, they say that you can't really trust the press: The Germans are censoring everything in the news!

Thank goodness for our neighbor to the left, Mme

Chavignat. She is lively and cheerful and she has a loud, catching laugh. I love to listen to her talk. She has definite ideas about everything. At first, Papa and Maman were a bit cautious around her—if you're Jewish, you can't help it—but it didn't last. "It's quite simple," she had said the first time Maman had invited her in for coffee. "In France nowadays it's no more the left against the right, or the capitalists against the working class. Either you are for Vichy—that is, for the collaboration between France and Germany—or you are not."

"Frankly I'm not all that sure myself," Papa remarks. "Maréchal Pétain is a nice man—a hero of the Great War. But all I ask is that he protect the Jews."

"Well, it certainly goes without saying!" snaps our neighbor with a catching conviction.

Tuesday, October 8

My sisters and I are quite delighted now about school. We were, in fact, in for a pleasant surprise.

The school is located not very far from Pigalle, the area where—as our neighbor to the right, Mme Lelièvre, warned us—"ladies of the evening dance in the nude and even try to lure men." It is rather exciting for Denise, Lily, and me to walk four times a day through these very streets where a mysterious and forbidden life takes place at night.

As everyone knows, the neighborhood is rather quiet—almost sleepy—in the daytime. Instead of rushing home as Maman always asks us to, we linger by some of the nightclubs to look at the 3-D nude pictures, or we stop at some of the fancy shops: shoestores showing glittering spike heels and velvet slippers with huge pom-poms, or lingerie boutiques featuring black and red underwear rimmed with soft feathers.

Together we try to figure out which part of the body a flimsy piece of fabric is meant to cover—or to show off.

Sometimes our laughs stop abruptly: We think we recognize a passerby. There's no way we are going to tell Papa or Maman about it—we don't want to be sent to another school!

Wednesday, October 9

"What's playing tonight?"

I know that Papa's question is the prelude to a pleasant evening at the movies. The program changes every Wednesday. Going to the cinema—Grand'mère staying home, of course—has become a favorite family activity and my new hobby. When I look at the screen, I forget about everything.

I don't even mind the occasional power failure, during which people make jokes and stomp their feet in the dark—except when we don't get to see the end of the movie!

Once in a while we even spot our landlord, M. Deschamps, a distinguished but extremely quiet gentleman. He greets us from a distance, barely nodding his head and moving his lips. But his presence is enough. It makes my evening complete.

There are three light knocks at the door.

"Who could it be at this hour?" Papa wonders, wiping his mouth with his napkin.

Lily rushes to open the door.

It is Mme Giroud, our concierge, out of breath from having climbed the five flights.

"Sorry to have to interrupt your dinner," she apologizes, refusing to come in. "The light is showing through your curtains, you know. They've been cracking down on us and giving out tickets right and left. . . . Excuse me," she continues, entering the living room and taking a closer look at the window. "No . . . I'm sorry to say that these curtains won't do. You'll have to find something else! Sorry . . . it's the rule, as you well know! You are not the only ones, by the way. Again, my apologies for interrupting your dinner. Good night—and *bon appétit!*" she says as she dashes out the door.

"She is absolutely right," Maman remarks. "I'm going to get a sheet—quick—before we get a second warning!"

"We can't even have a quiet dinner in this house! I'm starving!" I protest.

"So's everyone else!" Papa reminds me. "Remember, Mme Giroud has come all the way up to warn us and to keep us from getting into trouble. The least we can do is what we were supposed to do in the first place!"

Grumbling, I am forced to agree with Papa. The idea of the blackout is to get the whole city pitch-black to keep the English planes from knowing where they are. It must be strictly observed.

"Don't you think that a blanket would even do a better job?" Grand'mère suggests to Maman.

"Good idea!" Maman runs to the bedroom and returns with a blanket. Papa helps her to hang it across the window.

We sit around the table again—finally. But Papa fidgets with his fork; he can't seem to decide which piece of meat to pick.

"If you want to know," he says, moving his plate away from him, "I don't mind their insisting on a blackout. I am much more worried about the new rule they came up with, which orders every Jew to register with the police. It's no big deal, people may say, but I don't like their making such a fuss about us. And I hate the way they stamped the word JEW on our identity cards."

"I know . . . I know." Maman sighs. "Come on, eat now. . . . The food is getting cold. Don't get yourself upset over something you can't change. We've lived through other bad times; we'll live through this one too!"

But I can't take my eyes off Papa's fork, which still won't pick up any food. I don't feel hungry either.

Why can't they forget about us and leave us alone, once and for all?

Saturday, October 19

Papa has a new friend too: Max Rosenberg. They met the day they registered at the police station.

Papa tells us that Max is a tailor also. But more important, I think, is that he, too, likes to play cards.

Maman is not crazy about the friendship: She never liked Papa playing cards. It takes him away from us, she complains. She does not mind his having a game with M. Schrifft and M. Klein when we visit them on a Sunday: At least Maman can talk about the good old days with Mme Schrifft and Mme Klein. They are sisters and live next door to each other, and she knows them both from Hungary. The three of us are perfectly content to play with Jeannot Schrifft and his cousin Germaine, and to stuff our faces with poppy-filled pastries. Jeannot's two older brothers are usually there, too, but they are too old to play with us kids.

M. Rosenberg lives around the corner from us on Rue du Delta with his wife and four children. Most of the time Papa goes to their apartment to play. It is much bigger than ours, and they have a special table set against the window just for that purpose.

But tonight M. Rosenberg has come to visit Papa.

I can tell something is wrong. He refuses to take his coat off and to sit down. I'm glad that he gets right to the point.

"What do you think of the ordinance that requires that all Jewish firms be registered? I don't have my own firm, of course, but I do work from my home. I just wonder if the ruling applies to me or not."

Papa suddenly looks very tired.

"Something else to worry about," he says with a sigh. "They just won't leave us alone, will they? I wish I knew what to tell you. My boss isn't Jewish, thank goodness. At least I don't have to worry about that."

"But what should I do?" Papa's friend pleads. "They took away my citizenship, and now we are stateless— which means that they can put us in forced residence anytime they wish! What do you think?" he now asks Maman.

"I don't know what to tell you. You're damned if you do and damned if you don't!" she sighs. "It's probably best to inquire and to go by the rules. I just don't like the whole idea."

I don't like it either. I don't like it one bit.

Wednesday, October 23

Pépée tells me that she, too, has lived her own exodus last June, when Paris was declared "open city" and the Germans marched in.

"Everyone panicked and fled to the country—we didn't know what to expect from the Germans. Maman and I went to our cousins' in Vierzon. It took us forever to get there. The train stopped all the time. And you should have seen the roads we crossed: They were full of women pushing baby carriages, people walking along horse-drawn carriages or pushing wheelbarrows. . . . Everybody was running away—no one really knew from what or where to. Then one day they said on the radio that everything would be all right and asked everybody to go back home!"

"Did you get to see the Germans? Are there many here?" I wonder aloud, my heart pounding at the thought.

"I don't think that there are that many in Paris—I mean, troops in uniforms or anything like that. There are some, though. Maman says that they are mostly high-ranking officials—like the Gestapo."

"What is the Gestapo?" I ask.

"It is the German police." Pépée suddenly stops and looks straight at me. "Why are you so interested in the Germans?"

I lower my voice a bit. "Because the Germans don't like Jews!"

She opens her eyes wide, trying to understand, and then says as if it were the most natural thing in the world: "So you're Jewish. So what? You can't let that get you down!" She then takes my arm, and we resume our walk.

"At home we are very fond of Jews," she confides. "Maman always says that they are studious, hardworking people. Our neighbors, the Cohens, are Jewish too. We get along very well—Jeannette Cohen is my friend. You'll see!"

If we weren't in the middle of the street, I would fall on her neck and give her a big hug!

Still, whether the lousy *boches* are in uniforms or not, I am in no hurry to come face to face with any of them.

Friday, October 25

Mme Chavignat is all excited: She swears she spotted the word *confiance*, or *trust*, written in big letters in the sky by an English plane.

She has a new idol, Général de Gaulle, who has refused to surrender and fled to London with a bunch of Free French to continue the war.

43

In school, though, it is Maréchal Pétain who counts: His picture is all over the place. His eyes are very blue, and I must admit, he does look like a nice grandfather.

Still, since then, I keep watching the sky for more words from the English.

Thursday, October 31

"Let's try to skate while holding hands!" I suggest.

My neighbor, Jocelyne Chavignat, and Pépée and I are returning from the Square d'Anvers, racing down Avenue Trudaine on our roller skates.

Maman doesn't mind my going up and down the street—we stick mostly to the wide sidewalks. Nowadays, with the gasoline shortage, there are barely any cars; you need a special permit. Even buses have dwindled down to a very few.

I suddenly freeze: Just a few yards away, a tall man has emerged from Rue Gérando. He wears a military uniform—not the familiar one of the French, but one of a darker color, complete with cape and boots. It is no doubt a German officer, like those in the newsreels.

"A *boche*!" I try to say, but the words get stuck in my throat. I am scared to death.

"Come on, Renée! It's only a German!" Pépée says, pulling me by the sleeve. "It's not the first one I've seen!"

"Well, it's *my* first!" I manage to articulate, still rooted to the ground and unable to take my eyes off the man.

"They don't bite, you know!" my friend teases. "Just ignore him. Come on, let's go and catch up with Jocelyne!"

She takes my hand, and without a word we begin to skate.

Thursday, November 7

A long, plaintive sound tears the evening air. I shudder. It is an air raid, like in Mulhouse.

I shut my geography book, thinking, This is it.

Maman has stopped putting away the dishes, Papa's face emerges from behind his newspaper, my sisters drop their game of Nain Jaune.

I ask, close to panic: "What are we going to do?"

"First get Grand'mère. And you, Denise, run down to get your uncle, aunt, and cousins. But above all, let's keep calm," Maman says.

"Don't leave without me! I'll be right back." Denise rushes out the door.

The bedroom door opens, and Grand'mère walks in. "What's happening? I heard the siren."

"It's an air raid. Sit down . . . here," Maman suggests, taking Grand'mère by the hand and leading her to a chair. "Since we left Mulhouse, we have not had to worry about this sort of thing. What should we do, Oscar?"

But there's no time to wonder. The bell rings. It's Mme Lelièvre.

"Did you hear?" she asks, first turning to Papa and then to Maman. "If you ask me, I think our best bet is to rush to the cellar! Suppose a bomb falls on our building—one never knows. We're better off underground, wouldn't you say?"

I am getting more and more scared. Bombings are no joke—I've seen them in the newsreels. "They're not going to bomb us, are they, Maman?" I ask.

"I hope not. Of course, if there's an air raid, it means there are planes flying around, and there's always that risk."

By now Mme Chavignat is showing her head in the doorway. "My husband thinks it's best to go to the cellar. We certainly can't run to the métro. We're not allowed out!"

Besides, I think, if we do, we may get caught in the curfew and not be able to get out until tomorrow morning, since the métro stops running around eleven.

"That's what *I* said," Mme Lelièvre points out. "Let's hurry down, then; we can't waste any time. Mme Roth," she adds, sensing Maman's hesitation, "I have a folding chair for your mother. Let me get it."

"All right, then. . . . I'll get my husband and daughter. And I'll take a flashlight along," says Mme Chavignat.

I'm *really* scared now. In Mulhouse the shelters were all underground. But our cellar here was not built as a shelter. Why, if the building collapses, we'll be buried alive! I tell myself. But I don't have time to ponder it.

"Let's hurry now!" Papa urges.

I say to myself: "If we are to die, we may as well die together"—and I rush to join the others.

I am grateful about one thing, though: Here at least they don't force us to wear those awful gas masks.

I shudder at the memory. I still remember the sickening smell, the feeling of choking. We waited in line to receive the masks, with dozens of families before us in front of a desk set up in the middle of a large, poorly lit gymnasium. Rubber masks were piled up on a nearby table, looking oddly like skeleton heads, with their heavy hoses running down from the nose like the trunk of an elephant. The mere smell made me feel like puking.

When my turn came—right after Papa and Maman—I prayed that no one would hear the wild beating of my heart.

The instructor tried to slip the mask over my head, like a pullover. Afraid to make a wrong move, I froze and stopped breathing. After a few seconds—they seemed an eternity—I ripped it away from my face and over my head, trembling and breaking into a cold sweat.

"This thing doesn't work!" I yelled. "I can't breathe with it on!"

What I had really wanted to say was that I preferred to die, period, rather than choke with the mask on—which I was sure to do.

But I had to get used to it; there was no way around it. The air raids became more and more frequent. Our best bet, we were told, was to rush to the closest shelter, or ABRI—which had quickly become the most common sign in our town.

In school, on the radio, we were constantly reminded that everyone *had* to have a gas mask and carry it at all times—just in case the enemy should use gas as a weapon, as they did during the Great War.

One evening, tired of having had to drag that thing around all day, I asked Maman, "Why do they have so many air raids, since nothing ever happens? And why drag along these masks that weigh a ton, since we never get to use them?"

Maman looked at me as if I had said something awful.

"Touch wood, quick, you silly girl," she exclaimed. "Be thankful that we've never had to!"

For Maman, talking about something is just like causing it to happen.

———

We are rushing down the five flights, Papa carrying the folding chair, Grand'mère tagging on to Maman's arm, Denise and the rest of the family dashing along behind. Other neighbors join us along the way, groping in the dark, giggling, darting their flashlights in one another's faces.

"Careful!" someone warns. "Don't play around with the light. The police will come after you. They can see us through the stairway windows!"

Let them joke and carry on, I think. The novelty will wear off soon enough.

Wednesday, November 13

I can't help watching the two other girls in class who are like me—that is, Jewish: Suzanne Blum and Feigie Langmann.

Suzanne is much older than any of us—by at least three years. She comes from Poland and is behind in her classes. But she is very smart and very sophisticated. She wears high heels and lipstick and everybody knows that she smokes cigarettes on the sly.

With Feigie, it's a different story. She always hides in the last row and keeps very quiet—except to answer the teacher's questions.

She is not pretty at all: Her face is too narrow, her chin too pointed, her eyes too closely set. Worst of all, her name is Feigie. It's risky enough to be a Jew these days without being saddled with a name that isn't a celebrated saint on the French calendar.

I feel sorry for her. Sometimes I try to be friendly and I smile at her.

But she always looks away.

Friday, November 15

It doesn't register at first. I am rushing back to school after lunch and I barely glance at the freshly painted black letters on the side of the corner building.

Then it hits me and I run back. My head hammers and my heart pounds as I read: KILL THE JEWS.

I can't keep it all to myself, and I drag Feigie and Suzanne back to the building after school.

"Don't pay attention to lunatics," Suzanne says with an easy shrug. "That's all they are, the people that write this nonsense—lunatics! I've seen these before. Papa says it will pass . . . it always does."

But Feigie can't dismiss the ugly, angry smudges so easily. "Just the same," she says quietly, "I don't like it one bit. Things like that give me the shivers!"

I can only think: *Kill* someone, simply because he's a Jew?

Friday, November 22

Pépée introduces me to Jeannette Cohen, her next-door neighbor, during recess this morning. Finally! She's been talking enough about her.

She is about my age and not all that pretty. She has a rather big nose and a receding chin. But she has long straight hair—lucky her!—and a beautiful smile.

Jeannette's eyes, it is obvious, are red from crying.

"I'm sorry!" she says, apologizing, and her face lights up as she attempts a smile. "It's Papa. Ask Pépée . . . I am not permitted to play after school or after dinner like everybody else. He wants me home, helping Maman or watching over Riri, my little brother."

Her voice trails off in a sniffle.

"There, there!" Pépée says, looking for a hankie. "Your papa is not *that* bad. He hollers a lot, that's true, but that's just his way."

Pépée must see all fathers as she remembers hers: perfect. You can tell she hasn't had one in a long time. Jeannette's father doesn't sound that nice to me!

I watch my friend as she continues to comfort Jeannette. I hate to admit it, but I feel a little jealous. I am envious of their living next door to each other, of their mothers being good friends. I have to remind myself that I get to spend much more time with Pépée. We're in the same class, we walk to school every day, and we get together often to do our homework.

Friday, November 29

"We need some more coal, Renée. We're running low."

I make a face: I know only too well that we won't be warm unless I go to that awful cellar.

"We should consider ourselves lucky to have any coal at all these days," Papa reminds us.

Winter in Paris chills you to the bone. I don't remember ever being so cold in Mulhouse, even though we were close to the mountains. Of course, there we had a large kitchen stove, which would spit out flames to color our cheeks and warm up our hearts whenever you took the lid off. Long woolen socks and mittens—and, I guess, a more carefree life—took care of the rest.

The only warm spot in our apartment now is the living room, where the enamel stove presides. We never leave it except to go to bed.

I hate to go to the cellar, and I curse all the way down. "I wish it would hurry up and get warm!" I mumble to myself, shuddering at the odd sounds of my own shovel digging into our *briquettes*, scared of the strange shadows cast on the wall by the candle I'm holding tight with my other hand. The silly place is full of drafts, and I don't want the light to go out.

I rush out as fast as my heavy pail lets me.

At least I can look forward to stopping at our concierge's door for a minute or two before starting the long climb up the five flights. Mme Giroud is small-boned and has a high-pitched voice. From a distance she can be mistaken for a young girl. She's good-natured and doesn't mind that I pop my head in at her door a good dozen times a day.

"There's no mail for you this afternoon!" she says with infinite patience.

The truth is, I love to peep into the Girouds' apartment every chance I get. It's even smaller than ours, and for that moment, I feel so much more fortunate.

Nothing escapes Mme Giroud's attention—especially strangers entering or leaving the building.

"Mme Roth," she says when Maman and the three of

us return from shopping, "Mme Larmurier came to see you this afternoon. I told her that you'd be back by five or six o'clock. . . . By the way, there's a letter for you from Chambéry. . . . I believe it's from your cousin Mme Broder. . . . Isn't that where she lives? I don't know why it should have taken six days for a letter to get here!"

"A concierge certainly gets to know you better than your father confessor or your best friend!" Mme Chavignat laughs.

I wish I could find it funny, too, but all I can think of is that we're back to being watched again. What if things get to be really bad for Jews—if we have to flee in a hurry again, like in Mulhouse—and Mme Giroud turns against us?

Maman laughs at the idea. "For a little girl you are much too pessimistic. You've got to be more positive about things! Mme Giroud is very nice, and so are our neighbors."

Granted, there's nothing wrong with the Chavignats, or with our other neighbor, Mme Lelièvre, who keeps to herself most of the time and barely greets us in the hallway.

But who's to say?

———

Maman is waiting for me at the top of the stairs. "We'll have baked apples for dessert," she promises. I know it is her way of thanking me for the unpleasant chore.

I welcome the idea: I love to sit by the stove and watch the apples turn gold, then brown; to suck in the delicious smell—and to forget about the cellar for two whole days.

Most of the food is rationed now. Still, sometimes you can't even get what you're entitled to: Eggs, for instance, are impossible to find, and we haven't seen any potatoes for ages. As for meat, you're better off not counting on it.

The stores are open for business only part of the day, and they close as soon as the merchandise is sold. We wait in line for an hour, sometimes two, hoping that this time we won't leave empty-handed.

At home we have an understanding: If Maman is gone for more than an hour, we go to her rescue.

Too often, after we've stood in the cold tapping our frozen feet, the storekeeper says: "Sorry! That's all we have for today. Come back tomorrow!"

"They're playing games, the bastards! They can't possibly have sold all their stock," Maman fumes, breaking her own rule of no cursing and no slang. "I bet they're only selling a trickle of merchandise so that they can sell the rest under the counter!"

As always, Papa gives people the benefit of the doubt. "Perhaps people are afraid of a famine and are stocking up as much as they can lay their hands on. . . . I've seen it happen in my time!"

I am not angry at the merchants, but I think it's unfair that we don't have anyone in the provinces to help us out—like Pépée, who gets parcels from her cousins in Vierzon and Gien full of oil, cheese, and sausages; or Mme Chavignat, whose many sisters and brothers take turns in bringing food to her.

At home soup has become our staple: Maman makes

enormous tureens of leek, cabbage, lentil, even pumpkin soups—and, of course, potato soup when we are lucky enough to find any potatoes.

The one thing that is still easy to find is kidney—or tripe; I never remember which is which. I suppose it's because the Germans don't care for it. Neither do we, for that matter.

In the meantime we are getting used to rutabaga—and to that awful smell that lingers for hours after it's been cooked. The other day the owner of a vegetable stand refused to sell us a lousy bunch of carrots unless we bought some of her rutabagas too!

Friday, December 6

In class today Mlle Serin tries to explain the food shortage.

"We are—we were—one of the richest countries in the world, thanks to our colonies. We imported wine from Algeria and oil, cocoa, sugar, rice, and rubber from other colonies," she says. "We also imported meat from Argentina, wool from Australia, coal from Germany, and gasoline from the Middle East. But the war has, of course, stopped all that traffic—or at least blocked most of it."

Michèle Gaudron raises her hand. She never misses a chance to get attention.

"Yes, Michèle?" the teacher asked.

"Papa says that the *fridolins* also take a fair share of our crops and other things."

Mlle Serin turns her face to the blackboard to hide her smile.

"There's no doubt that our invaders make themselves at home here," she concedes. "But please, Michèle, from now on in class could you refrain from calling the Germans *fridolins?*"

"Yes, Mademoiselle, I'll try," Michèle replies.

Everybody in class laughs, except me. I think that *fridolin* or even *boche* is much too nice a nickname for the Germans. I wish we could come up with something mean and ugly-sounding—as ugly as *youpin*, which means "kike."

But Papa says that tit for tat gets you nowhere.

1941

The best thing about school is getting there. Now that my sisters have their own friends, Pépée picks me up every morning. There's so much to talk about, we don't mind the long walk.

She tells me about her older brother, Gilbert, who has been living with their uncle and aunt in Liège, Belgium, since the beginning of the war. She tells me mostly about her mother, who hardly lets Pépée out of her sight since her father died nearly six years ago.

"I know my mother is not mean or anything, but I can't stand her worrying about me all the time—about my walking to school, about my having the right kind of friends, about my grades. At least she trusts me with you and your family. She is convinced that all Jews are sensitive, intelligent—and often very rich!"

"Well, *we* are not rich, that's for sure," I say, laughing.

I think in a flash: Who's to say? We might well have been by now—had we stayed in Alsace, but I keep the thought to myself.

"But you *are* one of the smartest in class," Pépée replies. "I bet Maman hopes that you will rub off on me."

We giggle. But I giggle the loudest: If either of us is rubbing off on the other, it is Pépée on me!

Her two years over me give her a definite head start— not to mention her well-developed breasts and her tiny waistline. Besides, she knows much more about boys, babies, and what happens in the dark than my sisters and me put together. I bet that's why Guy Le Quintrec and Michel Lesueur of the boys' school, Lycée Rollin, like to keep her company.

She has come home with me this afternoon, and she's telling me about something we never discuss at home— making babies and all the rest.

As usual, my friend and I are looking out of the window, our arms resting on the sill. Maman insisted on letting in some fresh air for a few minutes and, confident that we are chatting about girlish things, she has left us alone.

Eager to pursue a discussion we started yesterday, I whisper, "Are you saying that a man and a woman lie in bed together to make a baby?"

"That's right. The woman has an egg and the man has something that helps it become a baby."

"But how does it work? How do the two things get together? Do the man and the woman have to touch?"

"Of course, silly! Certain parts of the body *have* to touch! How else could it happen? And that's why the girls have their periods and the boys their *zizis*."

Now, I know as well as the next person that boys and girls are built differently, but what has one to do with the other? I wonder.

I try to picture Papa and Maman lying close together in their large bed—they do it every night. Then what? I can't imagine anything beyond that. Still, I reason, babies grow in their mother's bellies. That I know for a fact. They have to get there somehow. But touching seems so chancy. . . . What if you touch the wrong part? What if you miss it?

"And kissing is part of it too. They say it makes it easier," Pépée continues.

I think of the many kissing couples we see daily—in the street, on park benches, in the subway, in the movies. They don't seem to be worried about having babies.

Still, does that mean I won't be able to look forward to kissing when the time comes?

I feel crushed. I don't want to hear any more about it—or to grow up, for that matter!

"It's getting cold, don't you think? Let's close the window. You don't have to tell me *all* about it today!" I say.

Just the same I continue to thank my lucky stars for putting Pépée on my path.

Saturday, February 22

For the last few days it's been bitterly cold. . . . They say that it hasn't been this cold since possibly the Middle Ages. They don't have to go back *that* far to convince me!

The trouble is, the supply of coal comes and goes. We heat up the apartment whenever we can—which is not every day. In the papers they tell us how to keep warm, like insulating our shoes and clothes with layers of newspapers.

I may as well sleep alone on these cold nights. Every time I try, ever so gently, to slip my leg against Denise's, she screams for dear life. I'm sure that Lily wouldn't give me such a hard time: She doesn't mind the cold that much!

Saturday, March 15

Today is Papa's birthday. He's over fifty—that's all he'll tell me. I worry too much about his age, he says.

For a long time I resented Papa's age. But then one day I found out he had had a life before us. He had been married a long time ago, but his wife died in childbirth—as did the baby. I learned about it by chance when I was perhaps six years old, from someone who had known the lady. I felt very sad for the lost baby—maybe it had been a boy—and I wanted to know more about it. "Maman, is it true that Papa was married before us?" I had asked.

I could tell from Maman's expression that she didn't expect the question. "That happened a very long time ago. . . . These things are best forgotten," she had said.

The words were like a door slammed in my face. I decided to leave it at that.

But I looked differently at Papa from then on and forgave him for being so much older than Maman.

At least it got him exempted from being called into the

Army to fight the war far away from us. Maman says that the fact that he has three young children helped too.

The family got together tonight. Aunt Fanny brought some of her puff pastries: "All they take is a little flour, a little bit of oil, a dash of sugar—and a lot of love," she says.

The family has been getting together practically every evening for about a week now. Papa has not even gone to his friend Max Rosenberg's to play cards. Sometimes he plays a quick game of gin rummy with my uncle—to do him a favor, I think—while Maman, Aunt Fanny, and Grand'mère chat in Hungarian. They all get serious and sit around the table and begin to whisper until they get into a disagreement. Then they stop, glance at me, and start all over again.

I think they're whispering so I won't hear. I can make out quite a few Hungarian words now—many more than Denise and Lily. It has to do with the Free Zone—that's all I know.

Whatever it is, it's driving me crazy. They forget I'm going to be ten in a few months—old enough to be treated like a thinking member of the family.

My sisters and cousins don't mind going in to the bedroom to play, as they're told, but I stay right here in the living room, pretending to be reading.

If something is going on, I've got to find out what it is!

Thursday, March 20

Tonight, as Maman is preparing dinner in the kitchen, Mme Chavignat rushes in—I guess she just can't wait to talk to Maman. I make believe I'm busy with my homework, but I am positive I hear our neighbor mention Général de Gaulle and Radio-Londres.

I can't blame her for wanting to keep that to herself. From what Pépée says many Parisians—and that includes her and her mother—try to listen on the sneak to the BBC every evening at 9:15.

They use short-wave radio and can hear Général de Gaulle in spite of the static. But everybody is scared to death of being caught and reported to the *Kommandanteur,* the Nazi command in France.

"Do you really think that we can believe in what they are telling us?" Maman asks. "With the Channel between us, how can the English fight off the Germans?"

A little later Maman confides—after getting us to swear that we won't tell a soul—that the Général has asked the Parisians not to give up hope and to write *V* for *Victory* wherever we can. Does he really believe in victory, then? I wonder.

Friday, March 21

Well, it turns out Mme Chavignat was right after all. The BBC must have hundreds of listeners. There are *V*'s all over town! This morning, Pépée and I spot three just on the way to school. We even see VIVE DE GAULLE and a Cross of Lorraine!

I am full of hope again! I could use some—especially after having heard from a girl in a higher grade that the school has been ordered to do away with any book or manual that has been written by Jews—like the history book by Mallet and Isaac.

How stupid and petty can you get?

This evening, when I take the garbage down, I make sure there is no one in the yard and the corridor—and I draw a *V* on the side of the door, right underneath the doorbell, with a rainbow next to it.

Friday, April 4

Ersatz products are everywhere, from artificial sugar to fake tobacco to substitute coffee.

At home Maman offers us concentrated grape sugar—sticky like anything—or suggests that we suck on an artificially sweetened candy to make our herbal teas more drinkable.

Maman and Mme Chavignat are making do with a cup of Viandox bouillon now—our last find; it is the next best thing to a soup, and it does warm you up.

Everyone has come up with his own *Système D,* or do-it-yourself system: Papa exchanges our wine tickets for cigarettes or oil from the Chavignats.

In school they give us cookies with casein—which I hate. I swap them for chocolate bars. Suzanne Blum barters hers for lipstick.

Today I notice a new brand of chocolate at the dairy store. Mme Durand sees me stare at the label while I'm waiting for my turn.

"This is new stuff!" she explains. "It contains vitamins—government orders. It's about time that they do something about the food shortage!"

"So what good is it?" an old man in front of me

remarks, suddenly coming to life. He is all bundled up, except for his shiny bald head.

The words, to my surprise, are coming from M. Minard, a retired postal worker—and a steady customer—who rarely speaks except to his dog, a perfectly ugly boxer.

"What good is it—you tell me!—if our government turns out cigarettes that contain no tobacco, leather that bears no resemblance to the material, and so on? Every time I hear the word *national* linked to anything, it means that it's crap! It only hurts our pride as Frenchmen!

"Ah! Our Great War was nothing like this, I assure you! Right, Nestor?" he adds in a much softer voice, pulling gently on the leash.

Long after he has gone, I wonder how anyone can prefer one war to another.

Wednesday, April 30

Maman says that our best bet these days to be on good terms with the shopkeepers is to get our food from the same store whenever possible. This way, they'll get to know us real well and maybe they'll let us in on the next shipment.

We go daily to the charcuterie Thévenin. Bare ropes hanging sadly from the ceiling, a stray terrine of pâté, a skimpy piece of ham, is all that's left of better days.

But from the minute Denise and I walk in to get our usual sausages today, I sense some unusual excitement.

"Isn't it a pity," an old lady is saying to the lady

standing on line next to her, "you can't find any tooth-
brushes! It's four times now that the pharmacy has asked
me to come back!"

"I'm not at all surprised. What about the milk? You
tell me: How can you expect a child to grow and get
strong on a quarter of a liter of milk a day?"

"Like I say, it was too good to last! That's for sure!"

M. Émile, another regular customer, grumbles when
told there's no ham left. I can't stand him. He never
smiles.

"What do you expect," he continues, "with so many
foreigners in our land? And I'm not referring to the
Germans, mind you! The few I've seen are real gentle-
men; they always give up their seats in the métro. Some
of us could certainly learn a lesson or two from them!
Besides, is it their fault if they won the war?"

He stops for a split second, as if to size up the people
waiting on line.

"No. . . . I'm referring to those people who weren't
even born here, who breathe our air and eat our food! *La
France aux français*—France for the French!"

"I'm glad someone's finally got the courage to say
how he feels," Mme Delorme exclaims. She sometimes
helps out the Thévenins during the busy hours of late
afternoon.

She has stopped serving the clients, and rests her hand
on her hip, obviously interested.

"Even if what M. Emile says makes sense, that's no
reason to stand here doing nothing!" Mme Thévenin
scolds. "Here! Why don't you weigh this slice of pâté for
Mme Pichard.

"There is some truth to what you're saying," she
continues, addressing M. Emile. "Come to think of it—

and counting only the shopkeepers nearby—there is the owner of the *parfumerie* across the street who is very pretty, but I'll be damned if I know where she comes from. . . . She has a half-baked Italian accent, but you can't be sure. And then there is the dry cleaner who's Armenian. Don't ask me to pronounce his name! Now, I have nothing against him, you understand. . . . He works hard and seems reasonably honest. And of course, there's the lingerie shop near Rue de Dunkerque, which is owned by Israelites." She pronounces the word as if it were in quotation marks.

Now a heavyset lady with a protruding jaw pipes in. "You can be damn sure that the Jews are not going hungry! They buy all their food on the black market. . . . They have all the money in the world. . . . Or else they have rich relatives. It's all the same! They come from God-knows-where, they can't even speak decent French, and they've got it made!"

I don't like her mean look or the angry words coming out of her mouth: She reminds me of a snake.

I feel my cheeks get hot. I wish I could strangle M. Emile with his scarf and yell to the old lady, "Stop it! Stop it! What you're talking about are lies! There was plenty of food before the war—with the Jews around. It's the Germans who are taking most of the food now! Everybody I know says so!"

But I'm scared, and I remind myself that I'm only a little girl who has no say in anything.

I clench my fist to contain my anger, but only manage to dig into my own flesh.

Denise kicks me for support.

"And what will it be for you, *mes petites?*" Mme Thévenin asks with a sugar-coated voice.

I bite my lips to keep from screaming, "It's none of your business, you two-faced witch!" and I dash out of the store, followed by my sister. She can keep her stupid sausages!

"What's wrong with her? What does she, what does M. Emile, have against foreigners and Jews? We haven't done anything to them! They act as if we were taking the food out of their mouths! God knows how hard Papa works to feed us all," Denise grumbles.

"What do they *all* have against Jews?" I ask, still shaky. "Including God, who doesn't do anything about it! You know, I really wonder about Papa and Maman sometimes. They keep telling us not to make any fuss, to try not to pay attention to anyone passing nasty remarks about the Jews. It's easy for them to say! I've had it with people telling lies and insulting us! Even Jews have limits."

"Well, Maman always says that there *is* a justice, and that means people will be punished in one way or another," Denise reasons.

"I certainly hope that someone up there is keeping score," I reply for Denise's sake.

I for one don't believe a word of it.

Wednesday May 21

I open the door with my usual greeting—"I'm starved!"—but there is no one in sight.

I dash to my parents' bedroom. There is Maman, lying on the bed, her face buried in the bedspread. She didn't even take the trouble of removing it. This is not at all like her.

Grand'mère is sitting next to her.

"What's wrong? Why are you lying on the bed? Are you sick?" My words rush out, but I'm so worried, they are mere whispers.

"What's wrong is that Uncle Maurice and Aunt Fanny are thinking of leaving Paris!" Maman says, her voice muffled by the cover.

I don't understand. Why would they want to leave now?

"But why? When?" I want to know.

"It's just that they're scared." Maman is sitting up now. I note that she has not been crying, but she looks worried and is rubbing the bedspread back and forth nervously. "They are talking about moving to the Free Zone. I'm terribly upset about the whole idea."

"But why the Free Zone? Aren't they better off being in Paris, like us?"

"Of course. And I would like for us to be together. Unfortunately we can't protect them from those anti-Jewish regulations that are hitting all the foreign Jews here. In the Free Zone at least there are no Germans—or if there are any, they leave the Jews alone."

Grand'mère is listening, her head bent.

"A friend of your uncle's was arrested last week," Maman continues. "And then two days ago Maurice and Fanny received a letter asking them to present themselves at the police station with the children, a set of clothes, and a blanket. Of course they won't! So they prefer to leave. I would, too, for sure. But what's going to happen to my sister?"

I wish I knew what to do to stop Maman from getting so upset.

"Nothing's going to happen to Fanny or to her family. They are doing something about it!" It's Grand'mère who is speaking now. Her face is turned toward Maman, her hand groping for Maman's hand. I notice her long fingers, her delicate nails, which Maman polishes every week.

"You mustn't worry yourself sick over that. You know how Fanny is. . . . She won't want to leave or do anything if she sees you in this state!"

"You're right, I'll do my best," Maman says in a little girl's voice. "But it's hard to pretend to be calm when everything is boiling inside!"

It *is* reassuring to see that Grand'mère—blindness and all—is still able to calm down Maman. Just the same I can't help wondering what would happen if we, too, had to leave Paris in a hurry—say, to hide somewhere or to flee to the Free Zone. Poor Grand'mère. No matter how brave she is, she can't possibly walk fast, let alone run. Maman would be a nervous wreck! Thank goodness we have Papa, who always manages to set things straight.

I walk toward the bed and sit down at Maman's feet, tailor style. "Maman, are you sure we are in no danger?"

"From what they say, we are not. Thank God, Papa and I are naturalized French—we have been for a long time. I did a smart thing, didn't I, insisting on filing for the papers? Everyone else in the family tried, but they gave up because of the impossible red tape and the endless waiting. Ask Grand'mère, she'll tell you!"

Grand'mère nods her head in agreement.

"Besides, the three of you are perfectly safe: You were born here!"

"And you, Grand'mère, are you French also?"

"No, I'm not. As your Maman says, they wanted too many papers that I didn't have or couldn't get. But at my age, and in my condition, who would want me?"

"Stop talking nonsense!" Maman scolds, adjusting Grand'mère's hair under her kerchief. "Whatever happens, you're going with us!"

I jump to my feet. "But what can happen to us?" I almost scream. "Will we have to leave too?"

"No, we won't. It's just a manner of speaking." Maman takes my hand. "You know how I am—sometimes I get carried away. The truth is, no matter how I hate the idea of my sister leaving, the Free Zone is still what's best. My cousins there, Paulette and Hélène in Chambéry and Périgueux, are doing fine—touch wood."

I ask for the last time—one more reassurance cannot hurt. "But you swear that they won't bother the French Jews?"

Maman smiles. "That's what they're saying. You've got to believe somebody!"

I wish I could share Maman's conviction. But then why don't they allow us—French Jews—to own a radio?

I really must think that one over!

Saturday, May 24

I can't wait for the recess this morning. I have to check out things with Feigie and Jeannette.

I decide to leave Suzanne out: She would probably shrug the whole thing off.

As soon as the bell rings I take Feigie by the hand and

69

explain that I have something important to discuss with her. But first we find Jeannette.

The three of us find a quiet corner.

"Have you heard of any Jews being arrested?" I ask.

"My uncle and aunt know someone who has been sent to a camp in the Loiret. And they've received a letter to report to the police. They're so scared now they want to leave Paris!"

"I haven't heard anything like that," Feigie says.

"I haven't either," Jeannette remarks. "My father says that they leave Jews alone as long as they don't break any rules. Anyway, he says he has good connections since he works for the French Army."

"That's funny. Papa, too, worked for the French Army—he made dozens and dozens of uniforms, just before we left Mulhouse," I exclaim, suddenly remembering. "But we still had to leave when the time came," I point out.

"But, anyway, my parents are naturalized French," I add. "Are yours?"

"I'm not sure," Feigie replies. "I know we come from Poland. I was about three when we came to Paris. I don't recall a thing about Poland, but my parents tell me that the Poles are very mean to the Jews. They say that the day they arrived in Paris was one of the happiest days of their lives!"

"Well, I can't tell you if my parents are French or not. All I know is that they were both born in Rumania, and that I was born right here, in Paris, at the Hôpital St. Louis," Jeannette informs us.

"Come to think of it," Feigie interrupts, "I remember now. My parents must have been naturalized, since the French took back their citizenship last year, when they changed the law—I'm not sure why. . . . My mother fought hand and foot to get it back, but nothing could be done!"

I can't bear to listen to all that. It makes me feel both scared and angry—especially scared at the thought of the French doing anything they damn well please with the Jews.

"What are you talking about?" I almost shout. "That's so unfair! Once you become French, it should be for keeps!"

"And what are the three of you so excited about?" A hand grabs my shoulder and I recognize Pépée's voice behind me. I'm glad that it is my friend who is snooping and no one else.

"Well, you, I guess, we can tell it to. We are trying to understand what's going on with Jews," I explain.

"My mother always says that if France is the first one to preach freedom and equality on paper, she manages to forget about it very quickly when it comes to the Jews," Pépée informs us. "I also heard her tell a neighbor that it was Maréchal Pétain—or someone in his government— who stated that the Jews could never be considered fully French—that there was something different about them. I think they used the word 'nonassimilable.' I sure don't like him anymore."

I'd never heard the word before, but it sounded mean to me.

Thursday, May 29

Maman is standing by the dining-room table, pressing. She flattens the garment with her left hand while her

71

right hand swiftly maneuvers the iron into the recesses of the ruffled sleeve.

She looks surprisingly young from the side, with her soft neckline and her short, wavy hair. She is humming *"C'est à Capri que je l'ai rencontré"*—"it was in Capri that I met him"—a sign that all's well for the moment.

I feel warm and cozy and, for once, I have her all to myself. I hate to admit it, sometimes I get very jealous of the attention she pays my sisters.

I am sitting next to her, leafing through my French History book, afraid to break the spell. But I must ask the question.

I clear my throat first. "Maman, what does *assimilable* mean?" I finally blurt out.

Surprised, she looks up. "It means that something can mix so well with something else that you can't tell the difference between the two. You sure come up with strange ones!" she adds, resting the iron for a minute, a puzzled expression on her face. "I never can figure out where you get your questions from."

"Pépée's mother says that Maréchal Pétain—and other people in the French government—believe that the Jews are not assimilable."

"For God's sake, don't go by what that old goat—or the others—are saying!"

"But why would anyone say such a thing if it isn't true? We aren't different from anyone else, are we?" I ask, wondering what on earth can be the difference between me and Pépée or Maman and Mme Chavignat—other than their accents and their tastes in food and clothes.

"Of course we aren't, silly. But a lot of people need to believe that we're an inferior race. It gives them an excuse to feel that they're better—and to blame us for all sorts of things.

"But don't let it get you down—ever!" she adds, reaching for my hair and smoothing it with her hand.

I wish we had more times together like these, just the two of us. She is so much more patient and affectionate when there's no one else around.

Her eyes suddenly brim with tears. "Remember," she says, continuing to smooth my hair, "no matter how bad things may seem sometimes, you never give up. Even if I cry, it doesn't mean that I don't continue to struggle and to hope. You must never despair. . . . Evil never wins out.

"And now get back to your homework!" she says, her old self again. "A good education is still your best guarantee for a future. No one can ever take that away from you!"

Deep inside I know that some things can never be taught in school. But obediently, I open the book and read from the beginning: "Once upon a time, France was called Gaul and its inhabitants the Gaulois. . . . "

Now, I know that my ancestors were not Gaulois, and that they didn't fight at Bouvines or Marignan. But, heck, I'm just as proud as any of my classmates of our brave heroes and kings. That's all the past *I* know.

Saturday, May 31

They're gone.

Uncle Maurice, Aunt Fanny, Raymond, and Fernand left early this morning to go to Moutiers.

In a few hours, God willing, they will be in the Free Zone—safe.

I couldn't bear to watch Aunt Fanny and Maman standing at the door, locked in each other's arms, crying silently; Papa and Uncle Maurice hugging, Grand'mère telling my cousins to watch over their parents. Poor Papa—for him my mother's relatives are all the family he's got.

I couldn't stand the sight of a silent tear streaming down my uncle's frozen face. I wish he had sobbed or screamed instead.

I was about to burst into tears myself, so I ran to the bedroom. When I came back, they were gone.

I never thought I would miss Aunt Fanny so much.

Tuesday, June 3

Since Aunt Fanny left, Grand'mère has not been herself either. She seldoms talks now, unless asked a direct question.

Something strange is happening to her. She is eating less and less. When she does, she accuses Maman of putting too much salt in her food—which we know is not so.

Today, she accused Maman of poisoning her soup.

Later on Maman apologizes to us: "It's her blindness that causes her to act so strangely. She can't see, so she's imagining things."

I feel sorry for Maman, who continues—day after day, week after week, with infinite patience—to care for

Grand'mère, to clip her nails, to admire her smooth skin.

I feel sorry for Grand'mère too: Maman likes her more than anyone in the world, and she doesn't even know it!

Saturday, June 14

I couldn't fall asleep last night; I tossed and turned. I envied Denise's short, easy puffs next to me as I held my stomach to still the gnawing pains. I was hungry.

Dinner had been rather skimpy: two small boiled potatoes with the skins on, a couple of slices of tomatoes, a hard-boiled egg, a piece of fruit. Yesterday was a day "without"—that is, without meat.

It had also been a meal without bread: Our reduced ration doesn't last to the evening.

Unable to stand it any longer, I got out of bed and walked to the kitchen.

A shadow talked to me in the dark. "What are you doing here in the middle of the night?"

It was Maman. Was she also too hungry to sleep? I wondered.

I admitted to my hunger pangs.

"I thought that's what it was," she said, sighing. "I wish I had something to give you. Why don't you help yourself to Lily's leftover milk? You know she doesn't care for it."

Today, my sisters and I are given an extra piece of bread for dinner and will receive an extra one from now on. Maman and Grand'mère swear that adults can do with less food, since they're through with growing, and Papa says that the lousy cigarettes he's allotted spoil his appetite.

I know better: I overheard Maman say to Papa that she prefers to go hungry herself rather than see *us* go hungry.

I make believe that I didn't hear a thing.

Thursday, June 26

Germany has declared war on Russia. Nothing stops those *boches*, really! True, marching through Greece and Yugoslavia was a cinch, and they thought they could go on forever. But, as Papa says, getting into Russia won't be any fun. Especially if the war lasts until the winter— they're as good as dead! It gets brutally cold, Papa says.

At last hope springs up again. I do hope Papa was right!

Tuesday, July 8

The newspapers and Radio-Paris say that the Germans are faring well, but according to the BBC and other sources, things go from bad to worse for them. The Russians are fighting back—they have driven off the Germans, who are losing a lot of men. It's about time someone stopped them.

I quite agree with Pépée's mother, who asks, Why should the Germans succeed where Napoleon failed?

I admire Pépée's mother, Mme Larmurier, very much. She is close to Maman's age, but she is very slim and looks much younger. Like Pépée, she has a round face, wispy short hair, and a dimple in her chin. And she is always so elegant: Even at home she likes to dress in pastel-colored robes with laces and frills.

She does scare me a little. She has a sharp eye and insists on knowing everything: whom did Pépée speak to today, why didn't she get a better grade on her French History quiz, what is that new boil on *my* neck. But she is so pretty!

When I was very little, I believed that all mothers were more or less plump, with fat legs and fat knees—like Maman and most of her friends. Then I began to attend grammar school, and I realized that many of my classmates' mothers were not fat.

I finally worked up the courage to ask. "Maman, why are you—and Aunt Fanny—fat?"

"Why, that's a silly question! It comes from having children!"

I felt so terribly embarrassed: Was it partly my fault that Maman had lost her looks? Still, I wish I had dared to remind her that in her wedding picture, in her long, lacy dress, she was already quite full.

But now that I know Mme Larmurier—who has had two children—and a few other mothers in the neighborhood, I don't worry anymore. When I'm grown up, I, too, will have children and be slim and elegant.

Saturday, September 6

It's nice to be back home—food restrictions, feeling Jewish again, and all.

My sisters and I have spent the last few weeks in La Trinité de Thouberville—a village so tiny, you can't find it on the map. Maman found it for us through a Fresh Air Fund.

I didn't want to leave my parents and Grand'mère in the middle of everything, but now I'm glad we did.

Denise, Lily, and I lived in an old wooden house with a doting elderly lady who let us go on hay rides, pick ferns in the woods, run over prickly grass. We wished it would last forever.

Tonight Maman hums "*J'attendrai*"—"I will wait," a popular romantic song—as she is preparing dinner. She has good news from Aunt Fanny and from her brothers in Hungary—and she is happy to have us home.

My sisters and I are arguing about who is to set the table. Now I know I'm really back.

Saturday, September 20

I wish Maman didn't worry so much.

"All our money is going to the black market," she complains, more and more often. "And we're only getting the bare essentials: eggs, butter, flour—it's costing us an arm and a leg. The little money we've been able to take out of Alsace is disappearing so fast!"

"As long as I'm able to work, we'll be all right!" Papa corrects her.

I've never wondered much about whether or not we had money. It seems that it's always the others who are very rich or very poor. Of course, common sense tells me that our life here is by no means as comfortable as in Mulhouse. I also know, from what Papa and Maman sometimes say, that we had to leave most of our valuables behind when we fled.

"What's important is that we were able to escape in time, and that now we're all together, alive and well!" Papa reminds Maman on the days when she gets tearful about our good life before the war.

Common sense also tells me that if we had had the means, we wouldn't have settled for a fifth-floor walkup with no hot water and no private toilet—especially with a blind grandmother on our hands. Besides, Papa can't possibly make a lot of money working for someone else.

With a family of six to feed and high rent to pay, money *does* matter, I decide.

Thursday, September 25

Mme Chavignat is horrified by what she saw on the Grands Boulevards this afternoon. She happened to pass by the Palais de Berlitz, where there was this exhibit called The Jew and France. Not quite believing her eyes, she walked back and forth by the gigantic posters and the incredible slogans. What shocked her most was a poster of an octopus—supposedly the Jew devouring France.

She says that the worst seems to come out when the Germans and the French anti-Semites—and God knows there are many of those—get together. Still, she says she's ashamed that all this is happening right here, in France, the very land of the Declaration of the Rights of Man!

Papa sighs. "This is simply the result of a vicious anti-Jewish campaign," he says. "I expect that this is the work of only a handful of fanatics, and I certainly hope that the people who see the exhibit will have enough common sense not to believe a word of this nonsense."

I can't understand how such propaganda can be permitted. I'm rather curious to see this exhibit—if only from across the street. But Maman says, Why get dragged in the mud when we don't have to?

Saturday, September 27

Maman was so excited to find out about a canteen in Rue Richer that serves only Jewish people.

She took us there tonight. I was not all that eager to go: I'm as proud as the next person, and I didn't want anyone to see me and think that we needed a handout.

But when I met the Greifenbergs, who are quite well off, and the Shapiras, who live in a huge and elegant apartment in Rue Lafayette, I began to relax and ate without a fuss those awful rutabagas and turnips they served. We were there not because we were poor, but because we were hungry.

Now, though, I can't sleep. While we were waiting in line, I overheard someone say that in August a detention camp for Jews was opened in Drancy, just about five kilometers from Paris. Even more disturbing, a few days after it opened, a whole bunch of Jews were arrested in the eleventh arrondissement and sent there.

My parents didn't say a thing; they must have their own reasons for not getting into a panic. They must have known about it—even without the radio or anything. But I keep wondering: How long will it be till they get to us?

Friday, October 3

They blew up seven synagogues last night. I go back and forth to school, which has just started again, but at home we are afraid to move. They say that a man named Deloncle was involved, but I'm sure that the Germans have something to do with it. Papa says that they must be furious because they no longer have the upper hand on the Russian front *or* in France.

It is true that there are more and more murders attempted against the Germans—always ending up with hostages being shot and vicious retaliations. Of course, they're putting only a little of the blame on the Communists and a lot on the Jews.

I really can't see what we've got to do with all this.

Wednesday, October 22

"Mlle Roth! Come to the blackboard, please!"

I stop fumbling with my pen-box. I do anything to avoid Mlle Serin's eyes, though I knew that my turn would come.

I turn as red as a beet. If I could, I would disappear under my desk.

I don't like what's happening to me. I'm ashamed of my name now. In Alsace it didn't matter as much: *Roth* could pass for a local name. But I've been feeling ashamed of many things lately: of my parents' foreign origin, of their marked accents, of Grand'mère's wig—of not being like everybody else.

I get up from my desk and walk toward the blackboard, facing the unmarked giant map unfolded over the blackboard—a favorite of Mlle Serin. I look closely at the familiar shape of France, the shady areas of the mountain ranges, the fine tracing of the many rivers.

"Tell us what you know of the resources of the Bassin Parisien and show us the major rivers and cities."

Now, I am always prepared for class—geography in particular. It allows me to dream about exotic, faraway countries such as Mozambique or Madagascar, or cities like Tombouctou or Tegucigalpa: The more complicated the name, the more promising it seems to me.

I take the stick that the teacher is handing me and I begin.

Thank goodness I don't have to worry about my Alsatian accent: It's all gone. But I am still uneasy about speaking in front of a class.

Just get it out of the way! I tell myself. And so I speak in a low, hurried voice.

Fortunately this year Pépée is here. As usual, she is moving her arm in a gesture imitating the four-beat tempo—a signal that means "Slow down a bit!"

Her knowing look, her friendly smile, always get me through the ordeal.

Today, strangely enough, I almost welcome the discomfort that always comes with being asked to the blackboard: It tells me that at least this part of the world is still the same—untouched by the outside events.

More than ever I enjoy the smell of the glue, of new erasers, and the stiffness of the new books. I don't even mind the dull gray smocks that we had to get for the new school year.

I want so much to feel that things will go on as usual, and I grope for reassuring signs: Here they are.

Friday, November 14

Since our return to school, Michel and Guy wait much more often for Pépée and me on Avenue Trudaine. Sometimes they walk us all the way to Rue des Martyrs.

Michel has shot up quite a bit during the summer, and he likes to show off the new shadow over his upper lip that he calls a mustache. He only has eyes for Pépée.

Guy has also grown. But his voice is what throws me. It goes up and down—mostly down. While Pépée walks ahead with Michel, Guy talks to me. He tells me about his school, about Brittany and the many towns that have been bombed by the English.

I can't bring myself to tell him that I am Jewish. Maybe he has guessed it by now.

"Let's not tell anyone about Michel and Guy," Pépée decides. "If Maman ever finds out, she'll insist on walking me to school every day."

I have no problem giving her my word.

Sunday, November 23

The series of murders against the Germans continues. This time they've blown up the German library.

As a result the Parisians are forbidden to go out between six o'clock in the evening and five in the morning until further notice, and the restaurants and other public places are closed. Big deal! The curfew will only last a few days, anyway.

And Paris has been fined a million francs.

Also anyone caught in the street after the curfew will be taken as hostage.

If only they would stop their killings. All it does is to get poor innocents into real trouble and make the Germans tighten their grip even more.

Monday, December 15

This time, they have arrested hundreds of Jews—many of them influential people—to retaliate against the recent events, and we hear they have been interned in the Drancy camp.

When I think that our Government in Vichy did not even lift a finger, as Papa says!

One cheerful piece of news, though: The United States has declared war on the Germans! *At last!* England must no longer feel alone. I hope they hurry up and end this awful war.

In the meantime I bet that the Germans can't sleep tight anymore with all that's going on. Serves them right!

1942

Tuesday, January 6

It is cold and damp, and my hands feel cold even with my gloves on, but I don't care.

I am in heaven!

Today Guy commented on how he liked the plaid bow on my white shirt and the way I part my hair.

He also wants to know more about me, my sisters, and my parents—and our life before Paris.

I still haven't told him that we're Jewish.

He is so nice that I'm thinking of marrying him when we are old enough. By that time the Jews and the French will have made their peace.

Feigie and I are about to become friends—real friends. The day before yesterday she walked up to me in class, holding her books under her arms. She looked so sad that I didn't even notice her homely face.

"Papa says we should become friends," she said, without even bothering to say hello. "How about coming for dinner after school?"

My heart stopped. Perhaps she has no friends?

"Sure . . . I'll ask my parents," I said.

"We live at Number Twenty-five Rue de Bellefond," she added, and walked away.

———

"Here's where I live!" Feigie says, ringing the bell.

A pleasantly plump lady opens the door, wearing an apron over her dark dress.

"You must be Renée!" she says, smiling and shaking my hand with obvious affection. "Come right in."

She speaks with an accent very much like Papa's, but she does not seem the least embarrassed by it.

As I look around, I notice a long table covered with large bolts of fabrics and various patterns as well as a collection of irons. Against the wall, there is a three-way mirror and a mannequin. I suddenly recognize the familiar odor that grabbed me when I came in—a mixture of chalk, fabric, and paper that I thought was buried forever deep in my memory.

So just like Papa, M. Langmann is a tailor!

I feel very much at home.

"I'm glad you came!" M. Langmann says as he joins us. There are two deep lines across his forehead that disappear when he smiles. But his large dark brown eyes remain sad.

"We keep a kosher home," Mme Langmann explains later, as she serves us boiled beef, sweet carrots, and a compote of prunes. "Do you?"

I barely manage not to make a face: It doesn't look all that appetizing.

"When we lived in Alsace, before the war, I think," I reply, recalling vaguely the special set of dishes we used on certain occasions and Maman's refraining from cooking on Friday nights and Saturdays. "But not now."

"Feigie tells me that you are one of the top students in class. She happens to be a good student too. But she is much too shy. I'm glad she likes you. Perhaps you can become close friends. In times like these, it's best to stick together," M. Langmann comments.

The two wrinkles have reappeared on his forehead.

Both Feigie's parents speak with a definite Polish accent: They substitute *i* for *u*. At home, behind closed doors, Denise and I sometimes make fun of it.

I don't feel like doing it anymore.

Feigie is not saying anything, but I can tell from the way she listens and smiles at me from time to time that she is glad I'm here.

"What nationality are your parents?" her mother asks.

I explain how Papa and Maman had settled in Alsace before they met, having both come from Hungary at different times, and that Papa was born in a small town in Poland.

"But they are French citizens—and the three of us were born here!" I can't help boasting.

"Well, our circumstances are rather complicated," M. Langmann sighs. "But frankly I don't fool myself anymore. I believe that all Jews—French or otherwise—are in trouble. I guess we're all asking ourselves the same questions: Should we stay here—where we know we can make a living—and hope for the best, or should we consider moving elsewhere? And where should we go? And how do we know that one place will be safer than another?"

Why is he telling me all this? Is he really that upset about what's going on? It seems to me M. Langmann is even more upset than Papa and Maman. Now he's getting me really worried!

"Well, perhaps we can all get together soon—with your family, I mean," he suggests as he walks me to the door.

When I say good-bye, he keeps my hand in his forever, and I wonder what his eyes have seen to look so sad.

Wednesday, February 11

I am climbing the stairs two by two, cursing my mother for getting me to promise to return early tonight from Pépée's house. Granted, I do hang around till late sometimes, but what's wrong with wanting to stay with my friend? Our homework always gets done.

When I come in, Maman is wiping over and over the perfectly clean table around which the family is sitting as usual.

"There you are!" she remarks, walking toward me. "I was waiting for you. Sit down." She takes my arm and forces me into a chair. "I have something very serious to discuss with all of you tonight." Her eyes move slowly from one to another, as if to stress the importance of what she is about to say.

"There's a new curfew. This time, we won't be allowed to leave home between eight o'clock in the evening and six in the morning! And we can't move without notifying the police!"

I am stunned. I think: There's no way that they're going to keep me from going to Pépée's in the evening!

But then I start to feel uneasy. Like the day when I heard about the Drancy camp for Jews.

"What are you talking about? It's incredible!" Papa explodes. He stops sketching the coat he is drawing for my sisters and throws the drawing across the table.

Then he gets up and begins to pace back and forth, his hands behind his back.

"We've got to do something quick! Say, Marguerite, why don't you speak to Sister Louise, in Clichy? Remember, she told us not to hesitate if we needed her for anything! I'd go first thing tomorrow morning!"

"Don't get so upset, Papa," Lily says, taking his hand and getting him to sit down again.

Maman falls into the chair next to him. "My God!" she exclaims, as if she has only just realized the meaning of it all. "What's going to happen to us?"

I can't stand to see her this way. I run to her and put my arm around her shoulders, trying very hard to ignore my own panic.

"Don't worry, Marguerite," says Papa. "The main thing is that we're all in this together. You'll see! We'll live through this. Why, it can't last forever."

It's what Papa keeps telling us.

"And the children? It is them I'm worried about!"

Maman continues, as if she hadn't heard him, her chin trembling as if she were about to cry. "They keep telling us that the French Jews have nothing to worry about, but each time I open the newspaper or Mme Chavignat tells me about the latest news bulletin, I'm shaking. If only we could leave here and hide in some faraway village. But how would we manage without your working?"

"That's precisely why we must do something *now*," Papa replies. "We'll see what Sister Louise has to say."

I remember Sister Louise. We all met her at a bazaar given by the Patronage—a youth center that she runs.

I protest, "But we can't possibly live at the Patronage!"

"I don't want to go to live at the Patronage either!" Denise echoes.

"And I'm staying right here," Lily decides, hiding her face in Papa's lapel.

"Oscar, I think we are making a mistake by discussing all this in front of the children," Maman protests.

"But there's nothing more to discuss!" Papa decides. "Sister Louise knows a lot of people. From what she told us I'm sure she'll help us out." Papa is calmer now, as he takes Maman's hand in his.

Maybe Sister Louise *can* find a hiding place for all six of us, that Papa could go to work from every morning, I think. When we met her niece, Sister Marthe, while attending the youth center in Zainvillers, she asked us to visit her aunt when we got to Paris. We have stayed in touch with Sister Louise since then; she is very kind. I'm sure we could convince her to help us.

"Maman, please let me go with you to see Sister Louise tomorrow! It's Thursday, and there's no school!"

"No, Renée—I prefer to go myself. This is no time to wander out unless it's absolutely necessary!"

"What about me?" Grand'mère asks suddenly. "Why can't you let me go to the Rothschild Home for the Aged? You know I've been wanting to go there for the longest time!"

We all look at her in shock: We almost forgot about her. We certainly no longer expect her to raise such an important question on her own.

Papa recovers first. "Grand'mère is right. Let's not get sentimental. It's as safe a place as any; we'll have to look into it. I'll talk to M. Shapira about it. He is familiar with the home and knows some people there."

Maman doesn't say a word.

Later on I ask her why anyone would want to go to an old-age home when she has a family that wants her.

"It's part of her illness," Maman says, sighing. I'm glad that Grand'mère can't see the sadness on her face.

Wednesday, March 25

In school Odile can't wait to tell me that she heard that the Germans now forbid anyone to speak French in Alsace. They have Germanized the people's names, they are burning or confiscating all of the French books in the schools and libraries—and they have renamed the Rue du Sauvage, Adolf Hitler Strasse.

I am glad we left and don't have to put up with that!

Maman has met with Sister Louise and Mlle Andrée Caban, her assistant at the youth center. But they haven't come up with any plan for us yet. That's fine with me.

Friday, April 10

I wish I hadn't gone to Pépée's today.

She showed me clippings from newspapers and magazines—all quoting important French people.

They read:

> Jews are a bunch of misfits. They're fat, filthy, loud, with fat lips and large noses. You can always spot them because of their broken French or the gibberish they talk among themselves.
>
> Jews are responsible for ruining France and must be eliminated if France is to survive. Death to the Jews and long live France!
>
> Jews wanted the war. Let them pay!

I couldn't read anymore.

What are they talking about? I asked myself. It's a bunch of dirty lies that have nothing to do with us or the people we know!

Now I really am scared: I know how ugly and mean people can be.

Tuesday, April 14

I saw a nun leaving our building this afternoon as I was coming back from school. I could swear it was Sister Louise.

She is very kind to take a real interest in us. How lucky we are that fate permitted us to meet with Sister Marthe in Zainvillers. Still, I don't like the idea of a stranger getting involved with us. They don't know much about us, and they probably won't think twice about disrupting our life—maybe they'll even take the three of us away. How can they understand that the family is all we've got?

With all this talk of hiding, it's a good thing we don't have to worry about Grand'mère. She moved out to the Rothschild Home and seems to like it there, though she's happy when we visit her every Saturday.

Anyway, I wonder what the neighbors and the concierge thought when they saw a nun come in and ask for us—of all people!

Saturday, May 30

I wake up with a start. The sound of voices—my parents' voices—is reaching me.

Whenever they raise their voices now, I panic: I can't help it.

I poke Denise with my elbow, and I run to wake Lily, who is now sleeping in my grandmother's bed.

"There's something wrong!"

We rush to the living room on tiptoe. I put my ear to the closed door.

"I won't! I just won't do it!" Maman says, pounding her fist.

"Calm down! Calm down, Marguerite!" Papa says.

That's when we decide to open the door.

"There we go! We woke the children!" Papa reproaches her.

"What's going on?" Denise and Lily ask at the same time.

Papa motions us to sit down. Maman does not move. She is hiding her face in her hands.

"'Calm down!' It's easy for you to say!" Maman protests, her face still buried. "I'm the one who's running these dreadful errands, not you! Every day, now, there's something else. I can't stand it anymore!"

I can't stand the sight of Maman, so I disappear into the kitchen, pretending I need a drink of water. I make sure I leave the door wide open: I must hear their every word.

Papa retorts, "I'm every bit as shocked as you are by what's going on, by the shameful, despicable way the French are treating us. They're being just as bad as the Germans!"

I feel more and more edgy. What on earth are they talking about?

I've got to busy myself: I turn on the faucet, turn it off, put the glass down, take the lid off a pot—anything to help me fight off the feeling of doom that is coming over me. I finally decide to return to the living room and take my seat between my sisters. They are not saying anything, but they're wide-eyed.

Maman starts again. "Just tell me one thing!" She uncovers her face, where traces of tears are showing. "Why did we leave Hungary, and then Alsace, to find ourselves in danger all over again?"

As Maman speaks the large vein in her neck swells dangerously. What if it bursts? I think. I wish she'd stop getting herself so upset.

"And one last thing," Maman continues. "Will you tell me why we went to the trouble of becoming naturalized

French, since it doesn't make the slightest bit of difference?"

This time Papa moves his chair closer to Maman. He puts his arm around her and speaks to her in a low, soft voice, as he does with us when we don't want to listen to him.

"Look, Mancsi. Don't you think that I'm tired, too, of being put down, humiliated, once more at my age?"

It hurts me to see Papa so resigned. For once, I would prefer to see him shout.

"And don't you think that I've been tempted to throw in the towel more than once? And then what? Can't you see? We have no choice, if only for the safety of the children! What would happen to them if one of us—or both—were to disappear?"

"It's not that I'm ashamed to be a Jew," Maman continues, wiping her eyes and suddenly becoming aware of us. "I just don't understand what's happening, that's all!"

But what on earth are they talking about? I don't know how much longer I can stand the waiting.

She finally gives in.

"Go ahead, Oscar," she says, sighing, as if exhausted. "You tell the girls. I just can't."

"No . . . no . . . you go ahead. You'll do a better job at explaining."

Maman crosses her arms on the table and looks us straight in the face.

"It's actually quite simple," she begins. "They've just ruled that all Jews must wear a Star of David on their coat or jacket at all times. Anyone who doesn't will be in serious trouble. Each family is to pick up their supply— three per person—at their local police station. They even have the nerve to ask for textile coupons in return!"

My voice has finally come back. "What will we look like, with this on?"

Lily wants more details. "But who's deciding all that?"

"Who?" Maman repeats, as if caught by surprise. "The Germans . . . the French . . . I don't know anymore." She makes a large, sweeping gesture embracing the whole world. "No doubt both."

Monday, June 1

There it is—black on yellow on gray—sewn tightly on my jacket and staring me in the face. The thick black border reminds me of a death notice. "We regret to inform you . . ." Perhaps it *is* a death notice. "We hereby condemn you until the end of your days . . ."

I never liked the word *juif*, Jew. Short, abrupt, cutting like a whip—probably because it is so often preceded by the word *dirty*. Ironically the gothic script gives it a decorative touch.

I far prefer to be called Israelite. It is less offensive, more neutral—almost respectful.

=====

Eight minutes left of my privacy. Eight minutes more, and the whole world will know that I am a Jew.

No one is around—a rare event for this time of morning. I look in the family mirror set over the mantelpiece, scrutinizing my face. It's all there: the narrow shape, the straight, long nose, the dark curly hair that I've tugged so many times to try to get it straighter.

But it's the sad look that gives me away, Maman says. She has strange ideas sometimes. Does she think only Jews are sad?

In my family, I'm the one who comes closest to what they refer to as the "typical Jew." The others—my parents, my sisters, even Grand'mère—have lighter skin. Their hair isn't as dark and curly, their features less pronounced.

LEARN TO RECOGNIZE THEM! a top newspaper proclaims. We are becoming public property.

I've come to hate the caricatures of Jews now posted all over Paris, like the one over the shoe store. Jews with hook noses and long, sharp claws that belong on vultures. Papa says that they are despicable, cruel distortions meant for hateful propaganda, but I still can't bear looking at them. They make me feel so ashamed.

Is this really how others see us?

In school the teacher said that slander always leaves a nasty aftertaste.

I tear myself away from the mirror.

Well, we'll see how right they are, these idiots. I am curious to see how many Jews resemble those outrageous posters!

I check the clock. Two more minutes to go.

Denise erupts from the bedroom. "How does it look?" she asks.

I turn around, facing her.

"I've fixed my scarf over it," she explains.

I lift the piece of silk and disclose the yellow star, identical to mine.

"Why, you know you're not supposed to hide it! So why not show it off, like M. Chavignat wears his *Légion d'Honneur?*"

Whatever came over me? I wonder. The last thing I want is to parade with my new emblem on.

I hear Pépée calling my name from the courtyard.

"I've got to go!" I say, as I grab my schoolbag and dash out the door. I run down the five flights.

"Whatever are you wearing here?" Pépée asks, staring at my jacket.

I'm not quite used to the new me. I'm glad she's the one to see me first.

"They want the whole world to know that we're Jewish," I blurt out.

"But I know you're Jewish! And so are the Cohens, my neighbors, and the Kauffmans on Rue de Dunkerque. So what?"

How I wish I could be so casual.

"I tell you what," Pépée says. "I'll carry your jacket when you get tired of it."

I can't help but smile. "With your upturned nose, your reddish hair, and your honest-to-goodness French name, you're pretty safe!" I retort.

We must rush to school, but I wish we'd never get there. I do my best to ignore the few people we pass on the street—especially the lady walking her dog on a leash, who stops to look at us. I talk a lot—about anything. I am afraid of the silences that would force me to look away from Pépée. Still, I feel a weight on my chest, and it grows heavier as we near school.

As we are about to enter the schoolyard Ginette Renard—a classmate of ours—stops me.

"What the devil is this?" she asks, pointing to the emblem on the jacket. I'm now carrying it on my arm, but you can still see the star.

"It means that the people who are Jewish must wear this sign from now on," Pépée snaps, pulling me away.

How brave Pépée is!

"I didn't know you were Jewish!" Ginette retorts, running after us.

"You never asked me," I reply, not liking the sharpness of my voice.

The bell rings. At last! Gratefully I line up next to Pépée, and two by two we enter the building.

In class I look for the other two "victims." They're both wearing the star. Suzanne is chatting with her neighbor as usual. She is so much more grown-up than I am!

Feigie doesn't look at anyone. Her arms crossed on her desk, she looks intently at the open book in front of her.

"Mademoiselle! Mademoiselle!"

Pépée is raising her hand urgently to try to get our teacher's attention.

"Yes, Gabrielle. What do you have to say that's so pressing?"

"It's about Renée, Suzanne, and Feigie's yellow stars. They shouldn't have to wear them to school!"

"You're absolutely right! Thank you, Gabrielle, for bringing up this very touchy point."

Mlle Serin gets up from her desk and begins to pace back and forth.

"God knows, I've always been a patriot," she says. "Yet I can't help feeling very sad about what's happening to our country. It's unthinkable that we are allowing ourselves to handle a group of people so cruelly just because they hold different beliefs. I'm warning all of you: I won't tolerate any derogatory comments in my class!"

For the first time in days, I am able to relax. I had expected enemies; I've found friends.

Wednesday, June 10

I am stuck here, in the middle of the school courtyard at recess, and I can't wait for the bell to announce our return to the classroom. Pépée is not here today, and I feel so alone. Despite the hope I felt on the first day I wore the yellow star, I have been getting a lot of stares and mean looks.

"Why don't you go back to your own country?" a blond girl from a lower grade asks me, point-blank, staring at the star. "My daddy says it's the Jews who are responsible for the war, and they should go back to where they come from!"

More girls gather around us. I feel a cold wave running down my spine, and I look desperately for a familiar face. None comes my way.

Thoughts are racing back and forth in my head.

Go back home? But I *am* home—here! Who is this shrimp who acts as if it were *her* France?

For the first time in my life I'm grateful that I'm not a boy and that this is an all-girl school: The only way out of this situation would have been a good fight.

I take a deep breath and I scream in spite of my shaking knees and my quivering lips: "Just who do you think you are? I want you to know that I feel every bit French, just like you do! If your father doesn't like it here, *he* can leave!"

I wonder how those words ever came out of my mouth. It's happened so fast, I'm just as stunned as my enemy.

I'm shaking like a leaf now, and all I want is to run far away from these murdering looks.

I run off, out of the yard into the street, which I cross.

I lean against a door to catch my breath, and as I look up I see the words engraved on the facade of the school:

LIBERTÉ ÉGALITÉ FRATERNITÉ

Something in me has just died.

"Lies! They're all lies!" I want to scream.

I feel lost. I don't know where to go, and I cross the street again. As I walk alongside the school building, children's voices are reaching me: "*Ce n'est qu'un au revoir, mes frères.*" "It's only good-bye, my friends."

I'm suddenly blinded by tears. I can't move. Leaning against the wall, I walk back to the now-deserted courtyard. Hugging the trunk of a tree, I let myself go and fall to the ground, shaking with sobs. We sang that song on the June morning when we left Mulhouse.

I remember looking intently at the milestones with a pang in the pit of my stomach as we passed them one by one, calling to myself the familiar names. I began to hum "*Ce n'est qu'un au revoir,*" but I had to stop. The tears invaded my voice.

I am wiping my eyes with my sleeve now. I'm afraid I won't be able to stop. I want to go home!

I want to be little again, I want to go back to that day in September in Villers-sur-Thur with the Peterses—I don't want the war to have broken out!

I want things to be like before.

Saturday, June 13

The whole building is in an uproar: Mme Chavignat heard that her neighbor from the next building over, M.

Berson, has managed to escape from Germany, where he was a prisoner.

His wife is deliriously happy, but scared. As a Jew, he must go into hiding. He is planning on joining the *maquis*—the underground.

I am all excited about M. Berson having played such a good trick on the Germans!

Tuesday, June 16

I have stopped counting the anti-Jewish decrees that keep pouring in on us.

We are forbidden to go to neighboring squares and parks, libraries, cafés, restaurants, swimming pools— even movie houses, for goodness' sake! As Maman says, they've thought of everything.

Papa is worried because from what his friend Max Rosenberg says, the new Frenchman who heads the Jewish Affairs Committee is very anti-Semitic.

What bothers me most is to see how some of our neighbors are turning their backs on us.

Take Mme Delmas: I hate to meet her in the hallway or on the staircase these days. She was never that friendly—it was mostly hello–good-bye. But now she totally ignores us. Perhaps it's for the best: Ever since Denise overheard her say, "The Jews? I don't feel sorry for them one bit. Besides, a little hardship is good for the soul." I feel like telling her straight to her face: "You idiot! How can you possibly understand? It's not *you* it's happening to!"

Actually, if I had my way, I would force people like

her to wear a star just like ours saying I HATE JEWS.

Maman reminds us that Sister Louise is working on a plan that should be completed soon. I hope to God that the war will end before that. I don't want to go live in a hiding place.

Thursday, June 25

Thank goodness for Mme Chavignat: She's always trying to cheer us up.

"Come on, girls!" she tells us, calling on us unexpectedly. "I'm taking you to the movies. There's a good film at the Roxy, and I'm going with Jocelyne. What do you say, Mme Roth?"

"Chic!" exclaims Denise. "What a great idea!"

"But they can't! You know we're not allowed into a movie house. And the girls can't go out without wearing their stars. . . ." Maman hesitates.

"I know, I know. . . . I've heard about the nasty rule. But once isn't every day, and the theater is only a short walk down the street. Besides, I know the cashier, Mme Huguette—I know I can vouch for her. Believe me, there's nothing to worry about. Just let them go without their stars."

Our neighbor has no trouble convincing me. "Please, Maman. We'll behave—and we'll come straight home, I promise!"

"How I wish my husband were here to help me decide. He's always so cautious. I don't think he would permit it!" Maman sighs.

"Come on, Mme Roth, I think you're making too

much of it. Since I'm going along, no one's going to stop us. Besides, it will do the girls a world of good and free you for a couple of hours."

"All right, then," Maman says.

I'm the first one out. I'm grateful for the diversion, but I'm also glad to get away from Maman's sad smile.

I settle with delight into the darkness, and in no time I get lost in the sad story that unfolds in front of my eyes. I cry hard for the little boy dying on the screen: At least I'm alive!

Too quickly the word *Fin*—The End—marks the end of our break.

Little by little my eyes get used to the light, but my panic returns immediately. I remember that not only are we without our stars, but movie houses are forbidden to us.

"I hope no one will spot us," I whisper.

I'm not sure Mme Chavignat even hears me: I am concealing my face in her sleeve to hide from the crowd walking with us toward the exit. What if a neighbor sees us and denounces us? All it takes is one gossip! I tell myself.

"Let's hurry—quick!" I take my face from Mme Chavignat's sleeve and pull at it.

Jocelyne, Denise, and Lily are walking in the back of us as usual. Why can't I be like them?

"Calm down! Calm down, *mon petit.* There's no reason for you to be so worried! I bet that no one's even paying attention to you right now. Believe me, people are mostly concerned about themselves!"

Now, which of us is right? Do I really see danger where there isn't any?

"Please, Mme Chavignat!" I implore again, convinced

that a hundred pairs of eyes are watching me by now.

I can't wait to get to the street, where I am still allowed.

It's the last time that I'll ever set foot in the movies!

Saturday, June 27

I hate the métro now. I no longer care about the safety gates closing like magic at the approach of the trains. I ignore the directional maps that light up when you press the buttons. I go past the gigantic posters on the vaulted walls. I look without seeing them at the shimmering asphalt corridors and hurriedly pass the handful of musicians in need of a few pennies.

I hate the métro now that we've been ordered to ride in the last car—humiliated once more. I no longer let my eyes linger on the passengers, and I've stopped wondering about the lives they lead on the outside.

Instead, I concentrate on the tips of my shoes, or pretend to be reading a book—or simply hide behind Maman. The car is a prison, and I can't wait to get out of it.

They don't want me in public places? Well, I don't want to be in them.

I'm tired of feeling naked when everyone else is fully dressed. They stare at me with searching eyes full of suspicion, disgust, or pity.

I am ashamed.

I no longer walk: I skim the walls. The few inches I've gained in height I am losing by shrinking.

I am ashamed.

More and more I stay away from friends and school-mates and neighbors—from all those people, "the others," whose carefree laughter hurts me.

"Our oldest worries me!" I heard Maman say to Papa today. "She hardly touches any food, you can't get her out of bed in the morning, and she doesn't even ask questions anymore!"

It worries me too.

Saturday, July 4

This time it's Papa's turn to be angry. I knew it would come. "I don't know if the woman is mean or just plain stupid!" He's trying to catch his breath. The long climb up the five flights is becoming a strain for him.

As usual, Lily has gone down to help carry up his packages. All he has to do is to whistle from the court-yard, and down she flies.

Maman has come out of the kitchen. "What's the matter, Oscar?"

"Well, Mme Chavignat just told me that a police-man—some sort of official anyway—showed up at the concierge's this afternoon looking for your sister and Maurice. As if that wasn't alarming enough, that moron told the man that even though they don't live here any-more, Fanny's sister does! How can anyone be so dense? She's throwing us into the lion's den! It's a good thing no one was home."

"This afternoon?" Maman says, panicking. "God help us!"

"How can we go to bed now, knowing that we have a

concierge we can't trust? How I wish Mme Giroud had not moved out! She was a gem compared to this one. What a day," he says, sighing, and he falls into the chair Lily has put out for him.

"Today has really been the day!" he continues. "Just imagine: In the window of a very reputable store, there was this sign. Not one of those graffiti, mind you. . . . It was a printed, quite official document . . . 'No Dogs—No Jews,' it read. Well, after that, anything is possible!"

I bite my lip to keep from blurting out what's on my mind—because it would only make things worse; from telling them that children can be just as mean, these days. Maybe hate is catching.

It's especially Odile that I am thinking of.

Now, I have been trying to stay away from her, as from the other troublemakers in school who make fun of my Jewish star. But she is often by herself, so that I—silly fool—don't have the heart to turn her down when she asks me to play hopscotch with her, as she did yesterday.

"You know?" she said, point-blank, halfway through the game. "If I wanted to, I could tell my daddy to have you arrested. He knows very important people!"

I continued to play, pretending I hadn't heard. But thoughts began to race in my mind.

To arrest me? What nerve! Wasn't it *her* grandfather who gave up his French citizenship because he chose to remain in Alsace when it became German? Why, this idiot boasts about it as if it were a feather in her cap!

I wanted to pull her braids, to scream at her and tell her that she was mean and stupid, and that next time she should find someone else to play with!

108

But I was too scared of her—of what she might do. So I swallowed the words instead. After the war, I promised myself, I'll spit it all back. I only hope it won't take too long.

In the meantime I took my rage out on the hopscotch marker and kicked it all the way to the far end of the schoolyard.

Friday, July 10

"I knew it! I just knew that woman couldn't be trusted!" Maman grumbles as she walks in the door.

I take the grocery net from her. Since Jews are permitted to go to the stores for only one hour—between three and four in the afternoon—we are all on edge.

"Do you know what this Durand witch had the nerve to say to me—just like that, in front of everyone in the dairy store? 'Sorry, Mme Roth! It's three minutes past four—you know the rule! I could get into trouble!'" Maman says, mimicking the storekeeper perfectly. "I was ready to strangle her! And do you know what she had the nerve to add: 'Come on, my dear lady, it's not the end of the world. You'll just have to get yourself better organized. Come back tomorrow!'

"Now, really," Maman goes on, "no matter how hard we try, how can they expect us to run all our errands within an hour? Especially since some of the stores are out of stock—if not closed—by the time we get there? You know, Oscar, I've had it! I've had it with Mme

Durand and everyone else! I'm tired of having to keep my mouth shut and swallow everything!"

"All right!" Papa sighs. "So she's mean, petty, and all that. But that doesn't mean that we should put everyone in the same boat. Take Mme Chavignat or Mme Larmurier or Sister Louise—they're very good to us."

Papa has a point. But then so does Maman. I think that we should send Papa marketing next time. Maybe he'll be a little less forgiving after he's been insulted once or twice!

Saturday, July 11

Since my sisters and I are off from school for the summer, we have been sent for Papa. He is, as usual, paying his Saturday morning visit to his friend Max Rosenberg.

"You know Papa! He always forgets about lunchtime when he is playing cards!" Maman told us.

The Rosenbergs live so close—practically around the corner, on Rue du Delta—that we decided to run over without our stars. Besides, it is much too warm to wear our jackets.

Mme Rosenberg greets us at the door with the baby in her arms. I offer to kiss the baby, but her mother keeps her from me. "Monique has a cold and is running a fever; you can tell from her running nose and her red cheeks," she explains. "I was about to put her to bed. Come in. . . . I think you're arriving just in time!"

Papa is not surprised to see us, as the game is over. He gathers the cards into a neat stack in front of M. Rosenberg, who sits next to him at the small table near the window. Then he gets up, glancing out to the yard.

Suddenly he points to the window and says, "I just saw two men walking across the yard—one of them looks like a policeman!"

My heart stops. The minute we hear the word *police* now, we run for our lives.

"Dear God, please help us!" Mme Rosenberg implores. "I hope they're not coming here! We're the only Jews in the building besides the Gamernes on the fourth floor in stairway A!"

"Goodness! The girls are without stars—all we need is for them to catch us!" Papa cries. "Hurry, now," he urges, pushing the three of us toward the door. "For God's sake, Max, you can't stay here. Run to your neighbors! Here. I'll take Monique if you want me to!"

But Mme Rosenberg refuses to part with the baby, and they stay behind.

The next thing I know, we are out of the apartment, my legs feeling like rubber. I keep thinking, One more minute—maybe two—and they'll be here! Time enough to stop at the concierge's to ask where the apartment is, and then walk up the three flights. . . .

Papa is standing by the staircase, hesitating. Then he pushes me forward. "Go up!" he orders. I'm glad he's here to tell me what to do. When I'm scared, I can't think. Papa is scared too; I can tell from the tiny droplets that are now all over his forehead. Then he grabs my sisters by the hand and drags us to the top floor—there are six—whispering to us not to make any noise.

I try to listen for any sound, but all I hear are my loud heartbeats.

As we reach the last step Papa stops, panting. That's when we hear hurried steps, then nothing. I look at Papa, wondering what to do next. He is looking at his watch, his forehead still wet with perspiration. He then leans out over the banister—so far that I'm afraid he'll fall over.

"Let's go home," he finally whispers.

We go down the staircase on tiptoe. As we reach the third floor, I can't help slowing down by the Rosenbergs' apartment, pulled by something stronger than myself. I could swear I can make out the strong voice of a man—one of the policemen, without a doubt—and I'm sure I hear Monique crying. My God: They *are* being taken away! I think I'm going to faint.

I give Papa an imploring look, but he grabs me and yanks me away. We walk down the last three flights with extra caution, but the stairs creak in spite of it, and I'm scared to death every time they do.

At last we are out. Papa is still holding my hand. With the other he is covering his Star of David with his hat. My sisters are walking ahead.

The few minutes it takes to walk up the street and around the corner seem endless. I don't dare look back. What if they're after us?

Papa knows my urge to rush home to safety.

"Don't run! You must never—do you hear me? *Never!*—let anyone know that you're scared!"

After dinner Papa learns from the Gamernes that the Rosenbergs were taken away. "Why didn't they leave, as I told them to, for God's sake? Maybe I should have stayed and tried to force them to leave!" Papa wonders, torturing himself before sinking into a long, hurtful silence.

"Don't talk nonsense!" Maman protests. "You know very well that you would have been trapped. You would have been taken away too—with the children."

I can't fall asleep.

I keep seeing Papa putting the cards into a neat stack on the table. What would have happened if he hadn't looked out of the window at that very moment? I shudder when I think that our fate had depended on just that.

And I keep seeing Monique, with her running nose and her red cheeks, and I picture her asking for her bed and her stuffed teddy bear in the crowded camp in Drancy where they all will wind up.

I tiptoe to the window and, leaning against the railing, I look intently at the sky and try to imagine God among the many stars—this God that Maman addresses so often, and who, she says, sees everything, knows everything, and has all the power in the world.

For the first time I talk to him directly: "Dear God, you've got to end this horrible war! What more will it take to convince you?"

Wednesday, July 15

"Is this your idea of a joke, Renée? Your sisters have been home awhile now. Do you know it's almost fifteen minutes past the curfew? Don't you think that we have enough to worry about?"

Papa is greeting me at the door, his eyebrows raised: This time I've gone too far.

I walk in without a word. Tonight for once—just once—I wanted to feel like everyone else, and I refused to rush home.

Maman is at the door in a flash. *Smack!* Her flattened hand on my cheek reminds me that I am still a child.

I glance at my sisters; they're mute. They know better than to give away my secret.

They know about Guy. They know how important he has become to me: He at least doesn't avoid me or make fun of my star. In fact, he looks for me in a crowd, in the street, or at the gate of the Square d'Anvers, since I am no longer allowed inside. When I am with him, he makes me feel that being Jewish isn't such a big deal.

My sisters tease me about his buckteeth. So what? He's handsome enough for me. He's also the only one who still gets me to laugh once in a while—not to mention the fact that he is the best roller skater around. Ever since he playfully etched our initials on the trunk of the widest tree in the Square d'Anvers two months ago—after I had fallen off my skates and he had picked me up—I know that I matter to him too.

I hate the curfew that spoils our meetings, especially now that the days are longer and we could walk around until late in the evening.

Truthfully I never thought that much about boys before—or about men, for that matter. To me they were pretty much people like you and me. For the longest time I couldn't even understand Maman's warnings against those strangers who lure little girls with candies. Maman has a habit of warning us against everything anyway.

Then I went marketing on my own one day, and a strange man stopped me. I remember he was well dressed and very politely tipped his hat while he looked at me with intense dark eyes. He asked me in a sweet voice if I wanted an ice cream—or anything else. I didn't answer, but I ran home as fast as my legs would let me. Fortunately I never saw him again.

But with Guy it's different. Of course, I'm a little older now—nearly eleven—and I'm finding boys much more interesting. Perhaps it has something to do with the changes I have been noticing about me lately: I'm growing to a fuller size, I blush even more easily than before.

"You'll turn into a young lady soon!" Maman predicts. She always thought that I was well developed for my age. Still, I know that my parents would not understand—let alone approve—of my friendship with Guy.

I just know what Maman would say; I know her like a book. "Have you lost your mind, Renée? How can you even think of befriending a Gentile boy—now of all times? Don't you know that he'll eventually turn against you, as they all do, in the end?"

I wish I could prove Maman wrong. I wish I could make her see that there are exceptions, and that Guy is one of them.

But what's the use? It would only spoil things for Guy and me.

Why couldn't I have been born in a regular family? Preferably blond and blue-eyed?

Papa and Maman's angry looks have turned to reproach. I would do anything to erase the hurt on their faces.

"I completely forgot the time!" I lie.

It's still early. The living-room window is open, and we can tell that it's going to be a warm, sunny day.

I love the summer. It's always the sun that wakes me up as it filters through the closed shutters. I like the way it slowly lights up the darkest corners of the room one by one and dispels the dreams and the terrors of the night.

In spite of our living in constant fear now, there's something nice about the prospect of being off from school for the whole summer. This morning Maman doesn't rush my sisters and me to finish our breakfast. Since Grand'mère left us, Maman doesn't nag us half as much anymore anyway.

As usual, Papa has gone to work.

There are three knocks at the door. We look at each other, wondering who it could be.

"It's Mme Chavignat!" a voice says through the door. "Open up, quick!"

Maman opens the door.

"Something is terribly wrong!" our neighbor explains as she shuts the door behind her. "They took away Mme Berson from Number Eighty! Poor soul! Her husband just left to go into hiding, and she's pregnant!"

"Mme Berson? This morning? But that's impossible!" Maman exclaims, falling into a chair.

"Well, Mme Michelet heard it from Mme Dutronc. She lives on the ground floor, and her apartment looks out onto the courtyard. She heard Mme Berson scream as they practically carried her away."

"Why would they want to take away a pregnant

woman?" Maman keeps repeating the question, looking at Mme Chavignat without seeing her.

I am glued to my chair. I can't move or think or anything. All I heard is that Mme Berson is carrying a baby. How is she going to manage in those forced labor camps where they're all being sent? I hope they won't work her to death!

I often wonder about those mysterious camps that exist in Germany and are now springing up in France too. Are people put into barracks surrounded by wire fences and under constant watch, and made to work in the fields all day, only to be fed stale bread and a bowl of watered-down soup in the evening? M. Berson, who was a prisoner in Germany, told us about this the time we met him briefly at a neighbor's.

What about the children and the older people who are not strong enough to work in the fields? I wonder.

———

The bell rings: a series of impatient sounds.

It's Pépée, out of breath. She doesn't even notice Mme Chavignat's presence.

"Mme Roth! Renée! They came to get Mme Cohen, Jeannette, and Riri!" she exclaims from the doorway.

"What are you talking about? Come in and sit down. I'll get you what's left of our *café au lait*."

No matter what happens, Maman always finds some food to offer.

Pépée sits down. She accepts the cup Maman hands to her with a nod of thanks and takes a long sip.

But I can't stand the waiting. I grab my friend's arm. "What happened? Tell me, what happened?"

Pépée takes another sip. "Well, there was such a commotion at the Cohens' early this morning that Maman decided she and I would knock at their door to find out what was the matter. We are used to their fighting, except that it's usually in the evenings."

My sisters have moved closer to Maman, who nods her head, whispering to herself: "No . . . I can't believe it. . . . It's simply incredible!"

"There were two men there, two Frenchmen—one in civilian clothes, the other one a policeman," Pépée continues. "They said they had received orders to pick up Mme Cohen and the two children. M. Cohen was ordered to stay, as they need him to make uniforms for the French Army, or something like that—Poor M. Cohen!" Pépée exclaims and bursts into tears.

I want to comfort her, but I am very upset too.

"Poor M. Cohen!" Pépée repeats. "I've never seen a man cry so hard! He was hugging and kissing his wife and Jeannette, asking them to forgive him. . . . Remember how mean he was to Jeannette sometimes?"

Pépée is addressing me now.

"Of course, I remember." I remember cursing him and wishing him harm for being so mean to his daughter when she came to school with red eyes. But I never, ever imagined him punished *that* hard!

I feel so sad for him now. I swallow hard, quickly, to fight the tears that are streaming down my cheeks.

"You should have seen him!" Pépée says, wiping her eyes with the hankie Maman had pulled out of her pocket. "He begged the two men—on his knees!—to take him along, or take him instead. They were all crying, except for Mme Cohen. She was so brave. She was sure it was a mistake—they had never done anything wrong in their lives—and that they would be back."

Maman does not say anything more. She looks suddenly shrunk.

"I really can't see how they can send children to a labor camp," Lily remarks, trying to understand.

"That's right! It doesn't make any sense," Denise agrees.

"What's happening here is totally beyond me!" Mme Chavignat comments.

"Did the men say where they were taking them?" Maman finally asks.

"They didn't know for sure. They were just following orders, they said. They weren't very nice really. They were rushing poor little Riri and getting impatient with M. Cohen. . . . Maman said she wished they were German, she would have been less ashamed! She asked M. Cohen to stay with us, but I couldn't stand it anymore, so I came here."

Suddenly Pépée grabs my arms and looks at me as if she is seeing me for the first time. "Maybe you should hide somewhere!"

"She's right, Maman!" I say, finally able to talk again. "They're practically next door! They'll be here any minute!"

"What are we going to do?" my sisters ask in unison.

"You know you can always count on us," Pépée offers.

"Or stay with us," Mme Chavignat echoes.

"Why not hide under the beds until Papa comes home? He has a key, so we won't have to worry about opening the door to anyone!" I suggest, panicking at the thought of the time ticking away.

Maman suddenly explodes, "*Istenem!* What am I to do? I can't even reach Papa at work! How I wish we had a radio. . . . Something horrible is going on, and we don't know a thing about it!"

I can't stand Maman's panic; it just makes mine worse. I need to do something. "I'll take a look outside!" I offer, dashing to the back bedroom. I open the window. At first glance I see nothing unusual on either side of our street, or farther out on Avenue Trudaine. I lean out a little more to be able to see if anything is going on around our building. That's when I notice a handful of people gathered at the corner of Rue du Delta. Among them is a man in uniform. A little girl—almost a baby—catches my eyes. It can't be, I tell myself.

"Maman! Maman!" I call out, frightened to death. "Come quick!" Maman rushes in, followed by my sisters.

"Istenem!" Maman exclaims, leaning dangerously out of the window. "It's little Michèle Jaffé of Rue du Delta—and her brother and sister!"

"But she's not even two years old. She can hardly walk!" I protest, feeling my knees buckle.

"That's not going to stop them!" Maman snaps. She slams the windows as if to shut out the cruel world. "God, please help me come to a decision!" she prays. "Maybe we shouldn't stay here one more minute. But then what's Papa going to think when he doesn't find us at home?"

We decide to stay, come what may.

===

When the bell rings again in the afternoon, my sisters and I look at one another, petrified.

Maman appears at the kitchen door, a finger on her lips. We are not to make a sound.

I clutch at my chair. That's it! This time it's *our* turn! The bell rings again, stubborn, compelling.

Stunned, I see Maman walks toward the door in spite of our despairing signs.

Ouf! We sigh with relief as we recognize Jeannot Schrifft. He is out of breath. I wonder what he's doing here alone. In the two years that I've known him I have never seen him without one of his brothers or at least his cousin Germaine. He looks suddenly quite lost and frail.

"But what are you doing here all by yourself?" Maman exclaims.

"It happened so fast. . . . I don't know anymore. . . . They took everyone—just like that—my parents, my brothers and then my uncle, my aunt, and Germaine next door. . . . They took me along, of course."

He stops to rub his eyes with his fist as if to erase the image from his mind.

"I was walking next to Papa. The others were walking ahead, between the two policeman. The Boulevard de Sébastopol was very crowded, so it was hard for all of us to stay together. As we passed in front of a large store Papa suddenly pushed me away from him into an open door. I didn't understand what he wanted until he whispered, 'Go! Get lost! Quick!'

"For a split second I tried to pull Germaine by the arm, but she wouldn't let go of my aunt's hand. So I disappeared in the crowded store without looking back. . . . I was too scared to stop."

"Istenem!" Maman exclaims, burying her face in her hands. "Vera, Ilonka! The children! What's going to hap-

pen to them! Will we ever see them again?"

But she catches herself and walks over to Jeannot. She takes him in her arms and hugs him.

"My poor child! I'm glad you came to us!" I barely dare look at Maman. A network of fine lines now maps her face. I would like to put my arms around her and Jeannot, and around my sisters, too, so that we may feel stronger and less afraid. But my arms won't move: They feel like lead.

"I remembered how to get to your house. I took the métro at Strasbourg-St. Denis. I didn't have any money, but the ticket clerk let me in."

"We've got to do something, quick," Maman frets, bringing her hand to her forehead. "I do hope my husband comes home soon. We can't stay here now!"

"How will they be able to write to me? They don't even know where I am! I shouldn't have listened to Papa! I don't want to be alone! What's going to become of me now?" Jeannot bursts into tears.

Denise, Lily, and I run to him and hug him for a long time. It speaks louder than words. But I want to scream. It's only the little people, like Mme Chavignat, who will help us Jews. When will somebody in power stop this madness?

———

We dash to the door even before Papa can turn his key in the lock. We don't feel half as scared anymore.

We all talk at once, and he seems hardly surprised to see Jeannot. He decides immediately that our little friend will take the first train to Nogent in the morning to stay with the Schriffts' cousin Belle—her husband is not Jewish, and they live in a big house. Jeannot's family had been planning to move in there—if only they already had.

"There's no way that we're going to spend another night here! We must do something—it's now or never!"

"But what can we do this late in the day? Curfew is just about an hour away!" Maman says.

Papa looks at his pocket watch and nods, sighing. "But isn't it tomorrow that you are to phone Sister Louise?" he reminds Maman.

Maman says yes. I can see that this time Papa is ready to take action.

The three of us girls sleep in one bed, Jeannot in the other.

All night long I keep hearing the bell ringing, Mme Berson screaming, and the policemen pushing us around.

Saturday, July 18

I'm helping Maman peel potatoes. I am doing my best to get paper-thin spirals. Maman doesn't even see that she is taking off thick pieces—a sheer waste.

Last night, for the first time, we slept away from home. We divided up to stay at neighbors'. We're no fools: It's usually in the wee hours of the morning that the traitors take you by surprise.

"How can they do such awful things and get away with them?" Maman keeps repeating with a new, tired voice, stopping for a moment and staring at the peel hanging from her knife. "From one day to the next our world collapsed! Why, God, why?"

For the life of me I can't see why she insists on keeping after this God, who couldn't care less about Michèle Jaffé, Jeannette, Mme Berson—or any of us, for that matter.

I can't stand to look at Maman; she has developed a twitch in her left eye that won't stop.

Papa rails against the French police and the other uniformed guards—all these "true" Frenchmen who, hand in hand, have helped the Germans along.

We're told that hundreds of families—Papa says more than twelve thousand non-French Jews in Paris alone—have been arrested in the last two days. Just like that. Taken to the Vel d'Hiv and then transferred to the Drancy camp.

"They got us, the clever bastards!" he storms. "The *boches* and the French. Who could even have imagined such a thing? One big sweep, and they're gone!"

What gets to me is that outside the sun continues to shine like before. It seems that the birds are even chirping louder than usual. I am tempted to scream: "Stop it! Can't you see that we're in pain here?"

I heard that the Langmanns were among those taken away. I can't believe it, and I keep expecting Feigie to walk up to me with her books under her arm.

Feigie, whose sad smile follows me everywhere.

Feigie, who doesn't even know how much I miss her.

I continue to peel the potatoes as best as I can, as if doing our everyday chores will guarantee us survival.

But then we've got to hold on to something, Papa always says.

Monday, July 20

The worst has happened.

Tomorrow—it's definite!—my sisters and I will be leaving.

Tomorrow! Tomorrow! I keep repeating the word without believing it. But how can I ignore Maman's getting together some of our clothes and things and putting them in neat little stacks, one for each? Or Papa not saying a word because there's nothing more to say?

I am positively shocked to see Papa and Maman so quick to send us off. True, we can't possibly think of staying in the apartment any longer, and we can't continue to hide at the Chavignats' or the Larmuriers' every night.

The verdict came today.

"I just talked to Sister Louise. You'll be leaving tomorrow night. It was a hard decision, believe me, but Papa and I feel that it's the only way that will get us out of this."

I couldn't listen anymore. Words were coming out of Maman's lips, but I couldn't grasp any of them. My eyes were burning. I felt a dizzy spot in my stomach.

"Tomorrow!" Denise and Lily protested in unison.

"The sooner, the better!" Papa sighed.

"You know that I've met several times with Sister Louise and Mlle Andrée. They both have been urging us, from the beginning, to get you away from Paris. We hesitated for a long time. But after what has just happened, we think it's the best solution."

I was dying to stick my fingers in my ears, to run away, but I wasn't going to cry or carry on in front of my kid sisters, so I clutched both sides of my chair with my hands and forced myself to listen.

"It so happens that Sister Louise has a close friend—also a nun—who runs a Catholic residence for women in a little town in Normandy called Flers," Maman continued. "With luck, you'll remain there until the end of the war. Papa and I ought to be able to maintain your upkeep there for that long."

"You must never, under any circumstances, tell anyone that you're Jewish," Papa emphasized.

"That's right. It's extremely important," Maman underlined.

"The Mother Superior—Sister Pannelay, Sister Louise's friend—will know about it, of course, since she is the one who's taking you in. But remember, the law is clear: Anyone who helps a Jew is as good as dead!"

"But why can't we all hide together? We'll manage!" Lily implored.

"All we really need is two beds!" Denise suggested.

I grabbed the idea for dear life: It was our last chance. "It's true! That's all we need! Please, Maman. You'll see, we won't be any trouble whatsoever!"

That's when I made a secret vow: I promised to do all the chores and to stop seeing Guy if it came to that. I'd do anything anyone wanted, as long as we could stay together.

I couldn't imagine living elsewhere—without Maman to force me out of bed in the morning, to keep my things in order, to eat slowly, or other such annoying things—and without Papa to reassure us and help straighten things out.

Maman shook her head. "Papa and I have gone over this a hundred times! What matters right now is to be able to hide, and it's much easier to do it when you are two than when you are five. Paris has become a danger-ous place—yet Papa has no choice but to stay here, since this is where his livelihood is. It's a good thing, too, that he still has a job and that—touch wood—his boss is a decent man. I can't possibly leave him here alone. At least the three of you have a chance to go to a safer place—you must grab it!"

"The war won't last forever. . . . The sun will shine for us again, you must believe that, just as I do," Papa added. But the cheer in his voice did not show on his face.

I gathered all my courage to ask, "And you, what are you going to do?" I had never imagined Papa and Maman without us.

"M. Meunier—Papa's boss—has helped us find a maid's room in Rue Rambuteau, near where he works. We'll move into it tomorrow. We're keeping this apart-ment, of course. And we'll try to get false I.D. papers, so that I can get around and visit you."

What if we wither away and die without you? I had wanted to ask. What if—what if you were to be picked up like the others and we didn't know about it?

But I said nothing. There was no use asking such questions anymore.

"At any rate it's all set," Maman continued. "Mlle Andrée, from the youth center, will take you to Flers. You'll each have to fit your things into a small bag so as not to attract undue attention. You'll leave at night."

"By the way, you must swear that you won't tell anyone—even your closest friends—what we've dis-cussed," Papa said.

"Can I tell Pépée, at least?" She, in turn, could tell Guy, I thought.

"No, not even Pépée!" Maman said sternly. "I'll tell her myself after you've gone."

It's so unfair! I raged to myself.

How could I leave without saying good-bye?

Tuesday, July 21

"Let's go marketing in Rue Cadet," Maman suggests this morning. I know Rue Cadet is much farther from home than Rue Clignancourt. I know Maman just wants to make sure that we don't run into friends or neighbors.

"At least let me look in the local shop windows one last time," I implore.

On the way back I press my nose against the windows of the bakery, the charcuterie—even the Durand dairy store. It takes all my willpower not to yell out, "We are leaving! Don't forget about us!"

"For goodness' sake don't look so sad, Renée!" Maman cautions. "Otherwise people will guess what we're up to! You've been so brave until now, all three of you. Keep up your courage! You will be needing all of it!"

This is it. . . . We'll be leaving in a few minutes. The three bags are ready, neatly set at the door.

We've had our last supper: sausages and paprika sauce on a bed of potatoes. The only sound we hear is that of the forks hitting the plates, of the glasses getting filled.

Lily is not hungry. She's nibbling from Papa's plate one last time.

Today we are still a family—something that goes beyond the worn oiled tablecloth, the mismatched pieces of furniture, the ordinary curtains, the family picture on the mantelpiece.

Tomorrow we won't be.

There are three quick rings. It's Mlle Andrée: I recognize immediately her long, heavy dark braid, her winning smile, her energetic presence.

Maman lets her in, but no one says a word.

"I see that you've managed to take along a minimum of luggage—good!" she says, ignoring our silence. "Actually we don't have very far to go. Someone's picking us up at the Café des Oiseaux to drive us to Clichy—where you'll spend a few days before leaving for Flers."

I can't help wondering how she managed to find a ride when there's a gasoline shortage and you need a special permit to drive a car. We are in good hands, I realize.

Her eyes fall on the three of us sitting around the table, motionless.

"I know you're going through very rough times, all three of you. At least you'll have each other!" she says.

Maman doesn't say a word, but she is crumpling a handkerchief in her hand, and Papa is now motioning us to get up.

I want to get it over with quick, yet I'm the last one to get up.

"Well, we should hurry now. Let's not keep our driver waiting!" Mlle Andrée reminds us.

We take turns hugging Papa and Maman. Even Lily doesn't cling to Papa.

For the split second that my eyes meet with Maman's, I can read in them a sad, tired resignation.

"Go ahead . . . it's time. . . . We have no choice," they say. And then, she breaks into a smile—a smile full of pain.

I would like to hug her one last time for all the times I won't be able to.

But Mlle Andrée rushes us out. I'm glad. I don't know how much longer I can hold out.

"Take care of your sisters" are Papa's parting words.

We are orphans.

I'm glad that the street is pitch-black, almost deserted. It makes it easier to leave.

I grab Denise's hand.

I know that Papa and Maman are watching us from the bedroom window, but I try my best not to look back.

Maman said we must save our courage, and right now, I need it all.

II

NORMANDY

1 9 4 2

We are walking up the street, away from the only cross-road in town, where the van let us off. The residence is a short distance from there, and Mlle Andrée didn't want to attract undue attention by having us driven all the way to the entrance.

Mlle Andrée is walking ahead, carrying Lily's bag with one hand and holding my little sister's hand with the other. Her long heavy dark braid is hanging down her back, flopping against her waist at every step.

I follow behind with Denise, taking my time. I pretend the valise is weighing me down. The truth is, I am in no hurry to find myself face to face with strangers.

What if they, too, hate us and give us a hard time?

It was hard enough to have to sleep away from home the last few nights. We stayed with Mlle Andrée and her mother in Clichy. They went out of their way to fuss over us, but I was in no mood for it. Then we had the long train ride here.

I stop and rest the suitcase on the sidewalk. I don't know about Denise and Lily, but I need a little time to wonder about Papa and Maman once in a while and to take in all that's been happening to us.

"Hurry!" Denise urges. "Look how far ahead of us they are! Let's not get lost."

But I continue to take my time. I know that the residence is just yards away. We are in Rue de la Planchette. All we need now is to find Number Five.

I take a closer look at the quiet cobblestone street with two- or three-story attached houses on both sides. We are passing by a wrought-iron fence; wide branches stick out from the trees behind it and tower over us. Then we come to a building where Mlle Andrée and Lily are waiting for us.

This is it: Number Five. The residence is officially called La Planchette, after the street, although I know it's affectionately nicknamed La Chaumière—The Little Cottage.

"Go on," Denise says, as she pushes me ahead the last few steps. "You're the oldest!"

I'm not going anywhere first, I tell myself, and decide to concentrate on the door we are now facing. It is made of two heavy wooden panels—one with a large brass doorknob, the other one with a slot for the mail. It looks like a fortress, a sealed wall, to me. I search in vain for a reassuring sign.

Let's just hope it's more cheerful inside! I think.

"Ready?" Mlle Andrée asks, her finger pressing the bell.

I park myself behind her, closing my eyes.

"Please, God," I pray, "make someone nice open the door!"

Within seconds a nun dressed in the heavy greenish-blue habit of the Sisters of St. Vincent de Paul appears in the doorway. "Yes?" she asks softly, not quite trusting us enough to open the door. She seems so young and fragile with her thin, pale face and her large blue eyes under the oversize wings of her *cornette*, her headpiece. Why, she seems so likable!

"Bonjour, ma sœur," Mlle Andrée replies cheerfully. "I am Mlle Andrée Caban and these are the *petites Roth*."

"Ah, yes, of course!" the young nun exclaims, relaxing somewhat.

"We've been expecting you. My name is Sister Geneviève. Come right in!"

I feel Denise's elbow in my ribs as we walk in.

"I am sorry that our Mother Superior, Sister Pannelay, is not able to welcome you herself. In the meantime I will take you to your rooms, so you'll have a chance to get settled before dinner, which is served at seven-thirty. Please follow me."

We rush past a tiled corridor and up the three flights of a narrow staircase.

"This will be yours," Sister Geneviève says as she shows us into a fairly spacious room. I note the three brass-frame beds and three tiny night tables, each holding a lamp. The beds face two large windows.

"You may put your things in here," she explains, pointing to an armoire between the windows. "There's a small mirror inside. And you'll also have this chest of drawers under the pitcher and the basin. By the way, the toilets are at the end of the corridor, to the right."

She turns to Mlle Andrée, who is to stay overnight before returning to Paris. "Your room is next door. Let me show you."

They both disappear.

Alone at last—and free to explore our new surroundings—the three of us dash to the windows. In the dimming daylight we can make out a vast courtyard. The far end is covered with flowers and bushes. The rest of it is a lawn bordered by low hedges. A graveled walk circles it all.

"A garden! A garden!" I exclaim, hoping that we might have roses or best of all, lilies of the valley and lilacs—Maman's favorites.

"Look at the white statue, right there, between the hedges," Lily points out. "I bet it's the Virgin Mary. I've seen it before."

"Could be," Denise mumbles, indifferently walking away from the window.

She is much more interested in picking out her bed right now. She is already taking off the bedspread from one and folding it methodically.

It's getting dark. I turn one of the small lamps on.

The walls are whitewashed and clean—almost too bare against the high ceiling.

"See this?" Lily asks.

I follow her pointing finger.

"There's a cross above each bed. Do you think it's all right for us to sleep under it?"

Now, how am I to know? "I'm sure it does no good

for Jews," I improvise. "But then I don't suppose it can harm them either."

I'm not *that* sure. What if Jesus comes down from his cross and converts the three of us while we're asleep?

"I guess not," Denise agrees, her usual unruffled self. "Otherwise the nuns would have done something about it. They must know what they're doing."

Reassured for the moment, I lift the thin bedspread to inspect the bedding—just as Maman does whenever we sleep in strange places. I can't help smiling: She would be pleased to see me now!

The sheets are made of ecru linen, stiff and coarse. And there's not even any pillow—just a long, skinny bolster. I feel positively cheated.

"How can they expect us to sleep without a pillow?" I demand, longing for the large fat one from home.

I suddenly feel out of place, in strange surroundings, assailed by strange smells. I'm close to tears, but the last thing I want to do is to cry—not with my little sisters next to me.

Thank goodness for Sister Geneviève, who appears at the door with Mlle Andrée behind her. "Mother Superior has just returned. She would like to see you now. I'll take you to her office."

My sisters dash out of the room, following the nun and Mlle Andrée.

I hesitate, not quite ready. My eyes fall on the cross hanging over my bed. Maybe—just maybe—Jesus on his cross could help me long enough to face Mother Superior.

But I decide that's not a good idea. Instead, I reach out to the armoire with my fingers, touching wood for good luck—and run out of the room to catch up with the others.

———

"Ah . . . les voilà! Here they are! Welcome to La Chaumière!" Mother Superior exclaims as we enter her office.

I tell myself not to swing my legs as I sit with my sisters and Mlle Andrée in a half circle around the nun's desk. She tells us about the excellent parochial school in town, the Pensionnat Notre-Dame, which the three of us will be attending, and adds that the headmistress will "know about us." She also tells us about the young women who board at La Chaumière and about how the war has forced the nuns to take in more people.

I am distracted by the fine fuzz over her upper lip, her straight elegant nose, her high cheekbones. She is doing her best to be pleasant and she smiles a lot, but I can't make up my mind about her yet.

She lowers her voice now, and pushing aside the pile of neatly stacked mail on her desk, she takes out three tan gold-rimmed leather-covered books from a drawer.

"Since you'll be going to Mass on Sundays, I thought it would be a good idea for each of you to have her own missal. Here," she continues, moving the books closer to us, "As you can see, your individual names have been engraved on each. I hope this will keep gossips from wondering about you since you will be the only children here."

She is the first person here who has alluded to our special situation.

Folding her hands in her lap, Mother Superior continues, "I hope you'll like it here. By the way, there will be someone to look after you, Mlle Marie-France. She will be teaching in town, but she has volunteered to spend all her leisure time with you. Unfortunately she won't get here until school starts. In the meantime Sister Geneviève will be your guide.

"Well, it's dinnertime now," she concludes, getting up. "You'll have a chance to get acquainted with the dining room—and with some of the people who live here. *Bon appétit!* And if you need anything, just ask for me."

"It's all right for me to stay with the girls, isn't it?" Mlle Andrée asks.

"By all means. Just make sure to tell M. and Mme Roth that I will do everything I can to make their stay here pleasant and safe—as much as is within my power."

———

Our first supper . . . how will it go? I wonder as the four of us walk past the two long rows of tables and benches of the crowded dining hall.

The tables are covered with shiny plaid oilcloth. Except for a huge wooden cross hanging between two windows, the walls are bare.

It's dark outside by now, and the room is poorly lit. An occasional candle helps give it a cozy touch. I am starved, and I'm dying to know what's on the platters, but I don't dare take my eyes off Mlle Andrée, who is preceding us. "It's rather clean, don't you think?" Denise asks. Evidently her priorities lie elsewhere.

"If you ask me, I would've preferred separate tables," Lily comments.

"At least we have our own room," I remind her, remembering to count our blessings.

The people are chatting away. For the most part, from what I can tell, they are women in their twenties. I sense many eyes staring at us, and the conversations stop at our approach.

"There's some room right here!" someone calls out.

We stop. Gratefully I sit on one side of the table next to Lily and Denise and Mlle Andrée on the other. At least we are *entre nous*, among ourselves.

"Here! Help yourselves!" a woman to my right says as she offers a platter to Mlle Andrée. It looks like a rather appetizing *hachis Parmentier*, like corned-beef hash. "It's quite good! Sister Madeleine, our cook, does her best to make the meals pleasant. By the way I'm Solange Niveau, and this is my twin sister, Yvonne," she adds, pointing to a woman at her side.

"I am Andrée Caban, and these are Renée, Denise, and Liliane Roth. We are all from Paris. I'm a friend of the family, and I know Mother Superior, so I offered to bring these young ladies here. But I must leave tomorrow."

I am thankful to Mlle Andrée for taking the lead, but I've got to muster up some courage on my own.

"Do you live in Flers all year round?" I ask, my heart racing at the thought of all the questions that may come up.

Brave enough to meet my neighbor's eyes, I see a thin, open face, surrounded by dark curls. Her twin's face, I note, risking a glance toward her, is somewhat fuller— just enough to distinguish one from the other.

"No, not quite. Our family lives in Le Chatellier, about ten kilometers or so from here. Both Yvonne and I work in town. I am a salesgirl and my sister is a seam-stress. You'll find that many of us at La Chaumière are from neighboring towns and villages, and so we often go home from Saturday afternoon to Sunday night. What about you? Will you be living here?"

My heart has stopped pounding. A little kindness goes a long way!

"Yes," I reply, feeling my cheeks return to their natural color and my confidence inch back gradually. "Our parents live in Paris where Papa works. We'll be staying here, but we'll be attending the Pensionnat Notre-Dame. We are originally from Alsace," I add, bravely taking the bull by the horns, hoping to forestall the inevitable question about the origin of our name.

"Oh, you've come a long way then!" Solange exclaims, smiling. "I can't blame you for wanting to come to Normandy!"

"Neither can I," her sister echoes.

Bless the Normans for their regional pride! It would take very little for me to throw a kiss at them. Comfortable enough to face the others, I let my eyes wander and notice someone smiling at me in the distance. I return the smile.

There is the good omen I've been looking for!

––––––

The lights are out. My sisters and I are lying in our own beds.

"It wasn't too bad, was it? I mean, our first day?" I ask.

"That's true. The nuns are nice. There's no reason to complain so far," Denise concedes.

"I agree," Lily remarks. "I only wish that Papa and Maman were with us tonight . . . just tonight . . . to tuck us in."

My little sister's independence has its limits!

"And give us a piece of candy before going to sleep!" Denise adds. "Remember?"

How could I not remember? It was only a few days ago!

Ever since we passed storytelling age, the three of us have been given a piece of candy at bedtime. In spite of the food restrictions Maman has always managed to scrape up some sweet to give us at night.

"Wait!" I exclaim, suddenly struck by a wonderful idea. I jump out of bed, and fumbling in my night-table drawer, I take out a rumpled piece of waxed paper.

"Here," I say, triumphant. "Help yourselves!"

I open the paper, which contains a few sticky pieces of broken candies, all I managed to scrounge of leftover cough drops before we left Paris.

"Gee!" Denise exclaims, as she and Lily get up and share in the unexpected treat.

"We'll be all right, you'll see!" I promise, feeling invincible as long as the three of us are together.

We hug, we kiss . . . and we cry a little.

"Back to bed now," I order, playing the big sister, and they obey.

It's quiet again, and I'm beginning to feel sad.

So I have managed to take care of my sisters today, as Papa has asked me to. But what about tomorrow? What about the day after tomorrow? How many days will we have to be away from home?

Remembering the cross hanging over my bed, I am grateful that no one has bothered us about praying.

No, we can't complain.

"Good night!" I say aloud. But there's no answer. My sisters are fast asleep.

Feeling alone and realizing that I am sleeping in my own bed for the first time in my life, I hug my skinny pillow as if it were a companion and bury my face in it.

"Good night!" I echo. "Welcome to our Chaumière!"

Sunday, August 9

We don't get a chance to breathe. Today is already Sunday, and the three of us are expected to go to Mass. I've already been inside churches—like the Sacré-Cœur in Paris—but I've never attended a service or anything.

"Be sure to wear your hats!" Sister Geneviève reminded us this morning when she woke us up. "Breakfast will be served at nine. Be ready to leave at a quarter to ten! We usually go to an early Mass at St. Jean's parish, close to here. But today is a special occasion for you, so we've decided to take you to High Mass at St. Germain. It's a bit fancier, and it has a beautiful organ. Hurry now!"

"How does it look?" I ask my sisters, putting my wide-brimmed hat straight over my head, without much enthusiasm: I wish we didn't have to go to church.

"You're supposed to tilt it to the side," Denise explains, adjusting it properly. "There! It looks rather nice with your curls."

Mother Superior bought us each a hat in a hurry yesterday. Denise and Lily settled for a more girlish plaid beret made of soft wool with a huge red pompon for good luck.

"Do you think Sister Geneviève *knows*?" I wonder aloud.

My sisters and I have learned to speak in code among

ourselves, knowing—as we have been warned time and time again—that "walls have ears."

"Why, she must! Why else would she bother to fill us in on so many details?" Denise replies.

True. Only this morning Sister Geneviève explained that women must always wear a hat when entering a church, out of respect for God. For men it works in reverse.

The bells start to peal—strong, melodious, inviting.

"Time to go!" Sister Geneviève calls out from the hallway.

"Remember!" the nun says as we walk briskly along, carrying our handbags and missals with our properly gloved hands. "Attending mass is compulsory on Sundays and holidays—and you must get to church before the Gospel is read, or you may as well not bother to show up at all!"

I can't help wondering what happens when one does miss a Sunday Mass or arrive late, but there's no time to think.

We have come to a gray building with square towers. I am disappointed. I miss the pointed spires of Alsace.

We climb the many steps to the main entrance.

"Let's go in through the side and find seats close to Mother Superior. She hates to be late, so she always gets here before the rest of us." Sister Geneviève motions us to follow her. Hesitant, I signal my sisters to go in before me.

"*You* go in first!" Denise whispers, pushing me ahead. I must remind myself that this is no place to argue or to pinch anyone.

I step in with utmost caution. I expect something to

happen. I am not sure what: instant conversion? Or to fall to the floor, struck dead by lightning for daring to step into this holy place where I don't belong?

But nothing happens. I take a second step and dare to look for Mother Superior. There she is, in one of the middle pews. She sees us but she doesn't smile. You're not supposed to in church, Sister Geneviève told us; God comes first.

I wish we could settle somewhere in the back, away from the suspicious stares, but Sister Geneviève points to four seats right in back of Mother Superior.

Following Sister Geneviève's lead, we put our missals on the pew and kneel down on the bench. The church looks as if decorated for a holiday: There are so many large paintings hanging down from the vaulted ceilings; tall statues; stained-glass windows letting in beams of light. It is so different from what I remember of our synagogue in Mulhouse—which was so dark, so bare.

Sister Geneviève signals us to sit down. The scented air, the soft music coming from an invisible organ, make me feel as if I'm dreaming.

The newcomers kneel down in the middle aisle before getting to their seats. I know it is to pay respect to the little house on the altar—we have one in our chapel too. Mother Superior calls it the Tabernacle. She says God is in there somewhere.

It suddenly dawns on me that Sister Geneviève got us to enter through the side door to spare us the genuflection. She is no fool!

"It smells funny, don't you think? Just the same, I like it!" Denise whispers as she greedily sucks in the air about her. "It's probably all those candles burning in the back!"

I like it too. But I'm much more interested in the people, all dressed up in fancy clothes.

At least here families can worship openly, I tell myself. I spot three well-behaved little girls—all blond, all dressed alike—sitting securely between their equally blond parents.

How I wish it were us!

My heart is pounding wildly now. I suddenly miss Papa and Maman, and I feel homesick. But I must not cry. I open my eyes real wide, bite my lower lip, and clench my fists tight. It does the trick.

I am grateful for Sister Geneviève asking us to kneel again on the bench—no doubt to get us to practice. But I get such a cramp in my left calf that I must shake it to get it back to normal.

I whisper to Denise what's bothering me, and together we burst into quiet laughter. Lily gives us a dirty look, but Sister Geneviève, still lost in prayer, has not seen a thing.

I direct my attention to the two young boys in long red velvet robes and white embroidered smocks who are now giving the last touches to the altar. The music suddenly gets louder: The priest emerges from the side in a long gilded robe, and everyone rises.

I like to watch the people when they sit down, kneel, and get up again, as if moved by an invisible choreographer, or when they pray in unison with the priest as he reads from a large red book. I watch the priest raise a gold cup, and one of the boys rings a little bell.

I am not bored at all.

I listen to the soft choir, which I still cannot see, and I look with envy at all these people who pray, their hands joined, their eyes closed.

It must be comforting to have someone to talk to who's really listening.

To my surprise an old lady a few seats away smiles at me. I am no longer afraid.

I know that I am not one of them. But so what? I feel welcome just the same.

If this is all that's going to be asked of me, it's going to suit me just fine.

Saturday, August 22

Of all the nuns I like Sister Madeleine, our cook, the best.

Still, I get scared when, at lunchtime today, Sister Geneviève calls out, "*Les petites Roth!* Sister Madeleine wants you in the pantry—immediately!"

Expecting God knows what, Denise, Lily, and I leave our barely touched salad and beef stew on the table and dash out of the dining hall, through the corridor, and into the kitchen. Gigantic pots are being stirred there by the expert hands of Sister Madeleine and her two fat helpers—Germaine and Thérèse.

They seem perfectly calm and continue placidly to stir the food—tonight's dinner, most likely—as we walk in.

"Don't look so frightened!" the nun says, smiling. "There's nothing in the world to worry about. In fact, I have good news for you!"

She lowers the fire under the pot and motions us into the pantry.

I liked her from the beginning. I like her narrow, bony face, her warm, broad smile, her energetic, friendly handshake. She is tall and skinny: Her wide apron is wrapped several times around her waist. Maman would definitely find her much too thin.

"I couldn't tell you in front of everyone why I wanted to see you," she whispers to us in confidence. "You see, I had some extra eggs left, so I decided to prepare a special custard for you. You'll have it after lunch. I just wanted you to know about it so you won't rush out for your usual walk. And what's more," she adds, "I have enough eggs and flour left to make a cake for your father and mother. What do you say? I'll send it tomorrow!"

She has—almost—wiped out all the hurt of the last few months. She even makes up for the fact that nobody made a fuss about my birthday last Sunday, when I turned eleven. I throw my arms around her neck with such force that she has to hold on to her *cornette.*

"I like you too!" she says, laughing. "Just don't tell the others about this, or else I'll get into trouble. Why don't you rush back so that no one will wonder. Can you keep a secret?"

Keep a secret! She must be kidding! Doesn't she know that we've become experts at it?

Sister Madeleine is definitely our friend, but even more so, mine.

Unlike Sister Geneviève, who pampers Lily because she is so skinny and the baby—or Mother Superior, who keeps praising Denise for the way she keeps her drawer and things in disgustingly neat order—Sister Madeleine doesn't play favorites. My idea of the perfect nun!

Madeleine isn't her real name, I know.

"When you take your vows," she explained one evening when the three of us were keeping her company in the kitchen, "you give up all you have to become a servant of God. To mark this new beginning, you get a new name."

She wasn't born in France but in Poland. The oldest of a large and poor family, she had settled in a small mining town near Lille as a young child.

She says very little about her early life in Poland, but one thing is certain: For reasons connected with her childhood she detests the Germans.

That makes Sister Madeleine even dearer to us—and I'm willing to bet we are dearer to her because of our secret.

Sunday, August 23

It's not enough to be the oldest—that is, to be sensible and set an example for my sisters. Mother Superior insists that I be the one to write our weekly letter to Papa and Maman.

I'm sitting at one of the dining-room tables, facing the blank lined sheet in front of me. My sisters are watching me closely.

I'm a good speller but that isn't everything.

I don't know where to begin. How do you write to someone you're used to talking to?

"Tell them about the cross over our beds!" Lily suggests.

"No! Don't tell them about that! Why give them

something to worry about?" Denise says. "Tell them about how nice the nuns are to us!"

"Since I'm doing the writing, I'll decide what to say." I start to write in round, well-formed, legible characters—for Papa's sake; he's a stickler about fine handwriting.

Dear Papa and Maman,
Everything is fine here. The nuns are very kind. Sister Madeleine especially is very fond of us and tries to spoil us a little so we don't get homesick. Imagine, she's like us: She, too, puts sugar in her vinaigrette!

I can't mention in the letter that Sister Madeleine is Polish—with the Germans controlling the mail, it could be dangerous for her. But this way Papa and Maman can read between the lines.

We'll be starting school soon, and now we're waiting for Mlle Marie-France, who will keep an eye on us.
They call us the petites *Roth. We have a cross over our beds, and we go to Sunday Mass.*
I think we will like it here. So please, don't worry.
Do you think you'll be able to visit for Christmas, as promised?

Love and kisses,
The three of us

Why bother to say that I miss terribly not being able to write to Pépée or ask if anyone heard from Feigie, Jeannette, or the rest of our friends?

Or to confide that every night now before falling asleep, I try very hard, with my eyes closed, to remember the details of my parents' faces or to recall the sound of their voices . . . and that the memories are growing dimmer and dimmer?

We each sign the letter.

Mission accomplished.

Tuesday, September 1

I do what I can to keep away from Mlle Suzanne—she is a gossip and so nosy—but tonight, she has decided to join us in the recreation room after dinner.

Her cat, Tommy, is sitting on her lap. She is holding it tight against her enormous chest to keep it from running on the keyboard of the piano next to us. For the life of me I can't see why she's so crazy about a fat gray cat that looks at you without seeing you—and isn't even friendly.

Mlle Suzanne is by far the oldest resident of La Chaumière. She has a round face that turns red in a minute and a rather short temper. Some blame the little nips she likes to take on those long winter nights.

She is rather plump; maybe because she doesn't move around very much. It isn't her fault. Her right leg is much shorter than her left, so that she has a marked limp. She's been crippled from birth, Sister Madeleine says, yet she hates it when people fuss over her.

When she stands up, leaning heavily on her cane, her curved spine makes her large bosom stand out and her derrière protrude. "She looks like a capital *S*!" I remarked the first time I saw her. The nickname "Capital *S*" stuck, and we call her that when we're in a joking mood. Sometimes, behind our closed door, my sisters and I try to imitate her.

Capital *S* has lived at La Chaumière ever since it was built—only God knows how long. "You should have seen me when I was young! I was the best milliner around!" she likes to boast.

It was obviously before anyone's time. According to Solange the only reminder of this glorious period is an extravagant collection of hats. All she does these days is some sewing for the nuns and crocheting for the poor.

She has moved her chair a little closer to the sofa, where I am reading. I make believe I'm totally lost in my serial, *"Semaine de Suzette."* She definitely wants to find out more about the three of us.

I wonder how much they all know about what's been happening to Jews in Paris and other big French cities? Mlle Andrée told us that there are probably very few—if any—Jews here in Flers. But that doesn't mean anything. People can hate Jews without even knowing any.

The lady must have stared at me for a long time.

"What do I hear?" she finally says. "Your parents live in Paris, and they've shipped you so far from home? Poor kids! It's just as bad as being orphans!"

I feel my cheeks turn crimson. I want to strangle the old *demoiselle*. I wish she'd mind her own business.

The trouble is, I've questioned my parents' decision myself a hundred times. Now, I don't doubt for a minute that they placed our safety before all else. But Uncle Maurice and Aunt Fanny, and Maman's cousins Paulette and Hélène—they all managed to stay with their children. So why couldn't we stay together? We're just as smart as they are!

But this is not the time to feel sorry for ourselves. "It wasn't easy—but they thought that the country had to be better than Paris, with the food shortage and all. We're lucky, I guess, that we had friends who knew Mother Superior. She offered to take us," I manage to retort.

Luckily by now Capital *S* couldn't care less: Tommy has fallen asleep in her lap. "There . . . there . . . aren't we comfy?" she whispers, patting the cat softly.

Relieved, I whisper to my sisters, "If everyone were as harmless as Capital *S*, we would have nothing to worry about!"

But I know it would be asking for the impossible.

Thursday, September 3

Mlle Juliette is another story. She has just walked into our room tonight to check on our sheets. We're trapped.

I knew I wasn't going to like this lady the minute I laid eyes on her. "She's a very efficient housekeeper," Mother Superior had said. "She's in charge of our linen and our bedding—and especially of our chapel—and she does an excellent job. We certainly missed her while she was on vacation."

There's nothing frail about Mlle Juliette, despite her small size. Her thick, blunt gray hair falls in straight bangs over gray eyes that pierce you like cold steel even through her thick eyeglasses. She has thin, unsmiling lips; a line cutting across her pale face.

Her head is tilted to the right, as if she has a permanent stiff neck.

"Serves her right! God punished her for her sharp tongue!" someone reported Capital *S* to have commented about her. They say that the two can't stand each other.

Mother Superior must have her reasons for liking Mlle Juliette—maybe if only to be a good Christian—but I run as far away from her as I can.

"What's your name again?" she inquires just before she leaves, having given us new sheets and removed the old ones. "I'm not sure I heard it right."

Here we go again! Alarm bells begin to go off in my head.

"Roth," I say, clearing my throat. "R-O-T-H."

"That's not a French name, is it?" she asks, turning around and directing her piercing glance at me.

"Well, it's Alsatian!" I lie, grateful for not stammering.

The old fear is twisting my stomach now, but I continue to meet her suspicious stare just the same: I am not going to let her get to me!

"My parents live in Paris now, but we orginally came from Mulhouse. Are you familiar with the area?" I am trying to change the subject. Let *me* be the one to ask the questions!

But she doesn't seem to have heard me. "Do you speak Alsatian then?" she asks.

"Of course. Well, I used to—we used to. We're speaking French at home now. It's been several years since we left Alsace."

"And your father, what does he do?" she continues, relentless. I try to fight off the panic that is rising in me. I only hope that she doesn't notice the perspiration that must have taken over my forehead.

I bend down to stretch my perfectly straight socks to gather my thoughts. Too many Jews are tailors, I decide. If anyone is going to make the connection, *she* is.

"He's working for a raincoat manufacturer," I reply, giving her a half truth.

"It is odd, isn't it, that your parents should send three little girls to a strange place all by themselves in these troubled times?"

Mlle Juliette is definitely getting too nosy—and steering me into dangerous waters.

I turn to my sisters for some support. A word, a

look—anything. But Lily is dangling her legs studiously, and Denise is concentrating on an invisible spot on her skirt. The cowards!

Better let the old maid misjudge Papa and Maman than give her more rope to hang us all, I conclude.

"Things had become too rough in Paris—with the food shortage, the air raids, and everything. . . . Some friends of ours knew Mother Superior and La Chaumière and thought it might be a good idea to send us here. They knew we wouldn't go hungry in Normandy! Besides, Maman will visit us as often as possible; she even promised to come see us for Christmas!"

This stops the investigation. Thank the Lord, Mother Superior would say.

———

After our enemy has left the room, I explode. "What happened to you two? Why did you both keep your mouths shut when I most needed you?"

"I knew you would get us out of it," Denise says.

"I did too. What else was there to say anyway? You said it all," Lily remarks.

"Baloney!" I protest, feeling totally alone and misunderstood. "You could've said something! Wait till she catches you alone and I'm not around to help you out!"

Just for one day let them be me, I think. They'll see what it's like to be the oldest, and to have brats for kid sisters! They won't like it one bit!

Tuesday, September 15

I couldn't wait for Mlle Marie-France to get here—if only to get that pesty Mlle Juliette out of our hair.

Well, she arrived today. She is tall and lanky, with legs as straight as telegraph poles. But she has a kind and pleasant face. I like her dark blue eyes and her chestnut hair, which she wears in braided puffs over her ears. She looks quite serious in her pleated skirt and her spotless white shirt.

"Mlle Marie-France will occupy the room next to yours. I expect her to supervise your homework and to make sure that you keep your clothes and room in order. She will take you on walks on Sunday afternoons. I hope you'll get along," Mother Superior said.

"I'm certainly looking forward to being here!" Mlle Marie-France replied. "I may as well warn you," she added, addressing the three of us, "I'm a stickler about homework and strict bedtime. Other than that you'll find that I'm fairly easy to live with."

"She seems fair enough," Lily concedes.

"We'll see," Denise says.

I'm quite sure she will do.

We decide to call her Mademoiselle.

Tuesday, September 22

Mademoiselle is well on her way to becoming a spinster. She will celebrate St. Catherine next fall. I love this custom, which makes a fuss over every unmarried young lady of twenty-five on the day of St. Catherine— November 25. But if you ask me, it doesn't make up for not having a fiancé or a husband! I certainly hope to be married before reaching *my* quarter of a century.

"There's an awful lot of old maids around here! Mlle Suzanne, Mlle Juliette—and now, Mlle Marie-France. Do you think it's got something to do with being a Catholic?" I wonder aloud.

"I certainly don't know many back home. Do you?" Denise asks.

I can't think of any right now," Lily remarks.

"The nuns are old maids, too, for that matter—even though they tell you that they're married to Christ. It does add up to an awful lot of wives, doesn't it! By the way, did you notice that they wear wedding bands?" I add, having just found out myself.

"What if they do?" Lily argues. "It's not the same as having a husband and children."

"That's for sure," I can't help agreeing. "They don't have to worry about a husband who gargles loudly in the morning and monopolizes the family sink because he needs a shave!"

I stop, mortified.

I can't believe that I said such things! Whatever came over me? It came out all wrong!

I know I'm turning as red as a beet. Never, ever in my life have I felt so utterly exposed.

I guess I did at times feel impatient with Papa. He was forever needing the sink to shave and all. But how can I blurt out such dreadful things, when I miss my father and the family routines so much?

I bite my lip—partly to punish myself, partly to keep myself from blurting out more nonsense—and wait for my sisters' teasing comments.

But there are none. I sigh with relief.

Spinsterhood or not, I think, I have plenty of time to worry about my future.

Friday, October 9

I love our new school.

It is really quite chic. It's an elegant gray building with ivy climbing all over some of the walls. There's a spacious yard with a lawn and trees and all kinds of equipment for sports and games. We also have our own chapel.

What a difference from our Paris school, which was all concrete and squeezed between two buildings!

They call us *externes*, all of us who don't sleep on campus. It's so wonderful to be able to come and go without my star. Since I don't need to hide or to be ashamed anymore, and can look up as I walk, I feel much taller.

My sisters and I are walking to class, arms linked, our schoolbags on our backs. We walk down our calm street to the Cinq Becs, the Five Corners, and the people we come across greet us as if they've always known us. Except for a few bicycles and an occasional car or truck, the town is rather quiet. There are no buses, like in Paris, or streetcars, like in Mulhouse.

I like the Cinq Becs, the most important crossroad in town, which points in all directions. I'm trying to get used to the names of the towns and villages in the area: Domfront, Argentan, Aigle, Messei, Caen—and especially Cerisi-Belle-Étoile and La Chapelle au Moine. It sounds so countrylike.

Denise—as anyone could've predicted—always presses her nose against the window of the bakery shop as we walk to school. I prefer to peep into the only café at the crossroad, where workmen in overalls are smoking a last cigarette or enjoying a *café crème*—coffee with cream.

Lily, losing her patience, usually pulls us both by the arm and reminds us that we're going to be late to school. Then we take Rue Blin and run all the way to school.

I also love my new teacher. Her name is Mme Prével. She is the headmistress as well; my sisters are just as happy with theirs.

Imagine: Even though they're nuns, they don't even wear habits. Lily wonders why we call them Madame rather than Mademoiselle or Sister. It doesn't bother me one bit.

On the first day Mme Prével said in front of the whole class that she was proud to have a Parisian student among them. I was so happy, I could have kissed her.

She does have a reason to be proud: I raise my hand for practically every question she asks.

I know I'm going to be a model student!

Friday, October 23

I am in our chapel alone.

I don't like what's been happening to us.

We've been at it again: getting into a heated argument over something that definitely should not concern us.

I'm the one who started the whole thing. "What do you think of God the Father being at the same time Jesus Christ and the Holy Ghost? I just can't see how it's possible," I had wondered aloud yesterday, as Denise, Lily, and I were getting ready for bed. The idea bothered me, and I had wanted to get to the bottom of it.

"But, dummy, isn't that what they call a Divine Mystery? Just like the Immaculate Conception! You're not supposed to question it!" Obviously Denise had been pondering it too.

"She's right. Sister Geneviève says that once you have faith, you don't need to ask yourself so many questions anymore!" comments Lily as naturally as if we were talking about a recipe.

I've come to hate these arguments about the Catholic faith; every time, I feel we are betraying Papa, Maman, our family and friends a little more. But I can't seem to stop them, even though I'm the oldest.

It's so unfair! Papa and Maman should have thought of this before. They forget that my sisters and I are not real Jews—not the way *they* are. A Seder here, a bar mitzvah there, some vague memories of celebrating Rosh Hashanah, does that make a Jew?

"Just don't pay attention. It's all nonsense!" Maman would say about our questions. She has a way of closing her eyes and ears to things she doesn't want to know about. I can't. I try so hard to push all the new stuff away. . . . I do my best to fight it off with Jewish prayers or Jewish stories. . . . But I can't come up with any. Even Grand'mère says that we were too little to learn anything before the war. And since then—three years already!—Jews have had nothing but trouble, and there was no time for learning.

"We'll catch up after the war," Papa had promised. I wish he were here now to tell me what to do.

My eyes fall on the statue of the Virgin Mary and the picture of St. Thérèse de Lisieux.

Jewish women can never become saints. They aren't even supposed to touch the Torah or to pronounce the name of God, and they don't count at all when it comes to a minyan, the quorum of Jews required in order to worship. It's Maman who told me this!

At least here God is nicer to women. He made Mary the mother of Jesus and little Thérèse de Lisieux a saint!

I look at the statue of Mary—her face soft and smiling, her hands stretched out and welcoming. I feel torn. I don't know which way to go.

———

"Please, Jesus, Mary, help me out, so long as it's not going to hurt Papa and Maman," I finally pray.

I feel much better now.

I will meet them all halfway.

I'll do my best *not* to let my imagination run wild or ask too many questions about the Catholic religion.

I will simply accept God's presence in the beams of light shining through the stained-glass windows in church, and I will talk to Him through the singing and the chanting.

If He is as understanding as He's made out to be, He'll accept me as I am!

Thursday, October 29

The other day Mother Superior called my sisters and me into the parlor after dinner.

"I think you could use a little coaching in religious

instruction," she said. "It's not that you're not learning fast—I hear that you are, in fact, picking up things very quickly—but I've discussed it with Mme Prével, your headmistress, and we both have come to the conclusion that memorizing the catechism would probably help you best. It sums up all the basic teaching of the Catholic Church. Since everyone around here is familiar with it from childhood, it will help you to feel less lost when someone brings up one pious topic or another."

I had nothing against learning the catechism. It would take up some of our free time, I thought . . . and it looked so easy.

———

Today I found out otherwise!

"What you are saying is basically correct," Mme Prével remarks after I have recited, almost word for word, my first lesson. "But you must memorize it in the exact words of the catechism."

My teacher is still smiling, but I don't like the inflexible, almost harsh tone in her voice.

So what's the difference if you say "all-powerful" instead of "almighty"? I want to scream. Isn't one word as good as another as long as the meaning remains the same?

I can't understand it. They tell you to trust God, to love your neighbor, and all those wonderful things, but you can't change one comma around!

Sunday, November 1

"We'll go to the cemetery after Vespers," Mother Superior announced at breakfast this morning. "It sure feels like winter, doesn't it?" she added, wringing her hands. "I think we'd better consider going to St. Jean's for the service. It's much too cold to walk to the Lande-Patry."

Attending Vespers has become a pleasant way to spend Sunday afternoons. We take a stroll with Mademoiselle—sometimes Sister Geneviève comes along—to the neighboring villages. We usually get there just in time to hear the bells peal.

I prefer Vespers to Mass, but I don't dare tell anyone; they wouldn't understand. First of all we don't have to worry about not taking Communion like everybody else, since we are not baptized. It would be a mortal sin, from what Sister Madeleine says. And secondly we spend most of Vespers singing.

I love these little churches, still untouched by the war. I know that no one will come to get us here, and I am happy to be able to blend with the humble parishioners, who look so much like the pink-cheeked statues that surround them. Surely God must hear the off-key singing coming straight from the people's hearts!

———

"We'll ask M. Jacques to take out the van," Mother Superior decides when Vespers is over. "There should be ample room for the eight of us."

I'm glad M. Jacques is coming along. I hardly know him, but I like him very much. He works for M. le Curé, the parish priest, and once in a while he helps the nuns with the gardening and other such things. Sister Geneviève says that, outside of our priest and his *abbés*, he is the only man allowed at La Chaumière.

It is obvious that M. Jacques is shy—and even sad, I think. He is very quiet, but he has the warmest smile. Sometimes, when no one is paying attention, he looks so sad that I am almost tempted to walk over to ask him what is troubling him.

Are his troubles the reason that he lives with his widowed mother rather than have a family of his own? I ask myself. Or is it his slight hunchback that keeps him away from people?

I, for one, like his smooth, white skin and the short hair that gives him a boyish look. I find him quite attractive.

I know that Mother Superior is very fond of him too. She calls him a holy man. I hope that he is not so holy that he won't get married. I'm sure he'd make the best father.

And I bet he'd like my sisters and me even if he knew that we were Jewish.

We all climb in the back of the van: Mother Superior, Sister Geneviève, Mademoiselle, Mlle Suzanne, and my sisters. I am allowed to sit next to M. Jacques.

Sister Madeleine has explained to us that it is a custom to visit the graves on All Saints' Day. I have been to the cemetery only once, when I was a little girl, before the war. It was in Alsace, at the top of a mountain. I was struck by the hundreds and hundreds of rows of white wooden crosses covering the fields as far as the eye could see. Papa had told me that they were all for soldiers, who had died for their country during the War of 1870.

===

It doesn't take us very long to reach the edge of town. M. Jacques stops the car in front of a wrought-iron gate, and we all get out.

Large gray clouds darken the sky. The wind sweeps the fallen leaves in spurts. We are crossing the entrance gate now. I walk on tiptoe as if afraid to wake up anyone.

There are several rows of tombs set closely next to one another. There are no wooden crosses here, but rectangles of stone or marble with various inscriptions and a large cross at the head of each grave. Some are decorated with wreaths or fresh flowers.

We are not the only visitors: In the next row there are two little boys holding the hand of a lady all dressed in black. And a little farther away there is a man standing, hat in hand, and a lady kneeling down like in church, her face covered by a black veil.

I glance at the surroundings. There is nothing but graves. Am I glad I'm not alone here! I'm afraid I would never find my way out. I shudder; it must be the cold.

"I'll be right back. My father is buried near here," M. Jacques says.

A wet cloud comes out of his mouth. It is cold. I raise the collar of my coat, but I continue to feel chilled—and uneasy. I can't wait to get home.

Mlle Suzanne has stopped a few feet away. "This is my parents' grave. . . . And this is where I'll be buried someday," she whispers.

She points to a neatly kept space covered with grass and green plants. She places the flowers she is holding at the foot of the wrought-iron cross.

I look at her, puzzled. She's not at all bothered at the thought of being here one day, unable to think, to laugh, or to play with Tommy—or at the thought of her parents lying here underneath the ground, stiff and lifeless, like the dead canary of our neighbor in Mulhouse. Does there come a time, when you're well on in years yourself, when you don't miss your parents anymore?

Without any warning the idea of Papa and Maman, dead and buried somewhere far away, comes to me. I try to push it away.

A small white marble grave with the statue of an angel on the side of the cross catches my eye. It must be a child's, I tell myself. Walking over the few steps, I read:

TO OUR LITTLE ANGEL, MARIE,
TAKEN AWAY AT THE AGE OF TEN.

Only ten years old and already dead? I shudder again. She must be cold, the poor child, with all this marble.

I suddenly feel lost and scared—and afraid to die too. I want my parents to protect me from this new world full of strange people and strange things, from the dead who are cold in their graves, from death itself.

The fear of Papa and Maman denounced, arrested, and—who knows?—perhaps dead, haunts me again.

I am beginning to shake—just like that day in Paris on the Rosenbergs' staircase. I think I'm going to faint. How long does it take to die?

I look for Lily's spindly legs, for Denise's woolen hat. They are safely holding onto Mademoiselle's steady hands.

I spot Mother Superior through my misty eyes and run to her—I don't even have the energy to pull her sleeve.

"I'm going to faint!" I manage to say. A cold sweat is running down my temples. I rush to sit on the nearest marble grave to fight off the dizziness.

"Good Lord! You're as white as a sheet!" the nun exclaims. "M. Jacques," she says, "I think you should take Renée to La Chaumière with Mademoiselle and come back to get the rest of us. A hot tea and a lump of sugar with a couple of drops of our Calvados will get you your color back in no time!" she adds, cupping my face in her hand.

———

As soon as I walk into La Chaumière, I feel much better. But I can't seem to catch my breath.

"Am I going to die?" I ask Mademoiselle as she tucks me into bed a little later. I've finally blurted out my secret fear.

"No, of course not! You've gone through very hard times, these last few weeks, and then you miss your parents, your home, and everything. It's quite understandable. . . . But it will pass, I promise. And with the help of God it will all work out all right."

It's good to know that I don't have to be the brave oldest sister in front of her.

Saturday, December 12

We have been summoned to Mother Superior's office.

"*Les petites Roth!* Hurry, it's urgent!" Mademoiselle said. "Mother Superior wants to see you immediately."

Nobody bothers to call us by our individual names anymore; we are one person divided into three. For once Denise is the one to hurry, and I am the slowpoke—I'm in no rush to find out.

The nun carefully closes the door behind us and motions us to sit down. She is holding in her hand a blue envelope like the one we get every week from Papa and Maman—our only link to them now. It's always Maman who writes. Papa simply addresses the envelope; he is just as ashamed of his French spelling as of his accent.

I know the letters by heart: "We are both fine, and so's Grand'mère. Papa's working hard, and sometimes I help out. . . ." We know it's much too risky to say anything more. No one must get an inkling as to where we are and why we are away from home. We have had to be cautious for a long time—for instance, no one in the family has used the word *Jew* aloud in a long, long time. Our code word for it is *szido*, its equivalent in Hungarian.

I notice Mother Superior's tight lips, her serious expression. Can our parents no longer afford to keep us here? I'm not sure whether I should be happy or sad.

She finally sits down. "Children," she starts, "I've just received this letter from your mother, handed to me by a friend of Sister Louise who saw your mother a few days ago."

She's fidgeting with the envelope and driving me crazy. I wish I could tell her to stop.

"The letter doesn't say much—there's always the risk of a search. All your mother says is that because of circumstances that would take too long to explain, she won't be able to come here for Christmas. In fact, she won't be able to come for a while. She knows that you'll be very disappointed—so's she. But she wants you to know that she'll visit just as soon as possible."

"It can't be!" I protest. "Are you sure that's all she says?"

I'm dying to grab the envelope she's still playing with. Why isn't she showing it to us? It's from *our* mother!

I feel a wave of anger shooting through me. Maman just can't do this to us. Why, only this morning I counted that there were twelve more days to Christmas—to Maman's expected visit!

My legs are beginning to swing angrily. I must keep from kicking. "She promised!" I want to scream. "That's all I was living for!"

Denise, our sensible sister, helps us out. "Does Maman say when she hopes to come?"

"No. She says only that she'll be here just as soon as it is at all possible."

"Maybe she doesn't have the false I.D. papers yet," Lily suggests.

"It's quite possible. If it's any consolation to you, we'll prepare a special package for your parents for the holidays—with Sister Madeleine's finest cake. And we'll try to make your first Christmas here a pleasant one."

"Can we keep the letter at least?" I dare to ask.

"No, we shouldn't . . . it's too risky to keep it. In fact, I'm going to destroy it right now. In the meantime all we can do is wait and trust the Divine Providence—and of course, pray!"

———————

I can't sleep after hearing this news. Pray! That's all Mother Superior ever says. It's her answer to everything.

Honestly I haven't had that much use for God—not like Maman, the nuns, or even the people in church—except when things go wrong: "God, make sure that . . ." The rest of the time, I forget about Him.

The saints are different. They are so much more real! The kitchen helpers, Germaine and Thérèse, invoke them all day long. The other day I did the same without giving it a second thought: "St. Antoine, please help me find my belt!"

I can't stand it anymore. I kick the cover and the sheet off my bed and I sit up.

"Anything wrong?" Denise whispers.

"I can't sleep."

"Neither can I," Lily mumbles from under her sheet.

"I just can't get used to the idea of Maman not visiting!" I sigh. "It takes forever to wait!"

"Knowing Maman—who would move heaven and earth to see us—something important must be keeping her," Denise points out.

"But all Mother Superior ever says is to trust the Good Lord, the Divine Providence. It's easy for her to say!" Lily protests.

"And even if we did pray, do you really know whom to pray to? The God that Maman and Grand'mère prayed to at home has a beard and snow-white hair—I remember it from my picture book in Mulhouse—and he looked so angry!" I say. "Besides, everybody was always so scared of offending Him. I think it's quite different with the God they're praying to here. The nuns seem very fond of Him and not scared of Him at all."

"What if it's the same God though?" Lily wonders. "Everyone here swears that there's only one God."

"Why don't we try praying to the nuns' God?" Denise suggests. So at last we agree to try.

Monday, December 21

I'm sitting in our chapel alone, carrying a package under my arm. No one knows I'm here. It is so quiet, and the clean smell of wax and incense—even the kind look of St. Thérèse in her picture frame—help me to think.

There is only one candle lit on the altar, solitary, as if forgotten. Its flame is flickering back and forth.

Cautiously I pull Jackie out of the pillowcase. No one must know I'm playing with her, not even my sisters. *Especially* not my sisters! I'm getting a bit old, almost eleven and a half, for dolls. A big sister should not waste time on kid stuff—Maman has said it enough times.

But, Jackie is no ordinary doll; we go back a long way. She's the only thing I have left of Mulhouse except for a couple of snapshots of Papa and Maman. I managed to sneak them all into my suitcase when I left Paris.

"How did you do it with so little space?" Denise wondered in awe when she found out about Jackie.

"No big deal," I bragged, even though squeezing the doll in after Maman's inspection had not been the easiest thing.

I sit Jackie down in the seat next to me and whisper to her. She always listens. "You know, we've decided to pray to the nuns' God—even though, to tell you the truth, I don't believe He's the same as the Jewish God. Not after Maman had to cancel her trip. To me it's just one more proof that He's let us down altogether!"

I think Jackie agrees with me. I sit her on my lap.

"I'll address the God they invoke here," I tell her. "But just to be on the safe side, and not to hurt the Jewish God's feelings—supposing they're *not* one?—I'll be very cautious."

I start with the obvious. "Please, God, make the war end soon!"

Next I ask Him to help the French and our Allies to win the war. And later on I ask Him to protect the

Jews—it's a sure way to get Him to keep an eye on my family.

———

Up ahead on the altar the candle is still flickering, hesitant, but never giving up.

I spot the harmonium, the reed organ, set against the wall. Capital *S* rehearsed the Christmas carols on it.

I get up from my pew, still holding Jackie, and walk over.

I hit a note timidly. No sound comes out. I hit another. There's still no sound.

Then I remember that air has to be pumped in. I sit down, and pressing my foot on the pedal to let the air in, I start moving my fingers slowly on the keyboard.

A vibrant tone emerges, then another, and still another. It feels wonderful—as if a new life is seeping into my fingers. It is hope, I think; the hope that will sustain me now.

1943

Monday, January 4

Christmas has come and gone. I couldn't get excited
about it, even though the nuns did their best to make us
feel a part of the celebration. We helped them with the
decorations—setting up the Magi properly in the crèche,
draping the huge Christmas tree in the rec room with
silver garlands and delicate gold-winged angels and
shimmering stars. And the three of us got many
presents: cozy flannel nightgowns, pink with tiny
flowers, all the way down to our ankles; woolen mitts;
and a hand-knit scarf. Still, I couldn't help thinking
about Maman—and Papa. Today is Maman's birthday. I
wonder if she's thinking about us all the time too. How
do my parents stand this endless separation?

I have a new scheme to ease my homesickness. I make

sure we leave for church early so that I have plenty of time to spot a balding man of medium height and a lady with short wavy hair. Then I find seats close by—even if I have to push some people on the way. I make believe that I'm their daughter, and for that moment I feel less alone.

Friday, January 22

I look forward to going to school every morning, especially now that I sit next to Françoise Delaunay. From the beginning my sisters and I agreed that it would be best not to get too friendly with anyone; we must be very careful to avoid arousing any curiosity, so we rush home after school.

But I miss my friends—like Pépée. I often think of her. I even try to sketch her in my notebook. Sometimes I also try to draw Feigie's narrow face, but I get to wondering where she is and I stop.

Yes, I miss my friends—but it's difficult not to like Françoise. First she definitely reminds me of Pépée: She has the same high forehead, the same full cheeks. And she is so helpful. She always lets me have her pencil when I can't find mine and lends me her blotting paper all the time. When she gave me a cough drop the other day, because I had a coughing spell, I couldn't resist talking to her beyond the usual smile or thank you. Since then we've been chatting a little, and I always sit next to her. I get the feeling that she would like to be friends with me. God knows, I am tempted! But I ask myself: How can you be friends with her when you must hide a big secret?

Today Françoise insists that I stay for a little while after school: There is someone she wants me to meet. Before Françoise even introduces me I know it's her mother; a pretty mother, who puts a warm kiss on her daughter's cheek, rearranges her scarf, and looks at her with sparkles in her eyes. "You should ask Renée home for snacktime!" I hear her say. I can barely whisper, *"Merci, Madame*—another time!" And I run away like a thief before their stunned faces, just in time to hide the tears that are blinding my eyes.

How could they understand? They have each other.

Thursday, January 28

Françoise has not given up on me. She hasn't asked me to her house again, but today she gives me a picture of her Holy Communion from last year. I put it in my missal with those of St. Vincent de Paul and St. Thérèse de Lisieux that Mother Superior gave us.

When Françoise asks me for mine, I am speechless for a few minutes, and I pray for someone to inspire me. Finally I explain that I didn't celebrate Communion because in my family, we are not practicing Catholics.

We leave it at that.

Wednesday, March 17

The three of us don't wear any cross or medal around the neck like the others—and, of course, there's no way we can take Communion. Our souls are tainted enough by original sin—erasable only by baptism, as they keep harping on in school—without burdening them with more sins.

But you can be a good Christian without all that, and being charitable toward your neighbor is one way. Sacrifices strengthen the soul and get you special graces and the indulgence of God. Even Sister Madeleine believes it. So every day now, I try to do a good deed. It's very easy—and you do feel good afterward. Yesterday, for example, I helped an old lady cross the Cinq Becs. And today I did two good deeds at once. I helped the same lady cross the street and I also carried her shopping bag.

In school today I also kept from doodling on my notebook even though I was dying to. Maybe God will take it into account and hurry up the end of the war. Sometimes I get impatient, and I feel like screaming at Him: What are you waiting for?

Sister Madeleine keeps reminding me that you get nowhere by screaming: People feel hurt, then angry, and they wind up sticking their fingers in their ears instead of listening.

But God isn't like everybody else, is He?

Thursday, March 25

I wish we would hear from Papa and Maman. I've been so worried since I heard that Paris had been bombed. Mother Superior says it's only a rumor. God knows, I want to believe her, but I can't get it out of my mind.

Why don't they write? Can't they see that we need to hear from them?

I turn the family snapshot, standing on the chest of drawers, against the wall: I'm too angry to look at Papa and Maman.

I can't hold my worry any longer.

"Do you think that something has happened to them?" I ask my sisters.

"What could happen to them?" Denise says. "They live in a safe place now."

"And we heard from them last week," Lily reminds me.

I wish I didn't worry so much. I wish I could still be like my sisters, concerned only about what's for dinner, forgetting each ordeal as soon as everything is all right again.

But I know better: I know that anything can happen to our parents, to any of us, or to anyone at any time.

Saturday, April 3

Good news! We finally heard from Papa and Maman. They were not affected by the bombing, which hit Boulogne-Billancourt, in the suburbs. Now I'm free to enjoy life again.

Right now I think I'm about to enter Paradise: We are at the residence of the Sisters of Mercy, where we have been invited for tea. We have come to a wrought-iron gate before a big white house with many windows, two gables, an elegant stoop curving down to a manicured lawn, and patches of sun shimmering between the tall trees.

I walk on tiptoe on the graveled walk behind the nun

who let us in—I don't want to break the spell.

The spell continues as Sister Charles—that is her name—escorts us around the rest of the community. A handful of nuns are walking leisurely about the wide lawn or sitting on white benches and talking softly to each other.

"Sister Pannelay has told us about you," Sister Charles says, after she has introduced us to some of her companions. "I hope you like Flers. It's a pleasant little town. I am from Alençon, but I am quite happy here."

She looks very serious with her metal-rimmed glasses.

I wonder how she can stand having her face squeezed all day in the tight, fluted, starched brim of her bonnet. But her eyes sparkle, and she talks with much excitement about the garden hose that leaked, the rabbit that got away, and the retreat they are about to go on. She preaches the virtue of silence, of looking into your soul without the temptations of daily living. I can't quite imagine her not saying a word for a week or staying put for more than a few moments at a time.

I keep looking at her as she goes from group to group with Mademoiselle.

"Don't you want to come with us? Denise and I have found a squirrel over here!" Lily calls out.

"No, thanks. I'd rather stay here," I call out.

Resting against a tree, I can't help wondering what Sister Charles would have done were she faced with our circumstances. Would she choose to be tortured for her beliefs, like the early Christians? Or would she go into hiding, as we did?

I see two of the nuns burst out laughing as they play tag. I have the odd feeling that my sisters and I are old and wise and that they are the children.

"How about playing charades?" Sister Charles asks, appearing at my side. "We have a few minutes before our tea."

I have no trouble whatsoever guessing the right word, and I blush with delight as they all applaud.

I envy them. Their life is so simple: a total devotion to God and some sacrifices from time to time. Most of all, it is trouble-free. I wouldn't mind it a bit!

When we sit down to our snack of cookies and apples, I confide to my sisters: "If it weren't for Papa and Maman, I could see myself spending the rest of my life here!"

Startled, Denise looks at me. "Are you crazy? What would Maman say if she heard you?"

Just then Sister Charles comes to our table. As she pours the tea into my cup she whispers to me, "It's so nice here, isn't it? Who needs to be married?"

Then she's gone. I panic: Why, she must have read my mind! Does she want me to follow in her footsteps?

Sister Charles has seriously shaken my little world. As if it wasn't confused enough!

Sunday, April 25

For the first time Sister Madeleine does not come to kiss us good-bye before we leave for Mass. We have a little extra time, and so I decide to go to her instead.

Voices are coming from the pantry. Mother Superior's sharp voice is unmistakable. "That's it! I won't discuss it anymore!"

Please, God! Don't let it be Sister Madeleine she's scolding so, I think.

Deep down, I know it can't be Sister Geneviève, who was simply born to live in a religious community—the way she blindly obeys Mother Superior and follows the rules to the letter. She is the only one who refers to "our" bowl or "our" umbrella rather than saying "my" like everybody else.

I wait for things to quiet down before venturing into the kitchen. Sister Madeleine is alone. She doesn't greet me with her usual cheerful manner but stares at the water draining through the huge sieve that she is holding with both hands, as if her life depended on it. She is sniffling and her eyes are red.

I can't stand to see her unhappy. "Are you sick?" I ask, not wanting to pry into something that, after all, is none of my business.

"No, no! Nothing like that." She finally breaks into a smile and rests the sieve on a pan. "It's just that life isn't always easy, even here."

I *must* know what happened, and I look at her with a question on my face.

"When you enter an order," she explains, "you take three vows: poverty, chastity, and obedience. Well, I happen to find obedience the toughest of the three. It's supposed to get easier in time, but after six years I still have a very hard time with it."

I don't know what to think. I'm dying to know if the argument had to do with the choice of the menu or Sister Madeleine using too much butter or the like—or whether it was much more serious. Surely only children—or at best, unreasonable adults—have squabbles.

Nuns have to come close to perfection! But now Sister Madeleine has proved that they are just as human as you and I.

Sister Madeleine has resumed her task. The storm is over.

I guess it isn't so much Mother Superior or Sister Madeleine who are disappointed in their community life: They accept it and live in harmony most of the time. *I am the one who objects to its imperfections.*

So much for becoming a nun!

Monday, May 10

Mlle Lucienne was not here for dinner tonight. It is nine o'clock now, and she still has not returned.

Unlike the others, I admire Mlle Lucienne. She's different. She comes from a big town—Caen—and is older than most of the other boarders. She wears very high heels and has long, thick black hair. Sometimes she looks sad; other times she laughs and sings, and nothing seems to bother her.

Now everybody puts in her five cents worth—starting with our nosy old housekeeper, Mlle Juliette: "She's got to be different, that one, doesn't she? To begin with her dresses are cut much too low, and she wears those open sandals with the spike heels. It's a wonder she can walk at all! And now she's coming home at ungodly hours! Really, I can't see how our Mother Superior can tolerate her!"

"Maybe she's working late tonight," Solange suggests.

"Unless she's been invited out! It's her right!" her twin says.

I, for one, like the idea of her having a date. If I were a man, I would like her dark hair; her clothes, which have a definite flair; her cigarette holder, which lets out rings of smoke that vanish in the air like bubbles.

At last Mademoiselle folds her knitting. It's time to go to bed. No use in trying to talk her into letting me stay up: Time is time.

I can't sleep. I leave the door half open, and I listen in the dark for the slightest sound. I wonder if Mlle Lucienne has a guardian angel? Everyone is supposed to have one, M. le Curé preaches from his pulpit.

Finally the bell rings. I hear voices, then the sound of heels clicking against the staircase.

I scramble to my feet and watch for Mlle Lucienne, who must pass by our door to get to her room.

"Why are you still up at this hour?" she whispers, patting my cheek.

"I wasn't sleepy. Everything all right?"

"Sure! We had to take inventory. It's been a long day. You get to bed now!"

I know that now I will have a good night's sleep.

Monday, May 17

I try not to fidget in the armchair as Dr. Dumesnil, sitting next to Mother Superior, examines my finger very closely. For a few days now, I've had a nagging pain in my forefinger, and the least bit of pressure makes me jump. It's an infection of the nail, according to the nun, which is getting worse as the days go by in spite of repeated boiling saltwater soaks. I dread them: They hurt more than the silly infection!

If Maman were here, she would probably say that none of this would have happened at all if the wash was adequately boiled or if we were kept immaculately clean. It is true that nothing is quite as clean here as it was at home.

"The infection can spread through the arm to the glands in your armpit and then you die!" said Claudine, a fool of a girl at school—as if the fact that her father is a physician makes her an expert.

Still, this morning, I could swear I detected a fine red line along my arm. Tomorrow, it will get to the armpit. I am doomed!

"It's an infected blister," the doctor finally says. "I'm afraid it will turn into a carbuncle. I must lance it."

I jump off my seat and instinctively hide my hand behind my back.

"Come, come, my child! It will only hurt for a short instant, and after that, you'll feel much better," he promises.

I let myself slide deep into the chair, looking away from the sharp knife that is going to save my life.

"*Aie!*" At the very moment that I let out a scream, a yellowish, gooey substance appears on my finger.

"Here we are. . . . It's all done! The dressing will have to be changed every evening. In a week, it will all be gone! But I'd watch over this young lady, Sister, if I were you. She's a bit anemic. I know you can't always find the proper food these days, but she needs to be a little stronger to fight all these infections!"

Friday, May 21

The infection has disappeared—but so has my nail.

To Mother Superior the best remedy is red meat. Just my luck!

Now, the nuns can't complain about us: So far, my sisters and I have not been fussy about strange new foods. We've eaten all kinds of pork dishes, even that awful, repulsive brown blood sausage. But they may as well get used to it: We'll never be able to stand the sight of a rare cut of meat.

Today the meat is not only dark red, it looks downright suspicious. Denise says it's almost purple. I find it much too stringy. Maybe it's cat meat? I shudder at the thought, recalling that Solange, who heard it from her grandfather, said that the starving Parisians had to resort to eating cat meat during the Siege of Paris.

"It's horsemeat!" Mlle Juliette volunteers, popping from her seat at the end of the table. "It'll make your blood redder. Come on, you should be grateful to get any meat at all—especially you, Renée. You need it more than anybody!"

I don't like the idea of having blood that is thin and discolored. I cut out a piece of meat the size of a button, and trying not to gag, I throw it into my mouth. I chew it slowly, then furiously. Nothing doing: It won't go down. I spit it back.

Nothing escapes the nosy old maid.

"You must try again! You know that Mother Superior insists on your emptying your plates!"

Mumbling against Mlle Juliette and the unfairness of it all, I cut a second piece of meat. This time, I manage to swallow it with very little chewing.

Lily has not touched her plate, but she'll get away with it. How I wish that I had a liver that acted up once in a while.

Poor Denise. She, too, is struggling. She has already downed several gulps of water without success. She winks at me in utter despair. Her morsel has now gotten stuck in her cheek and won't go any farther. She finally takes it out with her fingers and sneaks it into her pocket. Mlle Juliette has not seen a thing.

"It's no use," my sister whispers. "I'll give it to Castor!"

I think it's a fine idea: He is also anemic.

Castor is one of the two pigs that we are raising on the sly at the far end of the garden. With the food restrictions it is forbidden to raise animals on your own, but Mother Superior says that it is a good investment. I remember that in Paris, Mme Chavignat knew of people who raised rabbits and chickens in their apartments.

You can imagine what a catastrophe it was when Castor developed an enormous boil on his rear end—complete with redness, swelling, and pus. We were so concerned about losing the precious animal through blood poisoning that we included him in our daily prayers: "Saint Antoine, please make our pig well again!"

When Castor recovered, a good dozen of us, led by

Sister Madeleine and Sister Geneviève, went to St. Jean's church to light the tallest candle we could find in gratitude to St. Antoine.

Saturday, May 22

Well, Mother Superior stormed into the recreation room this evening to ask who dared give their precious meat to the pigs. "Such waste is unthinkable!" she shouted, her eyes black with anger.

She even deprived Denise and me of dessert for a whole week after we admitted to being the guilty ones.

Big deal! We can always count on Sister Madeleine to sneak a piece of fruit into our room.

But from now on I will be forced to eat the awful meat each week, and any extra winds up on my plate because of my condition.

Monday, May 31

This morning a blister appeared on another finger! Horsemeat did not do me one bit of good. If anything, it made my condition worse!

I'm so happy to have proved Mother Superior wrong—even if the ordeal costs me *two* nails!

Tuesday, June 8

Outside the hedges have grown full, and the warm air carries the fragrance from the freshly cut grass and the lilac bush. But I don't care anymore. Absentmindedly I skim through the *"Semaine de Suzette,"* sitting at the foot of the Virgin Mary, hiding behind the bushes.

When I feel this way—that is, when everything is gray inside—I like to sit by the Virgin. She is a mother, and she must surely understand.

"Come, come! You can't let yourself go this way!" Mother Superior scolded when she learned that I lost interest in the catechism and that I don't even bother to raise my hand in class. "You can't complain! You're getting your weekly letter, aren't you?"

If only she knew that twice I ran after someone in the street, thinking it was Maman, and that last Sunday I could have sworn that I heard Papa cough in church just a couple of rows ahead of me! Just this morning I woke up with a weight on my chest, near tears, and the Yiddish melody "Chiribim, chiribum," went through my head.

I had forgotten all about it. Papa used to sing it when we could not fall asleep—a long, long time ago when we were still living in Mulhouse.

Really, I am getting tired of having everyone say all the time that it won't be much longer now! Even the British are sending tracts promising a victory soon—but it never happens.

It isn't that nothing is going on around us. The nuns have a radio, and from time to time everyone gets excited about one piece of news or another.

For instance we know that the Americans—or is it the British? the Allies, at any rate—have landed in North Africa. They are fighting very hard to win the war. But that happened so far away, on another continent. So what good does it do us? It is so tiresome to get up day after day for nothing—without even the promise of a visit from Maman.

I listened with only half an ear when Mother Superior attempted to cheer us up this morning by announcing the arrival next week of a bunch of girls from the Patronage of Clichy—with Sister Louise and Mlle Andrée—to spend the summer with us. The poor kids will love the fresh air of Normandy and won't starve the way they do in Paris, she said.

My sisters are happy at the thought of seeing Mlle Andrée. But I'm not at all thrilled at the idea of finding myself surrounded by thirty nosy little girls to whom we will have to lie—or at least conceal the truth.

Tuesday, June 15

"Taratata! Get up, everybody!"

Paulette, one of my neighbors in my new dorm room, is singing reveille with her hand cupped over her mouth. "You can't go back to sleep!" she reminds me, pulling my legs and blanket out of bed.

Paulette is fourteen, the oldest of the girls from the Patronage. Because I'm among the oldest, too, I wound up in this dorm with her and six other girls. My sisters and I have been separated—Denise and Lily are in a room with younger kids. They have a chamber pot; we don't. We are big enough to run to the toilet on the floor below.

I didn't dare to protest the separation; this is not the time to attract attention by acting as if we were special. To be perfectly honest I was relieved at the thought of being without them for a little while. But I feel a little lost, as if I didn't matter to anyone anymore. What I miss most is that we can't confide to one another at night in bed now. At least they aren't very far away, since they sleep next door.

I prefer Paulette, my left-hand neighbor, to Ginette, who sleeps to the right of me. Ginette is about my age. Her skin is dark and her hair very curly—even curlier than mine. Her father comes from the colonies, they say.

She talks all the time. I don't mind too much, since I have to keep my thoughts to myself. But she has a lot to say—especially about America, where one of her uncles has settled. She swears that there you can get rich overnight!

"Someday," she predicts, "I'll go to America too."

Good luck! I think. I am not at all tempted by this country of wide-open spaces, where wild horses run freely and everyone kills everyone else in two minutes. I've seen it in the movies. All I want is for everything to go back to normal so that I can return home.

You would never know that Paulette is the oldest of us. She is redheaded, and her eyes always look surprised. I feel sorry for her; they say that her father died less than a year ago. But she never talks about him, or even cries for that matter. In fact, she is a perfect clown: She imitates everyone, likes to spit water through the little space between her front teeth when you least expect it, and flicks cherry pits in the middle of evening prayer. She always gets away with her mischief too!

Mlle Andrée calls her a tomboy. She plays rough—no one can top her at ball games or at races. She always prays or sings the loudest in church, and sometimes, too, she plays tunes on the harmonica that bring tears to my eyes. She must miss her father even if she doesn't show it. Does she cry secretly at night, I wonder?

With the arrival of the new girls we have been swept into a whirl of activities: early rising, prayer, exercise, breakfast, chores, naps, outings, dinner, and evening prayer.

I prefer the afternoons when we are all sitting on the lawn, listening to Mlle Andrée telling us, episode by episode, the fantastic adventures of Monique, lost in a jungle infested with mean sorcerers and every possible kind of wild animal. By the grace of God she wiggles herself out of the most incredible traps!

Mlle Andrée is a wonderful storyteller. She weighs each word, her eyes gazing at some spot in the distance—now whispering, now praying, now shouting with such conviction that we forget it's only a story.

"No! Not yet!" we scream when she suddenly stops at the very moment when something's going to happen and tells us, "To be continued tomorrow!"

Mlle Andrée likes to wear plain dresses, without waists or belts. She has the most extraordinarily mobile face. Her dark brown eyes have a life of their own—nothing seems to bother her really. She laughs even under the most trying circumstances—like when our bean salad turned sour in our tin cans on the day of the picnic, and we all got diarrhea and had to wait in line three times to go to the toilet and sit two at a time on the throne to hurry up.

I bet Mlle Andrée never cut her hair. When she undoes her braid, it reaches all the way down to her waist. She reminds me of Mary Magdalene, the sinner who loved Jesus, from our Holy History book—except that Mlle Andrée is no sinner.

Paulette says that Mlle Andrée's fiancé died during World War I. It's a beautiful love story: Mlle Andrée never stopped loving the man, a hero who died for his country, and she has remained faithful to him all these years.

I like to watch her in church as she prays, her head bent forward, her eyes closed, her hands joined. You can tell that she's talking to God, as M. le Curé would say. And when she sings, her clear and powerful voice reaches all the way up to the arches and the rose window.

I never leave her side. She is, after all, the closest thing to home. She knows Papa and Maman—and she knows our secret! I can tell from the way her eyes linger on my sisters or me sometimes, or the way she squeezes our hands, or even the way she stops by my bed at night, however briefly, that there is a special bond between us.

It's amusing to see how she defers to Sister Louise—who is so much older and quite wrinkled, with a hair growing out of a pimple on her chin. Her voice creaks, especially when she screams at one of us. And she can't see too well—even her thick glasses don't do the trick anymore.

So we fuss about her too. But deep down, we know that Mlle Andrée is running the show.

Thursday, June 24

Two by two our little group marches through the streets of the town, singing in perfect harmony: "Through mountains and valleys we're traveling, two companions. . . . "

I love those walks. They are getting to know us, the people of Flers. Even the sternest of them smiles as we pass by.

But today I stop in the middle of a sentence. How can we sing about brotherhood and friendship, how can we celebrate the beauty of France, our fatherland, when one Frenchman can denounce another?

Then I catch sight of Sister Louise and Mlle Andrée walking ahead. Haven't they—and all the nuns of La Chaumière—risked their lives to save us?

I resume my singing, almost screaming at the top of my lungs, determined in spite of it all to believe in friendship and the basic goodness of people.

Wednesday, June 30

I hate our naps—they're a sheer waste of perfectly good daylight. Staying in bed when you're not sick is being lazy, Maman would say. She never allowed us to stay home from school—except if we had a serious illness, like the measles.

I can't sleep during the day anyway. I need darkness—the pitch-black of the night—and preferably a fat pillow.

"Do you want to play?"

Dominique is at my side, all wrapped up in her blanket.

"Hush!" I whisper, a finger on my lips. "We're not supposed to make any noise!"

"I won't! Just watch me!"

Before my dazzled eyes I see Dominique turn into Sister Louise with her cane, Mlle Andrée telling us a story, and Charlie Chaplin with his ducklike walk.

It's mime, she explains; she learned it in school this year.

Within minutes Paulette and Ginette—as well as Lily, Denise, and Danièle from next door—have joined us. We contain our giggles as best as we can.

Then, as if wound up by an invisible key, I suddenly get up and grab my pillowcase, which I arrange as a coiffe over my hair. Then I take the umbrella standing nearby: I have become my favorite character, Bécassine.

I don't mind at all the sound of their applause. I never thought I would enjoy the new girls so much.

Tuesday, July 20

We are in trouble—serious trouble.

We are lined up two by two in front of Mother Superior, Mlle Andrée and Sister Louise. Mother Superior, her arms stiffly crossed over her chest, is looking at us with eyes darkened by anger.

"I'm simply horrified by what I've heard—and deeply disappointed too! It's outrageous to think that young ladies from good families and with fine Christian upbringing can lower themselves to stealing apples from someone else's orchard!"

Who let the cat out of the bag? I wonder. My mind flicks back to last night, when a bunch of us went to the Dumoulin farm to fetch some milk, eggs, and butter at Mother Superior's request. Germaine, one of the kitchen helpers—who knows the area inside out—was asked to lead us across the pitch-dark fields with a flashlight.

Just before getting to the farmhouse, we stumbled over hundreds of hard little balls that practically covered the ground. Germaine was the first to see that they were apples.

"Let's share in the wealth! There are so many of them; no one can possibly miss them," she remarked.

It took very little to convince me. Giggling, we stored the fruit in our socks, in our sleeves, under our sweaters. It felt cold against my skin and tickled so much, I burst into uncontrollable laughter.

"Hush! The farmers are going to hear us and wonder what's going on," Ginette warned me. "Don't let them catch us!"

"You know, stealing is a sin!" Dominique said, worrying on the way home. "How are we going to get out of that one?"

"So what's the big deal? At worst it's a venial sin— nothing that can't be erased by confession," Germaine remarks. "We'll tell M. l'Abbé, and that will be the end of it!"

She's a grown-up. She should know! I thought.

Mother Superior's thundering voice brings me back to the present. "You do realize, don't you, that you've committed a serious offense?"

I glance at Paulette standing next to me. She's looking at the tip of her shoes, properly repentant. I do likewise. I can't say that I feel that bad: I'm not a full-blown Christian like they are. Besides, most of the apples were rotten. Shouldn't that make a difference?

"I don't care who stole the apples!" Mother Superior

continues. "As far as I'm concerned, you're *all* guilty—those who stole apples and those who shared in them! There's only one thing for you to do now: You must return them. I want all of you—I repeat, *all of you!*—to go back to the Dumoulins with the apples that still remain. This very afternoon! Is that understood?"

Mlle Andrée and Sister Louise have not said a word and look at us with reproach in their eyes. I can't bear to look at them. I can think of no punishment worse than this!

Mother Superior is waiting for us when we return from the farm. We follow her to the chapel, where she asks us to face the altar and to recite an Act of Contrition.

"Peace be with you!" she says as she dismisses us one by one, kissing us on the forehead.

We are forgiven. *Ouf!*

Saturday, August 23

We are preparing a show for the community, to be performed in the parish hall. We will be singing in harmony and playing a series of holy scenes taken from the Gospel under the very able direction of Mlle Andrée.

I thought I'd positively die when they asked me to pose as Judas in the Last Supper because of my black curly hair. I'd like to know if Judas really did have black curly hair!

My sisters think it's very funny; they keep hiding my headband and the white sheet I wear as a tunic so that I'm almost always late for rehearsal.

It's hard not to show the apprehension that overcomes me every time. I know I haven't done anything, so why do I feel guilty?

I think I'm afraid that they'll put two and two together and come to realize that I'm Jewish, too, with my hair and my Semitic face—and that I'm a traitor as well, since I'm passing for a Catholic.

I've done some research though: Judas Iscariot was a thief, a man without scruples, before he became a disciple of Jesus. He betrayed Him because he wanted to. I, for one, don't have any choice. Besides, I'm not hurting anyone.

In the meantime everyone says I'm doing a fine job.

"He did a mean thing, Judas, didn't he?" Véronique, a pretty blonde with an angelic face, remarks in all innocence. She's playing John the Baptist. "I don't like Jews—any of them. They're the ones who put Jesus to death!"

I look at her in utter disbelief. How can she have such a lovely smile and not like Jews? Does she know any? I'd like to know.

"What's that I hear about your not liking Jews?"

It's Mlle Andrée's clear, resonant voice behind us. I feel her friendly hand on my hair.

"This is hardly a charitable statement, Véronique. If you refer to the handful of Jews who were responsible for Jesus' death, that's one thing. But you can't blame a whole race! And you're forgetting that Jesus was a Jew too!"

I feel sorry for Véronique, who has turned as red as a beet.

"Come on, my child. . . . Jesus has forgiven Judas

and the others. Why can't you? I suggest you both make peace with each other and forget about it."

"Ouch!" Véronique cries in pain as I squeeze her hand. If she only knew how close we came to being enemies!

Friday, September 10

I am in the garden alone, sitting at the foot of the statue of the Virgin Mary, hidden by the hedges.

I am holding a daisy in my hand, the flower Maman is named after—*marguerite*.

Slowly I begin to pluck.

She loves me. . . . She loves me not. . . .

I stop short at the last petal. She loves me not!

I knew it! I knew it! I scream inside my head where no one can hear me.

It's been two weeks since our summer companions left, taking along Sister Louise and Mlle Andrée. Two weeks that I have been in no mood to write home—a sure sign that something is very wrong.

We haven't heard from Papa and Maman in that time either. Why aren't they concerned about not hearing from us? I wonder.

It's worse now than before the girls joined us: The hole they left is bigger than the one they'd filled. Even being back with my sisters doesn't help much.

Please God—someone!—do something to get me out of this mood.

But I am like the skier in the story who screams for help at the top of his lungs from the bottom of the ravine where he fell. All he hears is the echo of his own voice; no one can possibly hear him.

I snap the last petal with my teeth and spit it right out.

Who cares anyway? No one's going to catch *me* crying.

Wednesday, September 15

Now I know why Maman didn't write for so long.

Aunt Fanny and Uncle Maurice have been denounced by a neighbor, taken away from their home in Moûtiers, and interned in a camp in the South of France—Rivesaltes, near Perpignan.

And many thousands of miles away Maman's two brothers and their families have been arrested and sent to a labor camp called Auschwitz.

It's Papa who wrote the letter to Mother Superior. She told me about it this morning. As the oldest, she thought I should be told. Papa knew he was taking a serious risk by writing all this, but he thought it preferable to keeping it from us.

Poor Papa; it must have taken him forever to write it! How I wish I could have seen the letter—it's the only one he ever wrote to us.

Maman must be quite upset if she can't even pick up a pen and drop us a few lines.

I'm simply horrified. So then all those sacrifices, all these prayers we offered to God, were they all for nothing?

It's the last time I'll bother to pray to Him. I should

have known He'd let us down, since He let His own son die. Why, then, should He take pity on us?

Granted, He knew that Jesus would rise again—but still, He didn't keep Jesus from being betrayed, humiliated, and all the rest. I can't bear the sight of Jesus' forehead bleeding under the braided thorns in the holy pictures. I always look away.

Yet if we take our trust away from God, there won't be anyone to count on.

God, please, I know you send hardships to those you love most—from what Mother Superior and even Sister Madeleine say.

Don't you think that our family has had enough?

Thursday, October 14

Nothing seems to faze Mademoiselle. I wish she'd rub off on me.

She swiftly presses her thumbnail down on the fine comb in an all-too-familiar gesture. The accompanying click has become just as familiar: It has killed the nit—the white dot that clings so stubbornly to my hair.

"One less to go!" she sings.

I wish I could share in her good spirits. But it is *my* hair that she's combing through, looking for nits—the eggs of lice.

Until a few days ago when I came home from school scratching my head, I had never seen any "inhabitants"—that's how Mademoiselle refers to the lice.

Mother Superior found out that there was an epidemic

in the school—to the horror of everyone. Françoise swears that she saw one jump from one of our classmate's head to another.

For once I am grateful for Maman's absence. She has always waged such fierce battles against germs and other suspicious creatures, there's no telling how she would have taken the news.

I don't mind Mademoiselle's patient search at all. In fact, I rather welcome it: I must do everything to save my fashionable curls—my only asset.

Monday, October 25

Mlle Lucienne has unusual ideas. She says that if God gave you a body, you should be proud of it!

Today she asks me point-blank, "Why do you always hide your smile behind your hand?"

I mutter that it's out of habit. I wish I could tell her that I don't want anyone to see my uneven front teeth and my big lips.

She forces me to look at myself straight in the mirror. "Just look at yourself," she says softly. "You have a very kind smile. You've got to show it! No one ever told you that?"

No. No one ever did.

The truth is, my assets have suddenly become very important. La Chaumière recently welcomed three unusual newcomers: Three boys have now joined our ranks.

"It's our duty to help our country. So what if we bend

the rules a bit?" Mother Superior apologized when she told us about it.

First there's Christian. Rather small for his age—ten— he is quick and always ready for games. But if you ask me, I think he could pay more attention to his little brother, Jean-Jacques, who is only five. He should have had an older sister instead of a brother!

Both boys are blond and blue-eyed with full, rosy cheeks—real French, like their name: Dupont.

"Poor kids!" Sister Geneviève sighs. "So young and already orphans!"

They're not really orphans, Sister Madeleine corrects, since they still have their father. But he's in the Resistance Movement. He's in hiding, fighting the Germans through sabotage and other secret means. Though he's a hero, the boys never see him.

I wonder how you can do without a mother when you're only five years old. Sister Madeleine believes that the little boy was so small when his mother died—he was three—that he can't possibly remember her. Is it possible to miss your mother even if you've never known her?

Jean-Jacques needs to be watched all the time. He never stays put, constantly bumps into things, falls, gets up—and starts all over again.

Yesterday he scratched his hand when he fell, and he cried a little. I cheered him up and kissed the sore part. He stopped crying. I was so happy. So was he, I think. For a moment I felt like I was his mother.

———

And then there's Marcel.

At fourteen he is almost a young man. He has a warm smile and green eyes. Pépée would find him quite distinguished-looking: She always goes for a pleasant face and fine ankles and wrists. My wrists are the only part of me that is distinguished.

He asked me straight out where we were from. He said that his mother sent him to live with his grand-mother in Flers because of the many bombings that were destroying his native Brittany. She stays with him at La Chaumière during the week. His father is a prisoner in Germany.

He also asked if I had ever seen the sea. I told him that I have not, but Papa has. He went to Juan-les-Pins once for his rheumatism. He even brought back an ashtray.

I pay much more attention to my looks now: I insist that Mother Superior allow me to wear ribbons to brighten up my curls, and I make sure that the pleat in my skirt stays in the middle. I also try to suck my cheeks in to give them a hollow look. But there's no miracle. I hope that Marcel will realize that, under this imperfect face and the crooked teeth, there is a bright and amusing girl who knows an awful lot about actors and movies, and that no one can beat her when it comes to knowing the songs of Charles Trenet.

Friday, November 4

I've never been so cold in my life. What can you expect when the only heated areas are the dining hall—during mealtimes—and the recreation room in the evenings? No matter how understanding Sister Madeleine is, we can't possibly spend all our time in the kitchen.

Poor Denise. Her lips are blue from the cold, and she has chilblains on her feet that won't heal. I do, too, but I can still slip my shoes on. Denise can't—Mother Superior got her to wear wooden clogs.

The doctor says that the chilblains can't heal because essential vitamins are missing from our diet.

Honestly I think it feels even colder since Mademoiselle left us. She had to go back home in a hurry to marry her prisoner, who has returned from Germany. She was so happy—and so were we—until we heard that Mlle Juliette was to look after us.

The worst time for me is at night—especially since we each sleep in our own bed and don't even have the comfort of a body next to ours, like in Paris.

Tonight my feet are so cold, they hurt. I'm sitting on my bed, my nightgown on, ready for sleep. I slip on my socks and try to wiggle my toes, but nothing helps. My feet remain ice-cold.

I am on the verge of tears. "I don't know what I'm going to do!" I complain to my sisters.

Denise has a brilliant idea. "Try to put your woolen mitts on—they may fit!" she suggests.

The door suddenly flings open and Mlle Juliette's sour face shows in the doorway.

"Time to go to sleep! It's past ten o'clock!" she warns.

"How am I supposed to fall asleep when my feet feel like ice?" I protest.

I should have known better: The old witch's ears perk up at the smallest challenge. All that matters to her is to rule her little world—the three of us, and the linen and the bedding of the institution; and to serve God—that is, attend her daily Mass and take care of our chapel.

She slams the door shut without a word.

"I bet she's going straight to Mother Superior to tell on us!" I say.

"So what? Let the old tattletale run to her! Anyway, I bet she's just getting ready for bed so she won't miss her precious morning Mass," Lily remarks.

She has now settled on the edge of my bed. "Let's see what I can do to help warm you up," she offers. I gratefully lift the sheet and blanket, take off my socks, and pull up my nightgown.

I can never understand how Lily's hands are warm on the coldest of days. She takes after Maman. At home the two of them used to walk around in short sleeves while Denise and I shivered in our long-sleeved sweaters.

Lily has now taken my left foot in her hand and is beginning to rub it vigorously.

"Careful with my sole!" I plead.

But I trust my little sister: She knows I'm ticklish, and she's not one to take advantage of it.

My leg is slowing coming back to life. I watch Lily as she continues to rub it, surprised, I think, to discover a maternal side in her.

"You're the best heater I've ever had!" I remark.

"Don't forget, I'm next! Don't take so long!" Denise announces.

"Your other leg now," Lily orders.

I lift my nightgown to change legs when the door swings open again. This time it's Mother Superior, a stony expression on her face, her arms crossed over her chest. Mlle Juliette is behind her.

"Mlle Juliette tells me that you won't go to sleep," she scolds. "Now, would you mind telling me what you're doing, holding your sister's leg with her gown raised?" she continues.

I don't like the accusation in her voice.

"I'm warming up her feet," Lily replies simply, with a what-else-could-it-be tone.

"I just won't tolerate your playing together in this way, do you hear me? It's in very bad taste! Don't ever let me catch you in each other's beds again!"

"But we're doing nothing wrong!" I try to explain. "I was—"

"I will not have this sassy talk, Mademoiselle!" the nun interrupts. She is addressing me formally now. How angry she must be! But I still can't see what this is all about.

"If your feet are that cold, why don't you sleep with your socks on!" she blasts.

"I don't think they will give you any more trouble now," she adds, turning to Mlle Juliette, who has not said a word.

"Good night!" she says as she leaves the room, followed by our enemy.

It happened so fast, I didn't even get a chance to tell the nun that wearing socks to bed doesn't help at all.

=====

The lights are out. I lie in bed, unable to fall asleep. I'm not cold anymore. My body is all tensed up, my eyes are burning with dry tears.

I don't understand. Whatever came over Mother Superior? Why this fuss about one of us comforting the other? Has she lost her mind? Doesn't she know that a sister is someone who's been with you all her life, someone you've watched grow day after day, someone who has no secrets from you—whose body is practically a carbon copy of yours because it comes from the same flesh and blood? Why, then, this strange outburst, turning a sisterly gesture into a crime?

I hate her! She didn't give me a chance to explain!

I hate all the grown-ups here—except Sister Madeleine. They don't understand anything.

But above all, I hate Mlle Juliette—that old tattletale who never finds anything nice to say about anyone.

I hate you, I hate you, I hate you! I scream into my bolster as I pound it with my fists, careful not to wake my sisters.

Saturday, November 5

I'm trying very hard to dismiss the whole episode from my mind, but Mother Superior's words keep ringing in my ears. I go over what happened, bit by bit, but I only get more furious.

I finally decide to run to Sister Madeleine. Even though she's a nun, she knows an awful lot about a lot of things.

I run to the kitchen, and at that very moment I catch her alone. I tell her what happened as fast as I can, keeping my eyes on the door: I don't want anyone to eavesdrop on us.

"Now, now," she says, smiling, after having listened closely to my story. "That must have been quite an evening!"

I let out a deep sigh: It can't be *that* bad if she's smiling. "I didn't do anything wrong then?" I plead.

"Let's step into the pantry," she suggests. "We'll have more privacy.

"Of course, you did nothing wrong!" the nun continues in the pantry. "Mother Superior probably got very uncomfortable finding you undressed—with your sister's hand on your leg."

Puzzled, I look at her. "So what?"

"Well, you see—this is not the easiest thing to explain—people very seldom talk about these things, and priests and nuns even less so." She pauses for a moment.

"Let's put it this way," she reflects. "You know about the vows we take—those of poverty, chastity, and obedience. Well, as far as chastity goes—I assume you know what *chastity* means?"

"It means not going out with somebody of the opposite sex—not getting married," I tell her.

"Something like that." Sister Madeleine smiles. "To be even more specific, to remain chaste means to stay away from situations that could get you into trouble—even in thought. So you can imagine how some of us can get nervous when those forbidden feelings are evoked in us!"

Now, I tell myself, I know that there can be sexual feelings between men and women—that is, in grown-ups—and maybe some pleasant feelings between boys and girls before that—I remember how I liked to be in

Guy's company—but what has that got to do with Lily and me?

"But Lily and I are sisters!" I protest, still at a loss.

"You are too young to understand that sexual feelings can exist between people of the same sex. It's rare, but it can happen!"

I think: So that's what Mother Superior was worried about! How silly of her! I feel so sorry for her.

I can't help recalling the hundreds of times I have touched and kissed my sisters. I wonder what Mother Superior would say if she knew that Denise and I slept spoon-fashion in Paris to beat the cold!

"I can't quite believe that Mother Superior actually thought anything was going on," I say. "But she certainly got nervous about it!"

"I guess I'm lucky. . . . The whole thing is much easier for me to handle. I'm from a very large family. There were seven of us—and since I was the oldest, I had to take care of my little brothers and sisters. Seeing them in the nude was no big deal!"

"Well, Mother Superior scares me a little anyway," I dare to confess. "Especially when she gets angry!"

"She can be difficult. God knows, I have had my run-ins with her. She does like to remind you that she's the boss—and she is! But you can get through to her after the storm has blown over. You ought to try." Sister Madeleine pauses and looks at me with a kind smile.

"Of course, when you're a kid, you don't always have a choice; you have to do what you're told, even if it chokes you with anger," she adds. "But you can always talk to me. My door is always open. And don't forget, praying is also a way of sharing your feelings and concerns with someone who understands."

How I wish Sister Madeleine were our *curé*! She would do wonders preaching from the pulpit on Sundays!

Wednesday, November 17

For once the three of us are in total agreement: Mlle Juliette deserves a good lesson.

Sister Geneviève was horrified when we asked her for advice about Mlle Juliette. "Poor lady, she is all alone in the world—and she's so terribly nearsighted!" she told us.

She gave us a wonderful idea.

"What if we hide her glasses? She's as blind as a bat without them!" I suggest.

"No, let's put nettles in her bed! She'll be uncomfortable for a long time," Denise says, speaking from experience.

"Don't be silly! She'll know that we did it," Lily protests. "How about hiding her missal? She'll hit the roof when she realizes she'll be late for Mass."

"Well, then, why not set her alarm clock two hours ahead?" I announce, finding the idea rather clever. "She'll hurry . . . and then she'll have to wait two long hours!"

"All right. You set the alarm then!" Lily declares.

"Well, you know how nervous I get. I'll probably push the wrong button in the dark!"

"Then Denise can do it."

Before Denise can respond, I say, "It takes her too long to figure things out, and then she'll check it a hundred times. All we need is for the old biddy to catch us in the act," I remind my little sister.

"All right then, I'll do it! But only this time," Lily says.

Thursday, November 18

I can't believe my ears.

"My alarm clock rang much too early this morning!" Mlle Juliette said casually. "There must have been something wrong with it. So I sat in the parlor until it was time for Mass."

She even smiled. She hardly seemed bothered!

Denise gave me a what-are-we-going-to-do look, while Lily kicked my leg for sympathy.

Friday, November 26

Mlle Juliette doesn't matter that much anymore. I have more pleasant things on my mind. I am watching for Marcel right now—I catch myself doing it all the time.

It's strange how my memories of Guy have become blurred, and how his face and Marcel's have fused into one. True, they are about the same age, they are both handsome, and they both come from Brittany. And just like Guy in the past, Marcel seems to enjoy my company.

I am getting more grown-up, I know. I think back to

the Sunday in Paris, a month or so before we left for Flers, when I found blood in my panties and Maman told me that I was a young lady now. Just like that. That's all she said. I was in no hurry to grow up, but there it was. I'd had so many questions to ask, but there had been no time—not with what was going on around us. No one even paid attention to the awful cramps that bothered me all day.

It has not happened again. But my breasts keep growing just the same. I still avoid looking at my face in the mirror, but I gladly sneak a glance or two at my breasts whenever I get a chance and no one is watching.

I think I'll need a brassiere soon. I hope Mother Superior has noticed.

I'm glad that for once I have something that my sisters don't have. Why, the other day, I caught Lily putting two pairs of folded socks under her sweater. She didn't see me, but I knew what she was up to!

———

It's funny how I always watch for Marcel. I can't help it; I'd do anything to keep our conversations going. He knows a lot about boats and the sea. He's not at all scared of big waves and storms, and he swims like a fish. His father has taken him fishing miles from the shore ever since he was a little boy.

As I listen to him I say to myself: God, just give us five more minutes!—and so I ask him another question. But his grandmother says he must get a good night's sleep to be fit for school the next day. There's plenty of time for him to dawdle and stay up late on weekends, when they return to her big house in St. Georges-les-Groseillers.

There's one thing I'm terribly ashamed of, though:

I've become very jealous of Marcel's friendship with Christian. I've come to resent their long, easy chats, their teasing each other. I feel so excluded!

I tell myself that if I were a boy, I, too, could laugh and carry on with him. No. I don't want to give up the warm feeling that quickens my heartbeats when he smiles at me or the disappointment I feel when he's not around.

Saturday, December 4

It all started with a nagging scratch.

"Just look at this!"

I showed my sister a maze of red lines on my arms and legs from the furious scratching that kept me up most of the night. Overnight it spread to my whole body.

Soon my sisters were complaining about it too. Within a few days scratching had become a way of life. All I could think of was when I could best sneak out and give myself a bloody, angry scratch—or else I'd look for the sharpest angle of the wall or the door against which I could rub my itching back. I kept praying that no one— especially Marcel and Christian—would notice.

Mother Superior decided to get Dr. Dumesnil to look at it. The visit to Dr. Dumesnil's office is sheer torture. The puzzled look on the doctor's face can mean only one thing: We're fatally ill and our days are numbered.

"The poor children scratch themselves day and night. They hardly sleep anymore. There must be something that can be done to relieve that terrible itch!"

The physician examines Denise's leg, then my arm with a maddening slowness, using his magnifying glass. If it weren't for Mother Superior's cooling presence, I would go raving mad.

"To tell you the truth, it's the first time I've come across something like this," Dr. Dumesnil finally says, replacing his magnifying glass on his leather-covered desk. "It's commonly found in animals—among sheep and cattle in particular. Scabies, they call it. It's a parasitic creature that furrows under the skin. It's catching, which explains why the three sisters have it. We can try sulfur baths daily for a week. . . . Let's see what happens."

"What does *parasitic* mean?" I ask, fearful as always of strange words.

"Well, it's said of an organism that lives at the expense of another. Now, don't you worry, and let us take care of you!"

Dr. Dumesnil's incorrigible optimism enrages me. How can he expect us not to worry when he's just finished telling us we have a disease that so far he's seen only in animals?

I make sure to press the palms of my hands—the most infected part—on the leather top of his desk, on his armchair, on the journals lying in front of him. I also make it a special point to squeeze his fingers hard during our parting handshake.

The disease is contagious? Good! Let him catch it!

Thursday, December 9

We're following the treatment to the letter.

We're delighted to be able to take daily baths. But,

most important, we are thrilled at the idea of being able to bathe without the supervision of Sister Geneviève. At least now we can step into the tub without our panties on, and we don't have to wait for the nun to modestly leave the bathroom while we do our *petite toilette*, wash our intimate parts.

Are the nuns simply repelled by our condition, or are they afraid to catch it? We hardly care. We're enjoying every bit of our new freedom!

We cheerfully take turns soaping and scrubbing, then splashing ourselves with gallons of water and eau de cologne: We must be absolutely sure that we don't leave the smallest trace of that vile, unbearable smell of sulfur behind us.

I'm not sure which secret is hardest to keep: Being a Jew or struggling with scabies!

Saturday, December 18

I usually have no trouble falling asleep after my bath. My skin is clean and can breathe while those bloody parasites are quiet, for the moment at least—the sulfur has done its job.

But tonight I can't sleep. I can't help wondering: Why doesn't God give us a break? He sends us one hardship after another.

Sister Madeleine makes me laugh: She insists that praying is not presenting God with a list of things we want, but learning to listen to Him and realizing that a wish or a prayer is not necessarily answered in the way we want it. The main thing, she says, is to know in your heart of hearts that He will always give us enough strength to get through. She says that I'm much stronger than I think.

I, for one, don't feel this mysterious strength she is talking about. As a matter of fact, I don't know how much longer I'll be able to hold out!

Since the beginning of the war, we've had nothing but trouble. First we had to leave Mulhouse, where we were perfectly happy. I know Papa likes to say that we were lucky to have had those few years of happiness. But it's sad that our luck had to stop, and besides, my sisters and I were too young to enjoy it!

Then we had to adjust to Paris in the middle of being cold, hungry, and having the Germans—and the French—come down harder and harder on the Jews until life became unbearable and we had no choice but to leave Papa and Maman.

And here we are now, struggling with scabies on top of it all!

I've thought it over.

If I were to be born again, and if I had my say, I would want to be a sea horse: The question of religion would not matter, and in the documentary they showed us in school, it was the daddy sea horse who gave birth to the babies. I thought that was wonderful!

1944

Thursday, January 13

Tonight I can't sleep, but this time it's because I'm so excited: Maman is coming tomorrow—for a whole week!

I look at the beam of light that the moon throws on the wall. I can't wait for daylight to filter through the shutters.

I wonder if we should bother Maman with all our troubles and tell her about the scabies and the rest. I'm rather glad that she didn't come for Christmas, what with the Infant Jesus in the manger, the Magi, the Midnight Mass—she would have been totally lost.

Christmas was sort of sad without Mademoiselle and

without Mlle Lucienne, who was called home in a hurry to take care of her sick mother. She wrote that she can't tell yet if she will come back. I miss her an awful lot. I hope that she finds a nice man to settle down with, like Mademoiselle.

At least we had Christmas carols: "Adeste Fideles," and my favorite, "Silent Night." Really when I sing, I forget about everything.

The best time of all was when I wished a Happy New Year to Mother Superior in Breton, which Mademoiselle taught me before she left. The poor nun! She was so moved that she almost choked!

Friday, January 14

"Is Papa going to visit us too?"

"How is Grand'mère?"

"How long is the war going to last?"

We are all talking at once. Maman is sitting on the cot that Mother Superior moved into our room.

Maman has not changed—at least not at first glance. A stray gray hair here and there, a hurt look around the eyes. What is striking, though, is that everything in her seems to work in slow motion—her gestures, her movements, the way she speaks—as if she's recovering from a long illness.

Sometimes I look at her on the sly and try to guess what she's not telling us. Has she heard from Aunt Fanny and Uncle Maurice? I'm dying to ask her, but I decide to wait until she's ready to tell us.

I had forgotten how she rolls her *r*'s and how she drops

the sound *one* at the end of a word, letting it hang in midair like a balloon. Unconcerned, she has spoken to everyone, even—imagine!—to Mlle Juliette and to Mlle Suzanne! Everyone seems to accept her accent, no questions asked. She comes from Alsace, and that's that.

Now that we are alone with her, she tells us the news. She and Papa have taken a new name: Benoit. I find it extraordinary that a simple word of two syllables can change someone's fate. I would have loved to try it—if only for a day. Would others see us differently?

Now that they live in Rue Rambuteau, they keep away from people. Maman manages to visit Grand'mère once a week. Grand'mère is quite used to her new home now, and so far—"touch wood," Maman says—the Gestapo and the French police have stayed away from old people's homes.

Maman goes to our apartment in Rue de Rochechouart at least once—sometimes twice—a week.

"By the way, I saw Pépée right after you left," she says. "I've told her about your being away in a safe place and not being able to write. She said she understood, and that she had learned from the concierge that we were all right. Really she's a good kid."

"Did you get to see Mme Chavignat?" Lily asks.

"I saw her only once. She wanted to keep me for lunch, but I don't like to linger. I always try to get there first thing in the morning so as not to come across anyone. You don't know how happy we are, Papa and me, to know that you are safe, and in good hands. Believe me, no day goes by without my thanking God for having allowed us to meet Sister Louise and Mlle Andrée. Being apart is hard on all of us, but only God knows what would have happened to us otherwise!

218

"Incidentally I do want you to know that our land-lord, M. Deschamps, told me that the police have come twice to our apartment to look for us. Just remember this when you get homesick or discouraged!"

<hr>

Maman refuses to eat blood sausage. She claims she's not hungry. And for the first time in her life—and in ours—she doesn't nag us to finish what's on our plates.

I think I know why she's allowing us to be so picky. Denise, Lily, and I are at the head of our respective classes for the Christmas term—as anyone can see from the gold medals we're parading on our chests.

I'm quite proud of the three of us. It's funny: I don't have that need anymore to prove that I'm every bit as good as my sisters.

I must be growing up.

"I couldn't have asked for a nicer present!" Maman had said, beaming. For her, doing well in school is just as important as food!

Monday, January 17

I stop my gesture halfway. Too late: Maman saw it!

"You keep scratching your head, Renée! Is anything wrong?"

Caught in the act, I remain mute.

"Let me have a look anyway," she insists.

"No! No!" I protest. "My hair just needs to be washed, that's all."

But Maman isn't listening. When it comes to our personal cleanliness, Maman calls the shots.

Reluctantly I fall into a chair while she towers over me.

"God!" I implore silently as a last resort, pressing my hands tightly together for more effect. "Since you can do just about anything, please make a miracle! Get the nits to turn black, the color of my hair, or get them to disappear altogether!"

Maman takes a lock in her hand. "No!" she gasps. "It can't be! Your hair is full of nits! My little girl has lice!" Maman shouts, lowering her voice as soon as she realizes that she can be heard.

I wonder how she knows about lice.

"I can't let you run around like this! Quick! Denise! Lily! Get me a fine comb!"

Denise rushes to her chest, opens the top drawer, and picks up one of the combs. There's no need telling Maman that we each have a fine comb of our own for daily use.

Maman begins to scour my head—hair by hair, it feels like.

"Your curls are full of nits. I'm afraid I have no choice but to cut them immediately. Otherwise, you'll have more tomorrow, and even more the day after. I can't let any child of mine walk around in this condition."

"Please, Maman! Don't cut my curls!" I beg, on the verge of tears. How can I ever appear in public without them? "We have a special shampoo we have that helps to kill the nits!" I exclaim, lying.

"Nothing will work as well as cutting them off. Come on, Renée, your curls will grow back."

"Please, Maman, please!" I continue to beg, crying by now, grabbing her arm. "It's *my* hair!"

Too late. Snip . . . snip. . . . Implacable, ignoring my

sobbing, Maman is now cutting my locks. Defeated, I stick out my neck as if for an execution. Tufts of hair fall on the towel she has hurriedly thrown on my shoulders.

"*Voilà!*" she says, calmer, as if the danger has passed. "Someday you'll be grateful for what I did!"

Grateful? She can't be serious! The way I feel now, I don't think I'll ever be able to forgive her as long as I live.

My sisters—lucky them!—require little trimming of their shorter hair. "Let's burn it all. The towel too," Maman says as she wraps it all in a piece of newspaper. "And let's hurry now, or else we'll be late for dinner!"

But I can't move. Mutilated as I am, how can Maman expect me to face the thirty-odd people with whom I share my daily meals? Surely the minute they see me, they'll know what happened!

I hate Maman. She spoiled everything. I wish she hadn't come.

"Here . . . why don't you wear a barrette," Maman suggests, "and make it look like a new hairdo?" She takes one from her own hair and hands it to me.

Reluctantly I take it. What's the use? I think. It won't do any good. Slowly I insert the barrette into my hair. It takes me forever to inspect my new face in the mirror. First I look sideways, then with one eye, then with both. My curls are all gone, and I can't even keep them as souvenirs!

Maman has done her best to cut my hair evenly, but I look as if I'd been hit by a windstorm.

"Why don't you try a part in the middle if you don't like it this way?" Maman advises. "That's always becoming on you! Here's another barrette. But let's get going now!"

Lily grabs my hand. "Come on, don't make such a face. It doesn't look as bad as all that!"

Honestly, I think.

Once in the dining room, I walk straight to my seat. Just like on my first evening, I avoid looking at anyone—especially at Marcel, who I know is sitting a few seats away.

I've hardly sat down when he's at my side. I *know* it's him, but I don't dare to look up.

"I see that you have a new hairdo!" he says, as if it were the most natural thing in the world.

I finally look up with imploring eyes, expecting a teasing comment.

"I liked your curls," he continues, "but this is nice too. Why, your hair is almost as short as mine!"

I finally break into a smile. I know that, from this moment on, I'll love him forever.

Thursday, January 20

Maman insisted on inviting us for a snack in town. I know she wants for us to be together one last time: She is leaving tomorrow.

"You wouldn't have a napoleon, would you?" she asks the waitress in a girlish, almost imploring voice.

For a moment her face becomes alive around her eyes, and then the look is gone.

I wish I could hide under the table. Maman must believe in miracles! How else could she expect to find napoleons with all the rationing that's going on?

"Of course not, Madame. We haven't had any in a long, long time. Why don't you try this biscuit instead? It isn't too bad. . . ."

Maman makes a face. "All right, I'll try it."

The three of us order something that resembles an apple tart—with many apples and very little tart.

"You're very quiet today, Renée. Don't you like it?" Maman asks as she sees me nibble without much enthusiasm.

She must have noticed that I didn't go out of my way to sit next to her and haven't bothered to take turns with my sisters to walk next to her in the street—as we usually do. The truth is, I still haven't recovered from the way she disposed of my hair.

I watch her as she carefully breaks a piece of her pastry and gathers the crumbs away from the rim of her plate. I suddenly see another side of Maman—a side that needs an orderly life with familiar objects, like the napoleon, to help her survive the upheavals around her.

Poor Maman! How did she manage to face all her hardships? How scared she must have been to see her world crumble little by little! How she must have dreaded sending us far away to a world she didn't trust—she who worries just to see us cross the street!

I note two new wrinkles on her forehead. Did I help put them there? I ask myself.

Poor Maman: She now looks smaller, more fragile, as if she needed protection herself.

I expected a perfect mother, and I discovered a human being.

"Let me taste a piece of your pastry," I say, raising my plate.

To Maman, sharing food is always a sign of love.

Sunday, February 6

Mother Superior seems so very worried these days and hardly pays us even a short visit at dinnertime. Sister Madeleine says that she gets on her bike almost every day now to scour the countryside with Mlle Raffray, a good soul of our parish with a square, hairy chin, who, we are told, knows all the farmers around.

We are running short on flour, vegetables—even dairy products can't always be counted on. Yesterday, for the first time, they came home empty-handed.

Sometimes Solange and Yvonne bring us a few tomatoes or even a cheese from home. But we're almost always hungry. Still, I can't bring myself to empty my plate at dinner today. We've been served noodles for the third time this week. The minute Denise lays eyes on them, she frowns and pronounces them stiff and sticky. What does she expect? She likes them swimming in butter and drowning in grated cheese.

It's Lily who first notices the tiny black balls. She wonders if it's a new dish. Suspicious as usual, Denise begins to align them on the rim of her plate. I don't know what to make of them. Are they peppercorns? I wonder.

Since it is Sunday, only Yvonne and Solange are left in the dining room with us. They must sense our hesitation. "I bet the noodles don't appeal to you tonight," Yvonne yells from across the room.

"You're right. Actually we were wondering what they put into it!" I reply.

Yvonne climbs over her bench and walks toward our table. "Well, I bet you'll never guess what these black things are," she whispers. *"Pouah!"* she adds, shuddering with disgust.

I wish she'd hurry and tell us about it instead of playing charades. By now her twin has decided to join us too.

"I went straight to Sister Madeleine," Yvonne says. "Frankly I wouldn't trust anyone else. Well, you may not believe it, but this black stuff is 'souvenirs' left by the mice. I understand that they have infested all our pantry!"

"But then Sister Madeleine knew what it was?" I protest.

"Sure!" Yvonne says. "They did what they could to take out all these awful droppings—of course, they boiled the noodles as usual—but it was impossible to do away with them all!"

"Why couldn't they throw them all out, then?" Denise grumbles.

"They thought of it, but that's all that was left, so the choice was that or nothing! You can see that all there is to eat tonight, besides this, is a couple of salad leaves, a compote of rhubarb—rather sour, since there's virtually no sugar—and a tiny piece of cheese. I was so disgusted, I didn't touch a thing!" Solange adds, making a face.

"Well, quite *entre nous,*" Yvonne confides, lowering her voice, "they say that—are you ready?—mice droppings are much cleaner than those of other animals!"

They both leave giggling.

The three of us look at one another in disbelief. With the same gesture Lily and Denise move their plates away.

But I am hungry. I look into the shapeless heap for a noodle that seems decent and roll it around my fork.

Pinching my nose, I stuff it into my mouth. But a hiccup brings it right up.

I prefer to remain hungry.

Friday, February 18

There are three new faces at La Chaumière. They're only in transit, Mother Superior announced. Rumor has it that they come from Paris.

Their name doesn't say much: Niego. But their faces betray them.

I can't stand to see little Nicole clinging to her mother's skirt as if she were afraid to lose her. Her brother is allowed to play with us just as long as he stays within earshot.

"Do you think they're . . . like us?" I whisper to my sisters. "I have a funny feeling that they are."

"Me too," Denise says.

I don't even dare ask what neighborhood they come from.

This afternoon Mme Niego smiled—it was such a sad smile. But I heard all that she couldn't tell me.

I returned the smile. It was so hard not to run to her, hug her, and tell her that things just had to get better someday.

I hope to God she understood.

I hope that this ugly hunting down of the Jews in France will stop and that we will soon go back to the time when the French were friendly and welcoming. I love France—it's my country. I want to be able to feel at home here like everyone else!

Mother Superior has just announced to us that Papa and Maman have given her permission to have us baptized. As simply as that!

I can't understand why Maman never discussed it with us. It must have come up while she was here.

"Now that we have German soldiers in town, we can't be cautious enough, in case they make an inquiry. M. le Curé will have to lie about the date, that's all!" the nun said.

I wonder how our parents agreed to it. It couldn't have been by letter—it would have been much too risky. Through someone else then? I'm afraid to ask: It would look as if I didn't trust her. A nun wouldn't lie, would she?

It is true that there have been Germans in Flers for several weeks now. Twenty or thirty—perhaps more. Sister Madeleine says that they have set up some barracks on the edge of town.

I am not as afraid of them as I was in Paris. First of all we don't have to wear the Star of David—and of course, the French police don't have us on record as being Jewish.

Almost every day we see them walk through the streets in combat uniforms, their boots hitting the pavement in perfect order, their hair blond and short. They are always harmonizing marching songs like "Halli, Hallo." Actually they sing rather well. But I hate to hear them, just the same. Aren't they ashamed to sing with such gusto while they are terrorizing people everywhere?

There was a funeral procession last week. A German officer died; I hoped he was killed. I watched them through the window, behind the closed curtains. They were marching slowly, dressed in their uniforms, as in the newsreels. There were many more of them than usual—they probably came from neighboring towns.

The music was sad. I wasn't. I remember thinking: Such a fuss about one single man. They certainly don't think twice about hurting and mistreating thousands of Jews!

Really I wonder how Papa and Maman can have made such an important decision without letting us know about it. Don't we count at all?

It's incredible: Everything has been planned very carefully, to the smallest detail. Our parents won't be here for the ceremony, of course, but Mlle Andrée will—she even agreed to be our godmother, while M. Jacques will be our godfather. And to kill two birds with one stone, there will be a double ceremony: In the privacy of our little chapel, my sisters and I will be baptized *and* we'll take our first Communion.

Denise and Lily are just as shocked as I was, but they recover quickly. "Imagine! We'll be wearing beautiful white taffeta dresses," Denise rejoices.

"I hope that we'll have a little crown and a veil too!" Lily remarks, excited.

"We probably will," Denise says. She turns to me and asks more pensively, "Do you really want to be baptized?"

"As if we had a choice!" Lilly retorts.

One thing really bothers me though: If Mlle Andrée agreed to be our godmother, surely she must be all for the idea.

The more I think about it, the more worried I get. Something serious must be going on.

Will we ever be able to get away from these damn Germans?

Thursday, March 9

I've stopped in front of the Virgin Mary—a white shadow against the blue drape of the night. I no longer pray to God; it's a waste of time. I prefer to address the Virgin Mary. I have come to like the women of the Gospel, the humble women—like Mary Magdalene, who so loved Jesus. I am sure He loved her, too, but he couldn't show his feelings—besides he had so much to do and so little time. I also like Martha and Mary, the two sisters who invited Jesus for dinner.

The ceremony is set for tomorrow. The two letters we received from home since we've been told the news didn't mention a thing.

I feel so totally abandoned—like a small boat carried away by the current without anything to hold on to.

Mother Superior's words echo in my head: "I hope you realize what joy is in store for you: Just imagine, you'll be the children of God, of the Virgin Mary—and the daughters of the Church!"

She doesn't understand. No one can. That's exactly the point: How can you adopt a new family without betraying the old one—the real one?

It's not that I don't enjoy going to church; on the contrary. I must admit, though, that I still avoid crossing myself, unless someone passes me some holy water and I have to. I can't help thinking that it would hurt Papa and Maman if they saw it. But I love the hymns and the

Gregorian chants, even if I don't know them by heart yet: I try to catch the words I'm familiar with and I hum the rest.

I also like the beautiful tales of the Holy Bible and the company of the saints. I always look for the statue of St. Joseph wherever we go. I have a soft spot for St. Joseph, even though nobody ever makes a fuss about him. He was so good to Mary—even after she had a son without him—and raised Jesus as if he were his own flesh and blood.

But to get converted is quite another thing! Once you are baptized, there's no going back!

Deep down, I am afraid that what they're teaching us in catechism is true: That, after we are baptized, my sisters and I will be forced to go to Heaven without our parents!

Saturday, March 11

"Do you feel different?" Denise asks me.

I think of yesterday. "I'm not sure . . . a little strange maybe."

We wore the taffeta dresses and braided crowns made of flowers. Mother Superior even borrowed lace gloves, and we had rosaries blessed especially for the occasion. Mlle Andrée's presence was comforting, although she had to leave right after the ceremony.

M. Jacques, quite proud and moved, said, "You look like a bride with your veil!"

I certainly would have preferred that M. Jacques give me away to Marcel.

In the meantime Mother Superior was carried away with joy. She didn't even realize that she kissed us three times—she who never kisses anyone!

I remember thinking, All that fuss for so little really: a mere few drops on the forehead, a few words from M. le Curé—and we are Christian forever. Deep down I expected something more.

What happens next? That's what Jean-Jacques always asks me, his eyes twinkling with expectation, when I read him a story or a fairy tale on Thursday afternoons.

All I have is this keen sense that something is shattered forever and we will never again be the same.

Tuesday, March 21

I wonder if Marcel has noticed a change in me since my baptism?

I do remind myself all the time: Beware of bad thoughts—they count now! But I laugh at Satan; I'm being a good girl, and besides, in his hometown of St. Servan-sur-Mer, Marcel was an altar boy. When I'm with him, we never even touch each other—except sometimes Marcel likes to fuss with my hair. We just talk to each other, and it feels like there is no one in the world but us.

I keep looking at him. I feel almost pretty when he looks at me with his golden green eyes and smiles at me—*me!* No one has ever really listened to me that way before.

Even Mother Superior notices that something is going

on. Today she asked me: "What do the two of you have to talk about that is so interesting?"

Marcel is so very poised: He speaks as if he has all the time in the world and as if what he has to say is very important. He says that they don't speak Breton in his home. He comes from Ille-et-Vilaine, which is a part of Brittany close to Normandy.

I wonder if he misses his mother, even though his grandmother is very good to him—and if he, too, would give anything to have her nag him a hundred times a day about sitting up straight, eating slowly, or looking ahead of him in the street.

Wednesday, April 19

I could hardly stand on my legs when I got up this morning to go to school. I went back to bed without even asking anyone's permission.

"It's probably a cold. A day or two of bed rest should take care of it!" Mother Superior said.

But I know better: I'm sick because of that awful split-pea soup she and Mlle Juliette practically forced down my throat yesterday.

Serves them right!

Saturday, April 22

But I haven't gotten better.

"I'm afraid it looks like jaundice to me!" Dr. Dumesnil declares, after Mother Superior asked him to come to my bedside in a hurry. He spent a great deal of time examining my nails and eyes. "The trouble is, it usually takes a long time to recover from it—weeks perhaps. She will need complete rest. Of course, going to school is out of the question!"

The doctor's voice—usually so cheerful—is awfully serious. I'm doomed!

As soon as I am alone, I run to the mirror. The whites of my eyes are yellowish, and the cuticles of my nails are beginning to turn yellow too.

I should be glad: They let me do whatever I want. I can read *"La Semaine de Suzette"*—Mother Superior even let me have one of the nun's large pillows—but my eyes hurt, and I have no energy.

Sunday, April 30

I'm still sick.

I miss school terribly—especially Françoise, who sent me a picture of St. Thérèse and a little note on fancy paper. I can't even go to church for the novenas and Vespers in the evening. And I was so looking forward to the Month of Mary!

Sister Madeleine comes in person to bring me vegetable soup and refuses to leave until the bowl is empty.

My sisters are allowed to visit me only after lunch, not to tire me. They chat about school. Christian and Jean-Jacques and Marcel visited me on Thursday afternoon and today after Mass. It's just as well they haven't come more often: I don't want anyone to see me the way I look now, with my yellow skin and my hair wilder than ever and sticking to my forehead.

Jean-Jacques gave me a fairy tale book. He wants me

to read it to him when I feel better. He is very excited now that he is able to spot the *x*'s and particularly the *q*'s—as in Jean-Jacques—when we read, but he gets annoyed with the *g*'s, which he always mixes up with the *q*'s.

When he leaves, he turns back several times to make sure I keep waving at him.

My only real distraction is Mme Catherine's visit in the early afternoon. She brings me whatever pastry roll or candy she's been able to spare at the bakery where she works.

She is our last recruit. They say that she is from Flers, but has lived many years in Argentan. When her husband left her, she decided to move back.

She is so different. First of all she never wears a medal or a cross around her neck, and you never see her with a rosary in her hand. The only jewelry she wears on her navy-blue dress is an old-fashioned pin with blue and red stones that used to be her mother's. She has deep wrinkles that spread out like a fan around her eyes and a front tooth that needs capping.

She is the only one who can still get me to laugh.

"That Mlle Suzanne. How do you like the way she pampers Tommy and cuts his food up for him? Don't misunderstand me; there's nothing wrong with liking animals, as long as you don't prefer them to people!"

Mme Catherine also likes to curse and to use bad language. The trouble is, her hoarse voice and her loud laugh make it easy to spot her in any crowd. She also whistles better than any man I've ever known. "Can't you try to behave? At least in public?" Mother Superior asks, despairing. But that's why Mme Catherine cheers me up!

Thursday, May 4

I'm going to die.

I can no longer go to the toilet unless someone takes me there or I can lean against the wall or the furniture on the way.

I know I'm going to die because my sisters are not allowed near me except for short periods of time. They put me in a room by myself and must boil my dishes, my nightgown, my sheets—anything I touch. I'm no better off than the leper in the Gospel.

I am scared to look at myself in the mirror. Just seeing my skinny yellow fingers scares me to death. When I show them to my sisters, they prefer to change the subject and try to make me laugh. But it's awfully hard to smile when you know you're going to die. It must really be the end: Even Mlle Juliette insists on seeing me.

Sometimes I drag myself to the window and admire the garden. I envy the trees, the hedges, the flowers that are growing and blooming while I'm wasting away.

I think, It's not for me that the leaves are greening, that the lilac is coming to life, that the sun—my best friend—is shining. I'll probably be gone long before summer comes around.

I cry, disconsolate, wiping my tears with my sleeve, expecting to find yellow stains where they fall on the fabric. Will my blood turn yellow too?

How long will Papa, Maman, and my sisters be sad? How long will they remember me?

I am not ready to meet my Maker—not quite. I hadn't planned to give it any serious thought until I was at least as old as Grand'mère!

As a brand-new Christian, my soul is pure and

white—I'm sure to go to Heaven. But I'm in no hurry. I don't know anyone there as yet.

I plead one last time: Please, God, don't let me down. You know I'm not cut out for the unusual!

But He continues to turn a deaf ear.

Tuesday, May 9

"Well, *mon petit*," Dr. Dumesnil says this morning. "We are going to be fine after all: But you need to take it easy for a long time."

Mother Superior cries, "It's a miracle!" Sister Madeleine admits she prayed very hard for me.

Perhaps God did try to test me once more, as only He knows how.

Wednesday, May 17

As the days pass I watch the yellow of my skin turn to white, then to pink.

I am living my own spring.

Sunday, June 4

Mother Superior must have lost her mind: She has once again invited a bunch of girls to spend the summer at La Chaumière.

"The poor kids, they'll starve!" Denise exclaimed when she heard about it.

"But it's so much like her. She figures that the fresh air

of Normandy and looking at cows grazing in the countryside are enough to impress city kids," I said, paraphrasing the nun.

Actually I rather welcome the change. And I'm curious: The girls are supposed to come from an orphanage in the Muette, which, as everyone knows, is one of the fanciest neighborhoods in Paris. I'm dying to rub elbows with kids born, no doubt, into "good" families, even though most of them have lost at least one parent.

So far, though, I've been disappointed. They wear quite ordinary clothes, their luggage has no fancy air about it—there were no trunks or hatboxes or anything like that. And they talk just like anyone else.

———

Marinette comes running into the parlor, where we're spending our free after-dinner time. Today her cheeks are pink, and her freckles are glistening with excitement.

"The Allies have sent tracts announcing an imminent landing on the Normandy coast! That's what Sister Madeleine told us!" she exclaims to Suzanne, the oldest of our dorm—a stocky, determined girl.

"What's a tract?" Colette asks, raising her pretty upturned nose like a question mark.

"Some sort of flyers that they drop from the planes," Jacqueline informs us. We can always count on her for common sense.

"It's not the first time they've sent these. Sister Madeleine says that no one believes them anymore. But what if they really mean it this time?" Marinette worries, covering her mouth with her hand, her eyes wide with awe.

"Why would they drop flyers over Flers rather than anywhere else?" I want to know.

"I don't know. Perhaps they want to scare the Germans, who have taken over the old wine market and filled it with ammunition. . . . At least that's what Sister Madeleine thinks!" Marinette continues. She turns to Suzanne and asks, "Do you think it's serious?"

"It's hard to say. Let's see what happens," Suzanne replies quite calmly.

"Still, how would the Allies know about our ammunition depot? I'm sure that there are many depots around the country that are more important!" I say. But Marinette's panic is getting to me in spite of myself.

"Dear God: If only Papa were here. I wouldn't be so scared!" Marinette cries. She is biting her finger now and looks smaller and more lost than ever. I wish I could comfort her, but I don't feel so confident myself.

Tuesday, June 6. Early morning.

I think I'm waking up from a nightmare. Then I hear people screaming.

"*Vite, vite!* There's a fire in town! You can see the flames from the window!"

I recognize Denise's voice, and I open my eyes and sit up in bed. It's still dark. There is no light: blackout regulations.

"But what time is it?" I ask, still wondering what's going on.

"It's one in the morning. Get up!" Denise orders, pulling me out of bed. "Didn't you hear anything? They've dropped a bomb in the center of town! Come and look!"

I suddenly become aware of the rumble of planes getting nearer, coming so close to us that they seem to skim the building. Instinctively I duck and then scream, "This one is for us! We can't stay here. Maybe they'll drop more bombs!"

Next to me Marinette falls to the floor and begins to pray frantically: "Virgin Mary, please protect us!"

The planes fly away—finally. I run to the window to join Denise and Lily and a handful of other girls.

In the distance I see long waves of flames tearing through several buildings like swords, sparks shooting in all directions. I think I can hear the crackling of the wood burning.

The air-raid siren wails.

Mlle Hélène emerges from the next room. She is in charge of the girls.

"They bombed the wine market!" she says. "They were right on target, our Allies, but unfortunately several houses nearby have been hit as well. Mme Raynal from across the street told us about it—her brother is a fireman. Tomorrow we'll know the extent of the damages."

"That's why we can't stay here! Suppose the planes come back?" I say, panicking.

Mlle Hélène walks over to me and puts her hands on my shoulders. "Where do you want us to go, Renée?" she asks softly. "There are no shelters here, like in Paris. So we may as well stay where we are.

"Let's keep calm," she continues, addressing everyone now. "And if possible, let's try to get some sleep until the morning."

"Are you going to stay with us? I think we'll sleep much better," I tell her.

She smiles. "If you want, I'll keep the door ajar."

Before returning to bed, I look out of the window one last time. I feel like shouting to our Allies, flying above in the sky, that we are their friends, for goodness' sake, and that they should be able to distinguish us from the Germans, their enemies. How can they drop bombs on innocent people?

The door swings wide open. This time it's Mother Superior. "You've probably heard that our wine market has been bombed. My poor children, you must have been terrified! I must say, we all panicked. But I think that the danger is over—at least for the moment. You all heard the siren. Thank the Lord, we're all alive! So why don't we say the Lord's Prayer and try to get some sleep? No one knows what tomorrow will bring, but we certainly ought to be rested and have a clear head in order to face it!"

I wish I could find some sleep. But I remain awake, jumping at the least bit of noise, waiting for the murderous planes to return.

Tuesday, June 6. Day.

Monique Jamet is dead—killed during the bombing last night; there were other victims as well. I can't get used to the idea. Didn't I see her just a few days ago, laughing, playing ball in the schoolyard? Why, she was the best swimmer in the whole school!

"Come on. Everyone in the yard!" Mlle Hélène

orders, clapping her hands to get our attention.

It's still broad daylight. We ate our dinner extra early: With what's going on, you have to be prepared.

The Allies landed at dawn!

It's Jacqueline who announced the news when she got us out of bed this morning. They have landed in Normandy, on the beaches at Calvados and Manche.

Lily jumped for joy on her bed. Denise clapped her hands and said, "Can you believe it? The war is going to end soon!"

I wonder if they know about it in Paris. Denise is ready to bet that they knew it even before we did. Jacqueline claims that nothing travels as fast as good news. But the danger isn't over yet—afraid of further bombing, many of the residents of La Chaumière have rushed home to their villages on their bicycles.

They say that if you listen very closely, you can hear the sound of the cannons!

I am very happy, too, of course—we are not very far from the coast, which means that the Allies will be here in no time. In my mind I can see them marching forward with their tanks and cannons. But with the Germans spread all over, it won't go all that smoothly.

"*Allez, allez!*" Mlle Hélène urges. "Everyone hold hands. Make a circle. Go ahead, get moving!"

I make it a point to stay next to the kitchen, where, I'm sure, the nuns have their ears stuck to the radio. I can't get Monique out of my mind. Was she hit by a bomb? Did she die instantly? Or was she burned in the fire—God, the flames were so high! Maybe she got buried under the rubble and suffocated to death?

I wonder if she called for her mother. Mlle Lucienne

once told me that one always calls one's mother when in pain or in danger—even soldiers on the battlefields!

It's so unfair that she died in this way, for nothing. She was just a little girl—a brave little French girl who studied hard in school and was waiting for the war to end. Why couldn't anyone save her?

I'm pressing my hands together, moist with sweat. I am praying without even knowing it.

"Come on, Renée! Don't stay in the corner by yourself—join in!"

But I can't move. My legs feel as if they're made of lead. The circle of girls is around me now. Denise yanks me into the round. My sisters knew Monique by sight; it's not the same thing. Still, Lily said: "Imagine, it could have happened to us too!"

My companions pull me, singing:

"Ne pleure pas, Jeannette . . .
Tra la la la la la la la . . ."

I really couldn't care less about Jeannette and her tears for her friend Pierre right now. I am hopping to the beat of the tune, like the others, but my body is all tensed up.

I am suddenly aware of the rumbling of planes in the distance. My ears perk up when I see, getting closer and closer, a group of planes forming a perfect triangle—just like a flock of birds. I don't like the sound they make; my heart is pounding like crazy. Maybe the sound will stop. The planes are slowing down—and now they stop moving altogether, but not for very long. As they accelerate their engines with a deafening noise, each plane dives toward us, one after the other, dropping something that looks like the paper birds we sometimes make in school.

"Bombs! Bombs! We are being bombed! Help!"

I'm not sure whether it is me or someone else who is screaming so. I've let go of my companions' hands, and I am rushing to the house, covering my head with my arms in a futile gesture of protection.

There is one explosion after another. The air and the earth seem to echo each other.

Someone yells, "Quick! Run to the corridor near the entrance door!"

We are crowding into the narrow corridor, screaming, crying. I push everyone in my way to join my sisters, who are clinging to Sister Madeleine's apron. The lamp above us is swaying. The wall clock crashes to the floor. Dédée, one of the youngest, screams with fright. The walls are trembling. There's no doubt: The house is going to collapse. We are waiting to die.

Marinette's voice can be heard over everyone's: "Dear God, please save us! I want my papa!"

New explosions follow, marked by screams and prayers alternating with deep sighs of relief when the danger abates. The siren is beginning to wail.

My terror comes and goes, as do the planes, but I can no longer control the trembling of my knees.

I pray like never before. "God in Heaven! Don't let us die! Not this way, not now! Please let us see Papa and Maman again. . . . I'll become a nun, I promise!"

Whatever came over me? The idea must have come from somewhere deep inside me. It is the least I can do—but also the most.

"For goodness' sake, open up!" someone yells from outside. "This damn door is stuck!"

The door finally gives in.

"Everyone must leave by tonight!" a policeman yells as he comes in. "They say that Flers will be completely destroyed. That's all we know, but you certainly shouldn't waste any time getting out!"

His sudden eruption instantly stops the intense flow of our prayers. As if propelled into action, Mother Superior takes over.

"You've heard, haven't you, children? So what are you waiting for? Get to your rooms, grab an extra set of clothes, a sweater and a blanket, and hurry back!"

Bumping into others on the way, the three of us climb the stairs two by two to our room.

Opening the armoire, I grab a cotton dress, a sweater, a pair of panties. There's no way I can take along an extra pair of shoes—it would be much too cumbersome. I take off my sandals and put on my good shoes instead.

My hands are shaking when I try to tie the shoelaces. I can't make a knot. "God," I pray, "please give us enought time to run away before the planes come back!"

"What should I take along?" Denise screams, wringing her hands.

"Anything! Your plaid dress!"

Denise and Lily bump into each other as they each try to pull a dress from the hanger or get a sweater from under their clothing stack on the shelf. Jackie falls on my head.

I pick her up, and tenderly I press her into my arms—discreetly.

"Are we going to take her along too?" Denise wants to know.

"Of course not! How can we? We'll come back to get her." I throw the doll back on the shelf and slam the door shut.

And how are you going to carry all this?" Denise wails.

"Just like this." I put the panties on over the pair I'm wearing and try to slip the dress on top of the one I already have on. My sisters follow my lead. Then my elbow gets stuck in the sleeve. "*Zut!*" I rage, close to tears. Lily helps me out with her usual impatience. "Leave it to you to get stuck at a time like this!"

"And the blanket?" Denise asks, stamping her feet. "Mother Superior said we need a blanket!"

I tear the blanket from the bed, fold it into four and then wrap my sweater in it. Denise, not at all her usual slowpoke self, is ready just as we are. I am suddenly full of remorse for the times I joined Maman and Lily in making fun of her.

This time Lily pushes us out of the room. "Hurry up, will you? We've dawdled enough!"

I caught a frightened look on Denise's face before her eyes blinked away from mine. I wish I could hug her, reassure her; another time.

I vow never to be mean to her or Lily again.

A plane rumbles above us. We dash out and rush down the stairs. On the way we bump into Marinette.

"Enough! Enough!" she screams, sticking her fingers in her ears as if to keep those awful sounds from entering.

Someone hugs her from behind and tells her, "Don't be frightened, Marinette! Nothing's going to happen to you!"

We join the others, who have now gathered around the nuns. Mother Superior pushes us out the door and orders us to line up on the sidewalk. Mlle Hélène counts the girls—twenty, besides the three of us.

The nun yells out her last warnings: "Please, children, get ready. You, Renée, stay with your sisters." She pushes me forward. "And you, Marinette, you will walk between Clothilde and Charlotte. Sister Geneviève, you will keep an eye on Jean-Jacques and Christian. . . ."

I can't stay put. I look to the right, then to the left. I want to know whether the other people in town are leaving too. Up the street a lady is rushing, pushing a pram, followed by a man pulling by the hand a little boy who refuses to walk. Farther down, near the crossroad, a few people have gathered and are arguing with a policeman.

I also watch the sky, which is now free of planes. But I don't feel safe at all: It could be the calm before the storm.

"All right, everyone is here now!" Mother Superior remarks as Mlle Suzanne and Mme Catherine come out of the building. "The main thing is for us to get away from town as soon as possible. We'll be walking toward the woods. . . . The Dumoulins are letting us have their barn for a few days."

She is carrying a bundle under her arm, like everyone else. A rosary is hanging down from her sleeve. *That's really her baggage!* I think.

"All right now . . . forward!"

We start to walk, three abreast, Sister Madeleine leading the way, Mlle Hélène walking last, while Mother Superior walks back and forth to make sure that no one falls behind.

That's when it dawns on me that Marcel is not with us: Just like most of the people at La Chaumière, his grandmother probably thought it best to go back to her own house away from town. And I don't even have his address!

As we are about to turn the corner I cast a last glance at what has been our home for two years. Mother Superior grabs my arm. "Do you want to slow everybody down now, of all times?"

I run to catch up with the others. There is never time for the most important things.

———

It's later—two hours, three hours, an eternity later. Our time does not go by the clock anymore.

We are at the Dumoulins' barn, safe for the moment.

Outside the sky is studded with sparkling stars. The air is very still.

But in my mind I keep seeing the bombs fall, the lamp sway, and my head still echoes with the deafening grumbling of the planes and the explosions, the frantic voice of Mother Superior yelling "Duck! Duck! Stay near the ground!" whenever a plane flew over us.

My head still hurts from straining not to look at the people we came across who were rushing around in a daze. I tried to ignore anyone that was not Marinette, Charlotte, and Clothilde in front of me, or my sisters at my sides, until we reached the outskirts of the woods and someone yelled: "At last! Now we can breathe again!"

Mother Superior had us stop three times to make sure no one was missing. Each time we had to wait for the latecomers: Mlle Suzanne—poor soul, she limped more than ever—and Mme Catherine, who was keeping her company.

When the old *demoiselle* arrived at the farm—a good while after everyone else—and she took Tommy out of the only box she was carrying, I felt very sad. I could have taken Jackie along too!

———

The barn is quite narrow. We have settled as best we could on the straw that prickles even through the blanket. I feel Charlotte's legs on my stomach and Marinette's arm on my shoulder. Poor Marinette! She looks sad even when she sleeps. They say she has lost her mother and that her father is an older man who is away a great deal on business.

Do you get to love one parent twice as much when the other one dies? I wonder.

How lucky we are: We have both!

I think of Papa and Maman for the first time this evening. I wonder if they have any idea that we nearly died at least ten times today?

Friday, June 9

It's morning again. I am waiting in line behind Charlotte. I close my eyes, liking the sun on my face. It warms me up from inside. I wish it could shine forever.

It's the third day that we are here. We are waiting to get washed in the chipped enamel basin that the farmers lent to us. It's a long line; the little ones get washed first.

We must fetch the water from the well, near the farm building about three hundred yards away. We use a large pail that two of the older girls carry to the barn, making sure not to spill any on the way. After each girl washes the water gets thrown out and must be fetched again.

So far we've been eating only cheese and apples,

except for yesterday: We had tomatoes with *crème fraîche* for dinner.

At least we can have as much milk as we want. It has a strange taste. Sister Madeleine explains that it is very fresh. Denise swears that she can taste the grass that the cow just ate. Disgusted at the thought, I give my share to Colette.

I fell under her spell from the start. She is about my age, but so pretty, with her almond-shaped eyes and her curly eyelashes. She likes to swing her long hair back and forth when she talks. And I like to listen to her: She lisps like a baby.

The poor girl, she is practically an orphan, abandoned by her parents. Her mother—a well-known actress, Colette likes to boast—has been touring the country for the past few months. "Do you want to see a picture of her?" she almost begs. We both admire the perfect smile, the complicated hairdo, the square-shouldered dress.

Sometimes I also talk to Marinette. Since the night of the bombing she has not been the same. She looks frightened, and every time she hears a plane, she sticks her fingers in her ears and screams, "Enough! Enough!" Fortunately Charlotte is always around to reassure her.

"Look!" Charlotte exclaims now. "Do you see the smoke, right there, to the right of us? Well, it's Flers burning!"

Her finger points to a heavy cloud that is darkening the blue sky. We are on a plateau, and when the weather is clear, we can see quite far in the distance.

I jump and grab her arm. "What are you talking about? How do you know it is Flers?"

"The farmer told it to the nuns this morning. He

heard that Flers had been totally bombed out."

I feel like screaming, like kicking: What's the matter with these crazy Allies? What's the point of wrecking our town?

The smoke is getting heavier and heavier and is spreading across the horizon.

At the news everyone begins to speculate. "Do you think that everybody had time to run away?" Lily asks.

"I think so! The police probably chased the other people out the way they chased us!" I say.

But deep down I know better: There must have been some brave Flérois who refused to leave their homes—just like the captain who refuses to leave his sinking ship.

The Jamets, for example. They couldn't possibly have left on the eve of Monique's funeral!

What about the Delaunays, whose youngest daughter was recovering from the measles? And M. Jacques?

=====

"Let's thank the Divine Providence!" Mother Superior tells us a little later when we are being served supper—a small portion of potato salad and a piece of sausage. "We are being offered a larger, more comfortable barn where we'll be able to settle down for a while. One of the nuns of Pont-Ramond found it for us. It is at La Crétine, the little hamlet near Le Chatellier."

She makes me think of Maman. She, too, always manages to come up with something when we think there's no way out.

I try to read her face, to detect the tiniest shadow in her look. She didn't say a word about our returning to Flers. I know her: She would have latched on the smallest ray of hope. There probably isn't any.

I'm no longer hungry.

Friday, June 16

We will be leaving early in the morning.

"May God be with you! Just watch the planes on the way and be very cautious. And be aware of the front line. It can't be very far away now!" the Dumoulins warn us.

The front—it is, I know, the firing line, the point where the Germans and the Allies are fighting each other. What's going to happen to us? Will we be caught between the two—overcome by bombshells or trapped in hand-to-hand combat, as in the newsreels, with dead bodies all around?

I am so scared. Battles are for men—soldiers who are young and strong and know how to defend themselves!

"What about Papa and Maman? With all this moving around, they won't know where we are!" Denise laments.

Lily thinks they'll figure out that with the landing and the invasion by the Allies, nothing's working anymore. "Why, Mother Superior says that even the Red Cross can't get through!"

I'm afraid that if they hear that we have been bombed, they will think that we're dead.

Saturday, June 17

"We made it—finally!" Colette says with a sigh, dropping her bundle on the ground and planting herself in front of the high gate to our right. "Mother Superior said we were to stop here!"

I look with disbelief at the elegant white house and the heart-shaped lawn at the end of the gate. Are we really going to live here?

It's enough to make me forget about our troubles. We have been walking—we forced ourselves to walk—for hours now. We were hungry and thirsty: an apple each, that's all we had, and nothing to drink, with this heat! The nuns must have been uncomfortable too. The perspiration was dripping down their temples; what can you expect, with their heavy pleated dresses that go all the way down to their ankles and their stiff headpieces?

Yet they didn't complain: Sister Madeleine kept an eye on the little ones in front, and Sister Geneviève and Mother Superior minded the rest of us, while Mlle Hélène watched the road. We came across several haycarts and we even had to squeeze to the side to let some cattle pass by. At times the smell of manure was so strong that the others had to pinch their noses. It didn't bother me one bit.

I look at my bloody feet. It's because of these silly shoes: stiff as anything because they are practically new. They have eaten holes into my socks and brought blisters to my heels and toes. I would have been better off keeping my sandals on, like everybody else, when we fled from Flers.

Sister Madeleine keeps telling us to offer our hardships to God so that the war may end sooner. I haven't kept a list for quite a while now. Besides, how do I know that He will actually trade one for the other? I don't have Mother Superior's blind faith. I'm more like St. Thomas, the doubter.

I was so frightened of being abandoned on the road that I didn't dare complain. It was Mme Catherine who first noticed my feet—she was walking way behind with Mlle Suzanne. They took turns carrying Tommy.

Mother Superior insisted that I soak my feet in a trough, somewhere on the way, after we drank from it. I walked barefoot the rest of the way. Never mind the gravel or the dirt road: Anything was better than walking with those shoes on!

When we entered this hamlet, we found it deserted. All we saw was a bike parked in front of a house, a wheelbarrow forgotten in the middle of a street, a pitchfork on the edge of a field. The villagers must have gotten so frightened, they ran away, Mlle Hélène thinks.

I thought we'd never get there. But can this mansion really be our destination? I thought we were going to another barn!

"I'm sorry to say that this is just Pont-Ramond," Mother Superior informs us. "What you see is an old folks' home. One of the nuns is going to take us to La Crétine, where they are expecting us. Come on, all you need is a bit more courage. We don't have very far to go now!"

A few moments later she comes back with a nun all dressed in white. We resume our walk again, following our guide.

As we turn into a dirt road we see three people waiting for us, leaning against a wooden barrier and waving. "Quick! Line up two by two!" Mother Superior orders, pushing us along. We line up two by two. We've got to make a good impression!

We are being introduced to the farmers—M. and Mme

Lafarge—and Mathieu, the farmhand. The farmer takes off his beret to greet the nuns.

Mme Lafarge wears a scarf on her head and has a thick apron around her waist. "Virgin Mary! All these little ones away from their mothers and fathers in such evil times!" she exclaims, walking toward us.

Jacotte has taken Mlle Hélène's hand. Suzette is holding on to her skirt.

We don't dare break the lines. I can't wait to sit down. In front of me Dédée is playing with her bundle, throwing it up in the air and catching it with one hand.

"Look at this darling little boy!" the lady continues, suddenly noticing Jean-Jacques, who is trying to hide behind Sister Geneviève. "My poor children, you must be starved and dead tired. Let me first take you to your home. After that, I'll bring you a dish of potato salad and hard-boiled eggs that I've prepared especially for you."

We walk past a wide one-story farmhouse made of gray stone. The stable, we are told, is right next to us. We finally reach our barn at the end of the yard—a large rectangular building. They have a hard time opening the heavy door. The farmers have covered the ground with straw and hay to keep us from sleeping on the bare ground. They apologize for not being able to provide us with a table or benches to sit on. We'll have to eat out of doors, in the yard—or better yet in the orchard. There at least we can sit on the grass.

"Don't you worry! We'll do fine!" Mother Superior says. "We are ever so grateful that you are kind enough to let us stay here! God will reward you."

We can't complain: Our new barn is at least twice as big as the old one. Here you can stretch out without bumping into your neighbor. We had to get settled in a hurry; we have no other light but the daylight from outside, and it is already past sunset.

We decide to sleep eight in a row, well wrapped in our blankets to protect us from the pricking straw. (How wise Mother Superior was to get us to take those blankets along, I think now.) They have divided us into three groups: the seniors (I am one of them), the intermediates (including Denise and Lily), and the little ones, who sleep nearest to the door to be closest to the toilets outside.

"Where are we going to put our things?" Denise worries. She is folding her sweater.

"Why don't you hang them on the pitchfork, right there in the corner. M. Lafarge will build us a makeshift shelf tomorrow," Mother Superior says. "I imagine we could also use the wooden beams under the roof for those things we don't need every day."

The three of us sleep in the last row; they've decided to let us stay together. Denise has spread her straw quite evenly and makes sure that no one intrudes on her space. I gather mine under my head to make a pillow. Mlle Suzanne and Mme Catherine have made a spot for themselves against the wall—with Tommy in between.

The nuns have their own quarters on a raised loft meant to store the hay. We call it Paradise. It can be reached only by ladder.

No matter how careful I am—I pull my cover all the way to my forehead—I must battle with bits of straw that find their way into my neck and my hair, and the strong smell of hay that surrounds us keeps me from falling asleep.

What's most important is that we're in a safe place, Mother Superior keeps reminding us. The fact is, we have not even heard a single plane since we got here.

Monday, June 26

We are waiting in line to get washed: We get our water from a pump in the yard, about midway to the farm. The pump is so hard to get started that we need four strong arms to get it going. Christian always volunteers. He *is* the only big boy among us—even if his muscles are no bigger than mine.

We get two pumps each: One to get our face and hair washed, another to rinse them out.

"I was first!" Jacotte insists, shoving Jean-Jacques and Suzette to the side. Nothing doing: She will have to wait her turn. The little ones always get washed first. The seniors help out the younger ones.

When it's the seniors' turn—that is, Charlotte, Colette, Mado, Dédée, Marthe, Jeanne, me, and of course, Mlle Hélène—we hold out a blanket to serve as a screen. We giggle at the idea, but Mother Superior assures us that it is the proper thing to do.

Since we have no towel to wipe ourselves with, we count on the sun to dry us off. It's a good thing that it's summer!

Mother Superior insists on our getting properly cleaned up. Sister Geneviève is expected to check out our nails and our ears. I think it's only for show: How can we wash up well without a washcloth and soap?

The other day Denise took me aside. "Where do you think the nuns get washed? There aren't too many places around. Can you picture them washing up at the pump, right in the open?"

"Maybe they get up in the middle of the night, when everybody else is asleep."

"Unless they get cleaned up at the farmhouse. They must have a tap in the kitchen like at home, in Paris."

I laugh to myself just thinking at what would happen if the farmer were to catch them in their underwear!

My sisters and I sleep in the loft now, next to the nuns. This way there's more room for the others downstairs.

The only trouble is that you must always remember not to bump your head against the slanted roof. "It will be easier to undress!" Lily exclaimed, rejoicing.

We got used to sleeping without pajamas or nightgowns fairly quickly, but even after all this time, it still feels strange undressing in front of everybody, so we always wait for the dark. We take off our dresses and our socks, and we slip into our blanket with our slips and panties on—quick, to avoid the prickly straw. The one who gets done first wins.

Right from the first night I began to wonder: "Do you think that the nuns get undressed, too, and that they take off their *cornettes*? I don't see how they can possibly sleep with them on," I whispered to Denise.

"I'd like to find out myself!" Denise giggled.

So we began to spy on them. We even tried to wake up early in the morning, hoping to catch a glimpse of their bald heads. And at night, just before the silly procession to the outhouse, I twisted myself around, taking advantage of the flickering light of the candle to catch them in the act. But all I ever got to see was their heads covered with skullcaps. We had to give up playing detectives.

What a chore the procession was at first! I was furious at being awakened in the middle of the night, like a baby, to grope in the dark toward a wooden shack, full of splinters, and a seat with a hole inside. Only one for all of us—that's all there is!

But then I decided to join everyone else. I'm not sorry at all: That's when we have the most fun.

It's Mlle Hélène who gives the signal. She is always ready first. She claps her hands and yells, "Come on, get up, everyone. Time to go to the toilet!"

She then lights the candle given to us by the farmer. I wonder how she remains so calm with Mother Superior worrying constantly about the candle falling on the straw or the hot wax dripping on one of us. Patiently she goes after the slowpokes or the lazy ones.

My sisters and I are up at the first clap of hands, and we slip on our dresses and shoes in a jiffy. I'm always the first one to step down the ladder. I hold on to both sides for dear life—it's unsteady, and I'm afraid I'll stumble on it.

While we're getting everyone together, Colette and Charlotte open the door, which squeaks every single time. We never fail to stop short, awed by the pitch dark and the frightening silence that surrounds us.

Charlotte always volunteers to run out first, hooting like an owl. Colette does the same. Then we feel much braver; courage is catching. And before we know it, we all rush out in single file, screaming, in the direction of the outhouse, over there in the dark, holding one another by the shoulder. We make believe that we're about to explore Treasure Island.

How lucky we are to have landed here!

Thursday, June 29

We are all lost in meditation, silently going over what happened during the day, as we do every evening during common prayer. The door of the barn is still open. The peace and the semidarkness from outside add to our introspective mood.

"Damn!" a hoarse voice interrupts.

Every head turns toward the impious Mme Catherine, who has let the word slip in the middle of our praying.

She is rubbing her arm, mumbling to herself, just as Tommy dashes out like a thief. Poor Tommy. He was probably tired of his mistress's tight grip and took it out on Mme Catherine.

"Catch him, for goodness' sake!" the old *demoiselle* yells out, unable to contain herself.

I bite my lips not to burst out laughing and turn to Denise who, like the rest of us, has her hands pressed together and is afraid to move.

Jean-Jacques finally begins to roar. Soon everyone does.

Mother Superior comes to our rescue. The Good Lord will surely keep in mind the hard times we have had these last few days and will forgive us, she assures us.

As usual we end the prayer by singing:

"Seigneur, encore un jour s'achève,
Le jour a dissipé tout bruit. . . ."

("Lord, another day is gone,
It's silent once again. . . .")

We sing with all our might—Colette screaming at the top of her lungs, her mouth open so wide, she could tempt the flies; Jean-Jacques stumbling on his words and looking to me for approval. Once in a while Charlotte hits Marinette on the head when she goes off-key.

It's as if time is suspended: There is nothing in the world but us, and we are singing the joy of being together.

———

The door of the barn has just been shut. We each have settled in our corner. We are allowed ten minutes to chat before going to sleep.

My ears suddenly prick up. I think I hear humming. I am not dreaming: It's a bunch of people singing.

I ask Lily, lying next to me: "Do you hear something too?"

"Silence, please!" Mlle Hélène cuts in, clapping her hands to get everyone's attention. "Can't you listen for a minute?"

Everybody stops chatting. There's no doubt: A group of men are singing quite close to us. I can't make out what they're singing at first, but then, in a flash, I understand one word, then another.

Frightened to death, I scream, "Dear God! They're Germans! *Germans!* What's going to happen to us?" I throw off my blanket and sit up, ready to do anything rather than remain at the mercy of our enemies.

"But where the devil are they coming from?" Mme Catherine asks. "And when did they get here?"

I crawl on all fours toward Mother Superior, groping for her sleeve in the dark. "Sister! Sister! We can't stay here! Not with the *boches* around!" I implore.

"Come on, come on, my child. Don't get yourself all worked up! You're not in Paris.

"Listen here, everybody!" she continues, raising her voice to be heard. "I'm sure we are not in any immediate danger. We'll know about this tomorrow. In the meantime don't worry and try to get some sleep. . . . God be with us!"

Long after the Germans have stopped singing, I ask myself, Does Mother Superior truly realize the danger we are in?

Sunday, July 2

A handful of us have decided to play hide-and-seek. We had the toughest time convincing little Jean-Jacques to stay with Sister Geneviève, who is always ready to do us a favor.

We had to swear to Mother Superior that we would remain within shouting distance—and especially that we'd avoid the Germans, who have taken up lodging at the Lafarges' farm. Her instructions are that we are not to speak to them and must hurry past them if we happen to meet them. So far they've kept to themselves and have left us alone.

There are six or seven young soldiers roaming around the grounds, dressed in worn uniforms. Blond-haired and blue-eyed—most of them so young, they probably don't need to shave yet—they look so innocent. But I know better than to trust them.

Our farmer says that there are quite a number of stranded German soldiers in the area. With the invasion of the Allies they have disbanded and are seeking refuge in various farms. "Our" Germans, he says, are not armed—all they have is a truck. The trouble is that they, too, have to be fed. The good farmers are already feeding us—thirty people who fell on them from the blue!

That's not all. These dirty *boches* have just painted a large red cross on the roof of the farm. I know it wasn't there before. "Another one of their tricks used to mislead the Allies," grumbles Mme Catherine. "An old trick that no longer fools anyone, least of all the Allies. If anything, it will make them bomb us. If the Allies want to aim at the farm, they'll get us too!"

It's my turn to lean against the tree. I put a scarf over my eyes to keep myself from cheating. I suddenly become aware of the increasing rumble of a nearing plane somewhere in the sky. I open my eyes—I can't help it—and spot it way above in the sky. Now, I *know* it's an English or an American plane—it has to be. So I spontaneously wave my hankie in a gesture of friendship. Our Allies can surely use some encouragement!

But I stop in midair: I have suddenly become aware of someone next to me, and I'm petrified. From the corner of my eye I first see what looks like a belt with something metallic attached to it. It must be a revolver! My eye then travels up the khaki shirt to the closely shaven blond head. It is one of "our" German soldiers. I know him. He often goes to fetch water at the pump. That's the end of me! I think.

I bite my lip and clench my fists to keep myself from screaming. Then I remember Papa's words: "Don't ever show that you are afraid!"

With surprising presence of mind I resume the gesture of my arm, still holding the handkerchief, and stretch my opposite leg to the back, like we do in school, making believe that I am dancing.

At first I avert my eyes. Who knows, he may guess, from my curly black hair and my frightened look, that I'm Jewish—and that would surely mean the end of us all!

Then I decide to look at him: He is very young. Maybe he hasn't had the time to learn to be tough and mean like his elders.

Why, he smiles at me—and then turns around and walks away.

I rush to the barn, shaking like a leaf.

Wednesday, July 5

My heart is pounding like mad. I inspect the sky: I look to the right, then to the left before I dare to step outside. I am especially listening for the new sound—a hiss that tears the air above us before we can say "*Boo.*"

We're at the mercy of bombshells now.

I decide to step out. I've got to get to the toilet!

"Are you sure it's safe?" Denise inquired, raising her eyes from the torn sock she is trying to fix.

"I think so. . . . The shelling has died down. I'd better go while it's quiet."

"Wait for me. I'll go with you!"

It *is* nice to have a sister. When there are two of you, it's easier to be brave.

Mme Catherine first warned us the day before yesterday: "Let me tell you—I've never been so scared in my life. This morning I was rushing to go to the toilet when suddenly—*vlan!*—I felt a wind blow over my head with a hissing sound. It barely lasted a few seconds. I thought that was it for me! It's not that I'm afraid to die . . . but it's not the way I'd like to go!"

From what our farmer says, and other villagers in the area, the bombshells are coming from the German Army, who refuse to surrender, and from the Allies, who continue to advance. There are also some clusters of French Underground who have joined in the battle, we are told, so that there are three fronts—with us in the middle.

The Germans at the farm are hiding. I think they're scared too. They've camouflaged their truck and stuck it between two trees. But I still don't trust them. In church at Le Chatellier last Sunday we heard that the Germans refuse to accept defeat, and that they are liable to do just about anything.

When the hissing begins, it's always the same panic: We scream and we bump into one another as we rush to the barn and lock ourselves in. But I don't feel at all safe. I can't help thinking that, with all this straw, the barn will ignite in no time if a bombshell hits it. Still, when Mother Superior pushes us in, yelling *"Vite! Vite!* We'll be safer inside!" I do as I'm told.

It reminds me of Mulhouse—the time that Denise and I were caught by an air raid as we were returning from school. We were smack in the middle of Place Franklin— God knows how gigantic it is!—holding our gas masks.

We got really scared; there was no shelter in sight. We fell to the ground, shaking with fright, until a police car spotted us and rushed us to a shelter.

With the front line approaching I'm always afraid I'll see a tank emerge from behind the trees, or find myself face to face with armed soldiers ready to shoot at anything that moves.

Even the cows are scared. They rush around frantically when planes roam overhead or the shells fly above us. Sometimes the farmers ask some of us to mind the animals. It was our turn yesterday. At first we found it funny to run after the animals and push them toward the hedge with a stick. Then all of a sudden a plane was on us and skimmed the treetops so closely that we fell to the ground and rolled in the grass, howling with fright. We dashed to the barn as quickly as our legs would carry us, forgetting all about the cows. Fortunately they had fled to safety.

With all that's going on, I'm especially worried about little Jean-Jacques. We don't know what to do to keep him inside.

If I were his mother, I would simply tie him down!

Thursday, July 6

We don't dare eat outside anymore—even if there is no shelling going on for the minute. Those shellings start just as they end: without any warning. So now we take our meals in the barn, sitting on the bare ground around the nuns, close to the open door.

Here comes Jacotte, complaining again. "Sister,

Suzette doesn't want to give me back my spoon! I can't eat my oatmeal!"

What a nuisance she is! She must have been spoiled before she landed in the orphanage—or else she had no brother or sister to teach her how to share. How dare she complain? She should be grateful that we're not starving. Mother Superior is quite right: We must thank the Divine Providence for the generosity of the farmers. Considering that our area has been devastated and that we are cut off from the rest of the world, the fact that we're eating at all borders on the miraculous.

We're so lucky that the Lafarges have cows, a handful of chickens, and especially a vegetable garden. So far we've never been wanting for milk, tomatoes, and carrots, and we're simply overjoyed when we are served potatoes. But nothing tastes as good as the bread that Mme Lafarge bakes for us when she can get her hands on some flour.

Sister Madeleine says that the *boches* don't think twice about helping themselves to our meager stock of food. I wonder how much longer we'll be able to hold out.

She prepares our food in the farm kitchen in a huge battered pot. It is so very heavy that Sister Geneviève helps to carry it all the way to the barn. Tiny as she is, she has incredibly strong hands, our little nun.

We clap our hands with joy as soon as the nuns appear with the pot. Funny how quickly we forget the danger!

We have just about enough plates for everybody, between the wooden bowls and the tin containers we gathered at the farm—but we don't have enough spoons. So, we let the young ones eat first, one ladleful for each. They always want more. We do too—but we can contain ourselves much better.

Wednesday, July 12

It's Wednesday today—the day on which we used to get our mail from Paris. When I was young, I used to believe that each day had a different color: Sunday was red; Wednesday, blue.

Now every day is gray. It's been so long since we had any news. We've lost all notion of time. One day drags aimlessly into another, and every morning we have to start all over again.

I close my eyes real tight and think of Papa and Maman. We've been apart for so long that all I can recall is Maman's ashen face the day we left and Papa's raised eyebrows when he is angry.

Sometimes I imagine us all back home, as before. I would never have thought the day would ever come when I'd actually miss doing the dishes or peeling the potatoes. After the war, I swear, I'll never complain again.

We are always hungry now. Still, today we can't complain: We had a potato each for lunch, with the skin on—in its jacket, they call it. I ate the skin first. It was delicious—eyes and all. I peeled it off slowly, carefully, with my nail, to make it last as long as possible. In fact, I could easily have swallowed the whole thing in one mouthful.

It's thanks to Sister Madeleine: She managed to strike a deal with the Germans at the farm. They always grab them first; everybody knows that the *boches* are crazy about potatoes. At any rate they agreed to give us a bunch of them—provided that we mend their clothes and resew their buttons.

At first I wondered how the nuns could even consider

talking to the Germans. But these pants and shirts are quite a sight: They are so worn at the knees and the elbows, they are beyond repair. How can they have gotten to that point? The Germans must be in serious trouble!

The little ones are always asking for bread. No matter how often we explain that we don't have any rationing cards and that it's not possible to get food like before, they keep asking, "Are we going to get some tomorrow?"

It's heartbreaking to see that they can't understand.

Saturday, July 22

Mlle Hélène is trying to distract us by getting us to draw dolls, using paper and pencils she collected at the farm. I'm good at sketching tall, skinny models wearing draped or pleated dresses, but my hands are bandaged because of new infections. Impetigo is the fancy name Sister Geneviève gives it. It's not surprising, Sister Madeleine says, that when you recover from jaundice, your body is not very resistant. They wrapped me up in rags to protect me from the straw that pricks me like thousands of tiny needles, and to keep me from the many little creatures that are all around us. But I think it's really meant to keep me from scratching!

Lily, Marinette, and Colette are beginning to be infected, too, but they don't need any bandages. I feel like a wounded soldier. At least it excuses me from some of the chores.

I'm getting a headache from being so hungry, so I decide to take a chance outdoors: We've had no shelling for almost twenty hours now. I may as well take advantage of it.

I walk out to the orchard and lie down under one of the trees, my head resting on my folded arms. A wasp buzzes around me, then flies away. I close my eyes and let myself be soaked up by the sun. It feels so wonderful. When I open my eyes again, I see a beam of white light quiver between the leaves and form into a cloud.

Come, come, I tell myself. Wouldn't it be nice, though, if the cloud were to open up and the Virgin Mary were to appear to me, as she did to St. Bernadette? She was only a year older than me. Please, Virgin Mary, I pray, I need a miracle!

I can't believe what's happening to me. I feel lighter and lighter, as if my soul were flying away. My hunger cramps are gone. Could it be that now I'm a saint, and in Paradise?

"Renée! Renée! What the devil are you doing outside?"

Damn! Lily's voice wakes me from my dream.

Tuesday, August 1

Thank goodness for Mlle Hélène. She is full of good ideas.

"How about setting up a scraping team?" she asked a few days ago. Two of us can take turns scraping the pot whenever we are served, she suggested.

We all welcome the idea—even Mother Superior. I'm worried about her these days. She spends all her time twisting her rosary around her fingers, and every time the hissing of the bombshells begins, she crosses herself quickly, as if she constantly needed new reassurance. Her *cornette* is all gray, and her wings no longer bounce. Imagine: Sometimes she even forgets to tell us to get washed.

It's my turn to scrape the pot today—with Charlotte. Armed each with a ladle, we kneel around the pot that has just been emptied, our eyes staring at the gray chunks of food that are still left on the sides. Within minutes we become the fiercest of enemies.

"Go ahead, Renée! One more!"

"Don't be a fool, Charlotte! Go faster!"

Our hungry companions, sharing in every mouthful that we scrape up, turn it into a match.

I can't believe it's really me who digs with such fury into the pot, forcing back Charlotte's arm and pulling her hair!

One thing is certain: Nothing ever seemed as delectable as the Sarrazin mush I lick off the ladle. I can't believe I ever hated that stuff!

———

All we can think of these days is food; it's become an obsession. We talk about all the things we will indulge in after the war.

My sisters play at imagining Maman in her kitchen, matching dishes to her guests. "You know what? I think Mlle Hélène and Charlotte would go mad over her goulash!" Denise declares.

"And I can picture Mme Catherine licking her fingers after she's finished Maman's stuffed paprikas," Lily remarks. "I bet she just loves trying new dishes!"

All that talk makes my mouth water. In my mind I am tasting the kugelhupf and the fruit tarts of the holidays, and I can smell cinnamon. All of a sudden Alsace comes to life, with its gingerbread and its mandarin oranges for the feast of St. Nicholas. I run away to keep myself from becoming homesick.

Once in a while I force myself to go to the orchard. If I'm lucky, I think, I'll come across a piece of fruit—even a rotten one. It's hard to believe that we're in the heart of Normandy, the country of the apple! I dig into two holes left by the shelling and come up with a piece of shining metal, which I drop in terror.

A little farther out I trace with my finger the deep grooves carved into the tree that was cut in two by a shell. One by one I lift the dead branches that are strewn on the ground like a lifeless hand.

I finally give up: Of the few apples that are still lingering on the ground, all that's left are rotten cores gnawed to death by the birds.

Once I was so hungry that I ventured as far as the main road and I tried to bite into a wild berry. It was so hard and so bitter that I spit it right out. Besides, Mother Superior keeps reminding us that one must be cautious. Just like with some mushrooms, you risk getting poisoned.

Bits of straw or grass are no better: It's dry, it pricks your palate and your tongue—and it doesn't take away the hunger one bit.

Still, I can't help it: I'm always looking for something to chew on.

Thursday, August 3

This afternoon Mme Catherine takes me aside.

"I have something for you. Here!" she says, taking a greasy white package out of her pocket. "It's a slice of bread. . . . I thought you needed it more than me."

I think, She must have saved her share from yesterday. I blush with pleasure at the thought of this unexpected gift.

But I quickly catch myself and manage to say in a small voice, "It's very kind of you, thanks. But I really can't accept it."

She takes me by the elbow and pushes me forward. "Come on, my child. I insist on it! Let's go to the orchard, where there's no one around. Nothing's happening outside for the moment!"

Maybe she is feeling sorry for me—what with my bandages and all that, I reflect.

We walk to the orchard. As we reach the nearest tree she hands me the package. I take it as casually as I possibly can and walk away, forcing myself not to run, all the way to the far end of the orchard. Here I finally can take my miraculous prize out of its greasy paper: a thin slice of gray bread with a thick layer of butter on top.

We are never wanting for butter. But what good is it, since we have nothing to eat it with?

I've wolfed down the last gulp when I stop short in shock: How could I deprive Mme Catherine of her one slice of bread? And the thought hadn't even dawned on me to share it with my sisters!

I hope no one will ever find out!

Saturday, August 5

We have dared to open the door a crack. At last, we can breathe a bit. Outside the sun is shining, there's not a cloud in the blue sky, the birds are chirping away. Above all, the air is quiet.

Yet we remain cautious. We are scared that it may start again, the bloody shelling—especially after the last one, a moment ago.

This time Lily was outside when it started. I thought that something had happened to her. I got scared like never before; for the first time I understood how real the danger is.

I dashed out, pushing back Mother Superior and Sister Geneviève, who were trying to hold me back. I ran straight out, screaming frantically, "Lily! Lily!" This time the hissing had seemed closer—hardly a touch over my head. Scared to death, I took refuge under a tree to catch my breath, trying to ignore the others who were yelling, "Come back, Renée. Don't stay outside! Are you crazy?"

All of a sudden bits of bark exploded above me. Frightened, I started to run again, praying aloud: "Dear Lord, make sure I find my little sister!"

Lily was waiting for me by the outhouse. I grabbed her arm, and without a word we ran as fast as we could—falling to the ground, noses pressed into the dirt, when another hissing sound tore the air. I counted one, two, three . . . waiting until the explosion came. "Hurry. Hurry, for goodness' sake!" voices were yelling from the barn. The short distance that stood in between seemed suddenly impassable. But I took Lily's hand, we looked at each other, and we ran nonstop to the shelter.

I'm still shaking. I'm telling the beads of my rosary, one Hail Mary after the other. It keeps me from thinking. Denise is still biting her nails; Lily is squeezed between us.

Marinette is hiding her head in her blanket—it takes her a long time to recover. Luckily Charlotte is always there to cheer her up. How I admire her! When I'm scared, I just can't be reassuring to others.

The juniors have gathered around Mlle Hélène. Suzette is sucking her thumb. The others are waiting; no one knows for what.

Our roof was hit by some shrapnel earlier. It made a frightening noise—like thunder. There's a big hole now just above Sister Madeleine's "bed." The farmer closed it with a piece of slate and gave us some more hay. He's also talking about bringing in some sandbags for better protection. But we don't feel safe anymore.

Mme Lafarge has brought us a big toilet pail. This time we are trapped.

Jacotte suddenly gets up and walks toward the door. Suzette is getting ready to follow her, but Mlle Hélène grabs her by her dress.

"Jacotte! Come back immediately! You know this is no time to go out to play!" Mother Superior has regained her voice and her energy. Funny how she always raises her voice when she's scared.

Our scatterbrains turn around. But Jacotte, frightened by Mother Superior's scolding voice, bursts into tears.

Soon, everyone gathers around her. Babette is frowning. She is going to cry any moment. The others are fretting too.

Mlle Hélène does an incredible thing. She intones, "*Aux couleurs du drapeau de la France* . . . To the colors of the French flag . . ."

Stunned, the little ones stop short. One by one the voices rise and join one another. A song of hope soars, shaking the walls of our humble shelter. We sing with all our might in order not to cry, scream, or die of fear.

How beautiful it is! I am no longer afraid. I wish we could go on singing forever.

Monday, August 14

It's Assumption tomorrow—a day to celebrate the Virgin Mary—and Mother Superior insists that the seniors accompany her to church in Le Chatellier: She wants us to go to Confession. We'll be right back, she assures us, since we've been ordered not to wander away; the farmer says that the Allies are very close now.

It's incredible how she is leading us straight into the danger zone. Really I think our Mother is overly concerned for our souls!

We've never missed a Sunday Mass. The tireless nun takes us on shortcuts through fields of corn or potatoes or makes us file in single line along the ditches of the road so as not to be seen. A couple of times we spotted a German truck in the distance, and we quickly hid in the ditch.

This time even Sister Madeleine protests. "But, Sister, you're surely not going to take the girls that far—even a mile or two is a lot under the circumstances. You may run into the front line!"

"That's nonsense. . . . Le Chatellier is not the end of the world. Actually it will be good exercise for these young ladies. Besides, I'm taking only the seniors!"

Aside from Mado, who is all ready and is always the

first one to do whatever Mother Superior wants, no one shows much enthusiasm.

Dédée tries a last time. "I have nothing to confess really. Since the Allies have landed, we haven't had much occasion to sin!"

Everyone laughs. Our Mother too. "I must agree. But remember, our souls are never pure enough. Come on, a little courage now!"

That's all she had to say. Now, the juniors and the intermediates run to Mother Superior and cling to her skirt.

"I want to go to church. Please take me along!"

"No, not this time, children. We must hurry. . . . Another time!" She looks around. "Well, girls, are you ready?"

Timidly I try to get out of it. I point to my arms and my newly bandaged leg. "Do I really have to go?"

"A big girl like you? Come on, you'll see . . . everything will go smoothly. In fact, who knows: Maybe you'll even get better sooner!"

On the way I can think only of rushing—and I stumble on the stones even more than usual. But I'm not complaining. I want to be worthy of M. le Curé of Le Chatellier, whom Mother Superior keeps praising, a holy man devoted to the soul and unconcerned about worldly possessions.

To be truthful I think he goes a bit too far: His habit is so patched up, I feel sorry for him. His bike is just as worn. Yet you should see him pedal away on the road; he covers three parishes all by himself, never mind the danger. Sister Madeleine says that his days are numbered: He has a terrible illness that eats away at his esophagus.

Does Mother Superior believe that we're going to die too? Did she get us here to confess one last time?

———

The church is crowded. The women, you can tell, have come in a hurry, a scarf thrown over their head, dragging their children by the hand. There are also men—many more than usual, in their dirty shoes.

Being frightened makes you want to be closer to God, Mother Superior says.

She rushes us to the confessional. I'm waiting for my turn. I nervously do and undo my bandage, which is beginning to unravel at the edges. I am not used to going to Confession; I've only been once since we got baptized. What am I to tell this brave priest, who doesn't know that I am a new Christian?

Charlotte walks out of the confessional. It's my turn. I kneel down under the curtain, my heart beating fast, and look through the grille at the strong nose, the protruding chin. M. le Curé breathes heavily. I close my eyes.

"Bless me, Father, because I have sinned."

"Go ahead, my child. I'm listening."

In a flash it comes to me: I tell him about the buttered slice of bread I did not share with my sisters.

"You'll say three Aves and one Our Father. . . . Go in peace, my child."

I feel so relieved. It's my turn to push Colette. She promises to hurry.

She has hardly come out when the head of the priest emerges from the confessional. "Hey, little girl," he yells, "I'm not finished. You forgot to say your Act of Contrition!"

Mortified, Colette does what she is told. Nobody dares to laugh. It's absolution we're after!

The priest finally gives us his blessing. He doesn't bother to talk to us from his pulpit; he addresses us from the altar. We have to hurry.

"And now, brethren, go back home and please, put your trust in the Lord. And of course, follow your common sense. . . ."

As he talks to us he is coughing hard and clutching his chest. He is in pain, for sure. Yet he is here, taking care of his flock.

Tuesday, August 15

Mathieu, the farmhand, has just informed us that there's no way we can go to church this morning, as Mother Superior had hoped to do. Someone told the farmers on the run that the Allies were next door. Furthermore rumor has it that the *boches* are mining fields and roads as they are forced to retreat.

The worried look Mother Superior gave Sister Madeleine didn't escape me.

"All right then, let's return to the barn," she says, pushing us inside. So here we are, sitting on the floor, circling the nuns once more.

I keep thinking: mined! That's serious. It's like these quarries, near Mulhouse, that they used to blow up with dynamite. I shiver at the thought.

"The mines are nowhere near us, are they?" I ask, looking desperately for reassurance.

"Dear God! We'll never get out of this!" Marinette

says, moaning, hiding her face in the straw. She doesn't even ask for her father anymore.

"Come, come, my child. Calm down. . . . Think of the little ones who will get panicky. Of course, mines can be serious—there's always the risk of getting wounded or killed—but only *if* you step right into one. And I'm sure they're talking about the main road and the neighboring fields where the troops marched, out there somewhere," Mother Superior explains, stretching her arm in a vague gesture. "Besides, I'm positive that the Allies are used to this and have the necessary equipment to detect the mines and to remove them. And—don't you ever forget it!—the Lord is here to protect us, as he has done so far!"

"In the meantime no one can tell exactly what is mined from what isn't," says Mme Catherine. "Which means that we can't feel safe anywhere!"

So we're trapped in this small barn in the middle of nowhere, until the Allies rescue us—if they ever find us.

I suddenly feel like moving, screaming "Help" for someone to hear us, to run for my life. But there's nowhere to run, so I sit.

Suddenly Jean-Jacques screams, "There's something in the sky!" and he dashes out.

Within seconds everyone has moved to the orchard, forgetting the warning to remain under shelter.

There *are* two white dots clearly visible against the cloudless sky, slowly coming down to earth toward us.

"It's the Assumption miracle in reverse!" Mme Catherine says in jest. "Something descending instead of the Virgin Mary ascending!"

Mother Superior ignores the impious soul. "They're parachutes," she yells. "*Parachutes!* Almighty God, please protect them. Make sure that there are no Germans around to see them!" she continues to implore, grasping her rosary.

"You know what Mathieu said: The Germans in the area have all fled, even ours!" comments Sister Madeleine.

I'm only listening with one ear. My eyes are riveted on the two white dots that continue to come down with maddening slowness, gliding at times, then coming down some more, as if they had all the time in the world. I would like to scream: "Hurry up, for God's sake. What if the Germans see you?"

I pray, I clench my fists, I count the seconds, afraid to see them shot down by some enemy hidden in a bush.

As they get closer to us, I pray: "Please God, make sure they don't get caught in a tree!"

An eternity later they finally land at the far end of the orchard—next to the beheaded tree. We all run to meet them.

They are English, we learn, and they're wearing their uniforms under their parachutes. On their armbands we read: 63rd R.I. Sister Madeleine explains that it means "Regiment of Infantry." One is blond; the other is a redhead, covered with freckles. They look so young. I am dying to touch them, to hug them. They're going to help us win the war—and they're going to help us get rid of these horrible Germans, for sure!

Still, a doubt starts creeping up. Will they really save us? There are only two for the moment—and I don't think they're even armed!

Jacotte wants to touch the parachute and the ropes, which have fallen on the ground like dead birds.

Babette asks if she can fly too. "Providing you become

a soldier," the redhead teases. Everybody laughs. "By the way, I'm Tom, and this is Pete," he says. In very bad French they manage to explain that they've been sent ahead of their troops, who should be following any moment now.

Mother Superior offers to take them to the farm, but they prefer to stick around in hiding and wait for their men.

As we return to the barn Mother Superior says, "Let's show our gratitude and celebrate the Assumption right here."

She starts:

"*Salve Regina, Mater misericordiae . . .*"

The air resounds with our cheerful voices. Mme Catherine sings the loudest. I'm so happy I don't even mind Tommy, who has landed in my lap.

M. Lafarge appears suddenly at the door, out of breath. "Sorry to interrupt you," he apologizes. "But my wife and I would prefer if you could move to the stable. . . . It's the only spot with sandbags. I don't want to sound discouraged, but frankly I won't feel at ease until I can see the Allies in the flesh."

"What about the two English soldiers from this morning? The others can't be very far away!" reasons Mother Superior.

"No doubt. And it is a fact that our *boches* have disappeared for good, it seems. But who knows? They may be hidden somewhere. No, really, Sister, we'd feel much better if you were all safe. I am a Norman, you know, so I'm suspicious!"

"But isn't your stable a bit small? How will we all fit

into it?" Mother Superior asks, her voice suddenly drained of energy.

"It *is* rather small, I don't deny it. But we'll manage. It won't be for very long anyway—a day, maybe two at the most," says the farmer.

―――――

So we've moved once more, each taking only our blanket—and our toilet pail, of course.

We hesitate at the door, intimidated as much by the intolerable stench—a mixture of manure and straw—as by the tiny space where we are to squeeze.

"It won't be any picnic!" Mme Catherine exclaims. "I bet there's not enough space for everyone to sit down!"

"Come on—one last sacrifice!" Mother Superior reminds us. "It won't be for very long."

The sun is going down. A graying light is still seeping through the dormer window.

"Let's try to sleep," Mother Superior suggests. "There's nothing better to do."

I would like to: "Who sleeps, eats," as the saying goes. We have had nothing to eat since the bowl of milk we were served this morning. But we can't sit or stretch, or lie down. The little ones are clustered, two or three at a time, on Sister Madeleine's lap or Mlle Hélène's chest. Jean-Jacques has taken full possession of Sister Geneviève's knees. The others have settled as best they can— back to back, curled up, legs intertwined. Everywhere we bump into sandbags which, in places, go all the way to the roof.

The stable is much smaller than the barn—and we have to share it with four cows to boot. Thank goodness they're tied to the wall and are separated from us by the manger. But it can't keep that awful smell from invading us.

"That stench is unbearable! Is there any way we can get a little fresh air in here? We're going to be asphyxiated, that's for sure!" Mme Catherine complains.

Charlotte offers to open the dormer and climbs on Colette's shoulders. It isn't nearly enough to air the stable. We decide to keep the door ajar.

"How long are we going to stay like this?" Marinette worries. "We're in the middle of nowhere! No one's going to know that we're here."

"I know, Sister! Maybe we should post a sign on the roof—or the dormer—to let the Allies know!" Mado suggests.

"What about the mines? No one's going to risk coming all the way here if they know it's mined!" Denise reminds us.

"We're going to die, abandoned, I'm sure!" Marinette continues, close to tears.

I feel like screaming at her, "Enough! Can't you shut up?"

Poor Marinette, she's a nice kid. But she manages to rob me of the little hope I have left.

"Come, come, children. Please don't worry. We're not going to be abandoned—not with the farmers in the area who know about us, and the two English soldiers who landed this morning. Come on, let's say our prayers and try to get some sleep. Tomorrow you'll see things differently," Mother Superior tells us.

Leaning against a sandbag in a corner, I feel that the world is closing in on me. I think of the *oubliettes*, those awful cells they mention in French history books where the prisoners could neither sit nor stand and where they died of pain, hunger, and cold, forgotten by their king.

I look at my bandaged hands and legs and fight back my tears by swallowing hard. The last time I counted the sores, which are all infected by now, there were twenty-eight on my left hand alone.

I have no struggle left in me.

I look in the dim light at the skinny little girl curled up against the wall across from me. Her arm is also bandaged up. It is Lily. Next to her Christian is playing absently with a paper bird left from Mlle Hélène's last game. He doesn't say anything; he hasn't for a long time.

My eyes then catch sight of a bony arm that someone is raising to adjust a barrette. I am not sure whose it is at first, but I recognize the dress. That scrawny girl is what has become of Denise!

Even Papa and Maman wouldn't know us now, I tell myself.

It's my birthday tomorrow. I know that no one will remember—let alone make a fuss.

Will Papa and Maman remember at least? Where are they now?

I can't keep my tears back any longer. They are streaming down my cheeks, my hands, my bandages.

I am still crying when, a little later, Mother Superior makes the rounds with a candle.

"Well, well, what's happening here?" she whispers, climbing over a mass of bodies and legs. "What's happening?" she repeats, towering over me.

"When is all this going to end?" I cry harder, wiping my eyes with my bandages.

"Soon . . . soon, I promise!" she replies softly. "You are not going to give up, knowing that tomorrow—or the day after at the most—we will be liberated? You heard what M. Lafarge said, didn't you?"

Deep inside me I think: Tomorrow we may be free, but we'll be dead, for sure!

"You know the two men who landed this morning? It's already a taste of victory! Come on, let me make you a pillow!"

She squeezes between Colette and me and sits down, leaning against the wall. She hands the candle over to Colette, who was dozing and has just opened her eyes. "Do you mind holding this for a moment?"

She then takes my blanket, folds it in two, then again, and rolls it into a pillow, which she puts on her lap.

"Here," she says, "rest your head here. Don't you feel better already?"

Her face is close to mine now. For the first time I notice her hollow cheeks, the deep shadows under her eyes that look sad and shine—I'm almost sure—with tears she is keeping back.

"Come now, try to get some sleep. Here, why don't you try to count sheep? Start at a hundred and count backward."

She takes the candle from Colette's hand and blows it out.

I try to close my eyes. But I can think of only one thing: How long will we be able to hold out—without food, hidden away in the middle of mined fields? We can't possibly get out of this alive. . . . This is the end!

"You must have faith, my child," Mother Superior whispers, putting her cool hand on my forehead. "Go ahead, close your eyes . . . and count sheep. . . . You'll see, it will help you."

I don't recall having counted beyond fifty-five.

"Renée, do you want to come along?" a voice whispers in my ear, dragging me out of my sleep.

I open my eyes. A stream of light is seeping through the dormer and shines right on Charlotte, who is shaking me. I look around, and everything comes back to me: We're in the stable and we're still alive!

The golden sunlight touches everything as by magic: It plays with the criss-cross beams above us, it pales the sandbags, it lights up the soiled straw on the ground. Even the stench we wallow in seems more tolerable.

My companions are still asleep—leaning against the wall, resting their heads on their knees or against one another's shoulder, as if frozen in the position they were in when sleep finally took over.

"It's M. Lafarge! He suggests that we walk as far as the main road to see if anything's happening!" Charlotte says.

I nod my head in agreement. Today is a new day, and everything seems possible. I disengage myself gently from Mother Superior and Colette. My sisters are resting on the other side of the nun, their heads together. Farther away Sister Madeleine and Mado are stirring— obviously getting ready to come with us.

We all work our way out, open the door latch, and step out as quietly as possible before the cows, who are becoming restless in their stalls, can start to moo!

Outside the morning sun is dazzling. The farmer and Mathieu are already waiting for us, flanked by an imposing, balding man with a hatchet face.

"This is Jean Pelletier. He owns the farm on the other side of ours," M. Lafarge says.

"Good morning, Sister," the man says. "I believe we've met before."

"Well, what are we waiting for?" M. Lafarge urges. "It's been two whole days now that everything is unusually quiet—"

"And that 'our' Germans have not returned to our farms," interrupts M. Pelletier.

"That's what I mean. Besides, they say that the Allies will be marching through the Domfront Road. If it's true, they'll be on the highway. I think our best bet is to go meet them. So let's go!"

I'm all excited. Just think! We are going to meet with the Allies! "But what if the road is mined?" I venture to ask.

"The child is right. Do you really think that it is safe to venture outside?" Sister Madeleine worries.

"Frankly I don't think there is anything to be concerned about as long as we are within the farm grounds. It's when we hit the county road that we'll have to be cautious."

We look at each other. Sister Madeleine decides that she'll go alone with the three men. "And you, girls, you'll wait here for us!"

"Please, Sister, let me go with you! I won't be any trouble. I'll be extra careful!" Charlotte promises.

"So will I," I echo, feeling braver now.

"Me too!" Mado says.

"All right then," the nun says with a sigh. "May God be with us!"

We walk through the yard in silence. I try to take long steps to keep up with the grown-ups.

As we reach the barrier giving out on the dirt road, M. Lafarge stops and turns to us.

"We are leaving the farm property now. From here on we've got to be careful. I'll be the leader. I'll walk first, as close as possible to the edge of the road. Just be sure to walk into my very steps!

"Ready?"

I hope no one notices how I'm shaking all over. I'm not sure whether it is from excitement or because I'm scared to death. I twist my rosary around my arm.

In front of me Sister Madeleine lifts her skirt.

We align ourselves behind the farmer. Our eyes are riveted to him as he lifts his right foot and puts it down a little farther out, hesitant at first, then settling down more firmly into the ground. After a short pause he does the same with his left foot. Still planted to the ground, he turns his head to us. "I think we can go ahead!"

We proceed with extreme caution. Everything vanishes that is not the precise, calculated footprints that we walk into one after the other.

At every step I feel more daring. I suddenly want to hurry, to run toward the Domfront Road.

"Careful! You're getting away from the line!" Mado yells.

We finally get to the end of the dirt path. To our right is a larger road, with trees on both sides. We all stop, and M. Lafarge carefully motions his foot to the right.

"Let's not lose our heads. We'll continue to be very careful. It won't be for very long now. The road to Domfront is at the end of this one, as you know."

We start to walk again, still in single file. My forehead is suddenly covered with perspiration. This road is much busier—perhaps the German Army passed through here and mined it!

With each step I feel I'm taking my life in my hands. How far are we from the country road—two hundred, three hundred yards at most? I start to count. There are about three steps to a yard. One yard . . . two yards . . . it takes much too long. I can't help looking for signs of mines to my side. I do spot something unusual. A red thread—or is it brown? What do those damn mines look like anyway? The perspiration is streaming down my temples now. I've got to stop so I can take a closer look.

"Renée! What's the matter with you! Are you crazy?" Charlotte yells at the top of her lungs behind me.

Everyone stops short.

"I think I've seen a mine. Right here!" I point with my finger to the odd-looking thing.

"My poor child. I think your imagination is getting the best of you. You really can't tell a mine from the rest of the ground. All right now, let's not waste any more time. We're almost there!" says M. Lafarge.

A wave of outrage comes over me. These *boches* are incredible! They think nothing of wrecking our soil, our land. They want us dead to the bitter end!

The last stretch, which we have walked so many times on our way to church, seems suddenly beyond reach. I can't walk any farther.

"Well, what the devil are you waiting for?" Mado says, pushing me forward.

I clutch my rosary harder and follow the others.

Our leader finally stops. We have come to the main road—a wide and paved way beyond which one can see large stretches of fields. I don't dare move. I merely crane my neck, trying to see.

M. Lafarge tries one step, then another.

"Goodness! Just look over there!" he exclaims, suddenly pointing his finger to the left. "What did I tell you? Isn't that the most beautiful sight in the world?"

I take tiny steps, brushing past our farmer and Sister Madeleine.

That's when I see, about a hundred yards away, this incredible sight: a German soldier, then another, and another still emerging from the ditch, their hands raised over their heads.

They're surrendering! They're being made prisoners!

I think I spot one of "ours." I'm glad he's not looking at us. They are all walking, eyes downcast, toward a handful of Allied soldiers armed with guns, who are motioning them to get into one of the military trucks parked at the side of the road.

We begin to scream, to clap our hands. I want to hug everyone.

"Careful with the mines, for goodness' sake!" Sister Madeleine reminds us.

I laugh. Nothing can happen to us now . . . nothing can happen to us anymore.

I look with all my might; I don't dare to blink, I don't dare to breathe. I don't want to miss anything. I look for me, for my sisters, for Papa and Maman—for all those who can't be here to see this.

It *is* the most beautiful sight in the world!

Tuesday, August 22

I had to see Flers one last time. It's my one and only chance: Tomorrow we'll be on our way to Paris.

It is thanks to "our" Englishmen—those of the 63rd Regiment of Infantry—that we have been able to find shelter in Flers, on Bank Street, one of the only streets that was not destroyed by the bombing. Sister Madeleine agreed to come with me. She is holding my hand as we cross an unidentifiable maze of ruins: singed wooden planks, blocks of concrete, occasional remainders of a wall, torn pieces of pipe strewn across a semblance of a street.

"It's hard to believe that I passed here every day on my way to school," I say.

Sister Madeleine doesn't answer. She merely tightens her hold on my hand.

As we walk on, I wish there were some way to hold onto her forever—her and the other nuns I've grown to love, Mother Superior and Sister Geneviève. But I know tomorrow we'll have to move on, even though it means leaving them behind.

"This is it, I believe," the nun whispers.

We have come to a shapeless lot, already reclaimed by untended grass and weeds. Was this really our home once—less than three months ago?

Oh! But here is part of the piano bench—charred by the fire. I touch it with my finger; it's covered with a fine black dust. And there, still standing between the hedges—now reduced to a scrawny bush—is this incredible thing, the statue of the Virgin Mary, white, intact, her arms still stretched out in a gesture of love and protection. It's a miracle.

I touch it with my hand: I want to make sure it isn't a trick of my imagination.

I bend down to pick up some sort of a clump—I think

I've spotted a bit of Jackie's black, curly hair, but it isn't that.

A fine drizzle is falling from the gray sky. I wipe the wetness off my cheeks. Rain or tears? It doesn't matter: The sky has the right to cry too.

I thought I had cried out all the tears in my body when little Jean-Jacques, our youngest—now our baby angel—died a few days ago, killed by one of those cruel military trucks that shuttle endlessly between Cherbourg and Paris.

He had crossed the street to get a chocolate bar. He crossed the street and he died. Gone forever are his babyish lisp, his bruised knees, his questioning eyes.

No one can hurt him anymore.

"Thank God! His face was untouched!" Mother Superior had exclaimed. She even added, "Dear God, may Thy will be done!" That's all she said.

I wanted to scream: "You mean God, you! All he wanted was a bar of chocolate!"

I remember their putting this white thing, the coffin, on the edge of the grave, and then I remember nothing.

Since then Christian walks around like a wounded animal, inconsolable. He wants to die too.

"One can't refuse life, my child," Sister Madeleine says now. "One must go on."

I know now that we each have our ruins, our private cemeteries. Memories of people who are no longer living, of places that no longer exist. Graves that no one can visit . . . *ni fleurs, ni couronnes*; no flowers, no wreaths.

I've become aware of the rain as it falls on a large wooden board, hitting relentlessly at a large stain in its middle, as if trying to wash it away. Rust? Blood? It's hard to say.

But the stain remains.

Friday, September 1

I can hardly believe it. We've just entered the hallway of our old building—Number Eighty-two Rue de Rochechouart. We're in Paris!

Denise and Lily are chatting away while climbing the steps two by two ahead of me, turning every so often to tell me to hurry up. Really they act as if coming home after two long dreadful years were the most natural thing in the world!

I wonder what Papa and Maman's reaction will be: They have no idea that we're on our way. How could they? They haven't heard from us in almost three months; since the landing of the Allies, Normandy has been cut off from the rest of France.

I'm still shaking from the straight-from-the-heart comment Mme Delmas let out when she saw us step out of the van a few minutes ago: "Hey! Look who's here! We thought you were all dead!" The war didn't change her, that's for sure!

The truth is, I'm scared. God knows, I've gone over this a hundred times during the long bumpy trip in the Red Cross car that Mother Superior found for us. It took us close to twenty-four hours, even though the distance is not more than a hundred and fifty miles, because of the many wrecked roads and bridges.

I keep asking myself: What if Papa and Maman aren't here? What if they were taken away and strangers open the door?

I pause for a moment on the banister. We are on the third floor. I recognize Mme Pérignon's apartment, with the business card still pinned to the door. Nothing has changed.

I slow down. I grow more apprehensive with every step. I'm on the fourth floor now—right by the apartment where Uncle Maurice, Aunt Fanny, and my cousins lived, just below ours. My heart skips a beat, and my thoughts begin to race. Where are they now? Has anyone heard from them since someone informed on them?

It takes me forever to climb the last few steps. Denise and Lily are arguing about who should ring the bell. They both hit it at once.

The door suddenly opens up wide, and Maman appears, smaller and much thinner than in my memory. She opens her mouth, startled, but nothing comes out. Then she howls, "My darlings!" and she grabs all three of us, hugging and kissing us all at once.

"God! How skinny you are!" she exclaims, taking a closer look at us. "Oscar! Oscar!" she then yells out toward the bedroom. "They're here!"

She yells so loudly, I'm embarrassed. What goes on in here is nobody's business.

Papa hasn't made a sound, but there he is, standing in the doorway, as if frozen. He, too, is much thinner—and he looks so old.

He breaks into a smile and opens his arms. I rush to him—for once I'm first, not Lily!—and he hugs me so hard, I am left breathless for a few seconds.

"Goodness! What are those bandages you have on your arms and legs?" Maman asks me.

"Did you see how they've grown?" Papa tells Maman.

"But they're so pale—and their clothes are all torn, poor lambs!"

Denise and Lily both talk at once—about the scabies, the impetigo, the bombings, the barn. Papa wants to know how we managed to find someone to drive us back in the middle of this chaos.

I am glad they're not paying attention to me for the moment. It's wonderful to be home, of course, but I feel oddly out of place. I can't help wondering about what Mother Superior and Sister Madeleine are doing, and I miss Mme Catherine and all the girls who are still stranded in Flers.

I look around. Everything is in place—yet it feels as if I need to get reacquainted with each object. I skim over the surface of the oiled tablecloth; I touch the fruit bowl on the dresser, the doily underneath it; I go over the family picture on the side of the mantelpiece. Here it's still yesterday.

The familiar faces of the past suddenly cross my mind. A lump forms in my throat. I run to the window, lift the curtain, and pretend to be looking out. I need time to compose myself.

"You don't say a word, Renée. Is anything wrong?" Maman's voice asks behind me.

I turn around. "How are Uncle Maurice and Aunt Fanny and Raymond and Fernand?" I finally blurt out.

My words are rushing out: I want to get it over with.

"We heard from them twice—briefly. They have been taken to the camp of Rivesaltes, in the Pyrenees. Uncle

Maurice was sick for a while. They should be freed by now, and on their way to Paris, shouldn't they, Oscar?" Maman pleads.

"They should, Mancsi . . . they should!" Papa replies, putting his hand on Maman's arm and keeping it there.

It isn't like Papa to be demonstrative for very long, and I feel rather lost with this fearful mother who is new to me.

"What about the others?" I work myself up to ask, trying to sound braver than I feel.

This time Maman's voice drops. "We have not heard from my brothers in over a year. Of course, with what was going on, the mail with foreign countries was not very reliable. But now that the Germans are out of the way, things should go back to normal!"

Sadly I wonder if, deep down, Maman worries that her brothers may never return from the forced labor camp where the Germans sent them.

Before anyone has a chance to say anything, Maman hurries on, as if she wanted to change the subject: "But we *do* have good news. Grand'mère is fine, and Mme Cohen and Jeannette and Riri were released from the Drancy camp a few days after you left!"

I'm also eager to know about the pregnant lady from Number Eighty; Jeannot's relatives, the Schriffts and the Kleins; Papa's friend Max; and of course, my little class-mate Feigie—not to mention all the other people we knew. But something tells me this is not the right time.

"Well, we'll try to forget about these bad times and pick up our life where we left it off!" Papa adds quickly.

I look at him as if he had stabbed me in the heart. How can he dismiss so easily what happened to all of us during this awful war, and particularly what my sisters and I have endured in the last two years? Do they even know that we've been baptized?

Why, even Sister Madeleine says that the three of us have been forced to try our wings much too early, and that people never forget what happened to them. They simply get used to it.

———

Maman puts the tureen of soup on the table. Lily is no longer sitting on Papa's lap; she is in her own chair next to him.

For a split second I think of saying grace, but I catch myself as my eyes fall on the small menorah. It's back on the mantelpiece after being hidden for so long.

Am I not Catholic anymore?

For the first time I feel the struggle in me. Will I ever be able to reconcile the two worlds?

Through the open window we hear the Chavignats' radio, just like before.

"Come on, Renée!" Papa urges. "You're the oldest and a big girl now. You do the serving."

I take the ladle he is handing me, thinking, No, it isn't yesterday here.

It's already tomorrow.